CLAIRE,
DARLING

CLAIRE, DARLING

A Novel

CALLIE KAZUMI

BANTAM
NEW YORK

Published in the United States by Bantam Books, an imprint of Random House, a division of Penguin Random House LLC, New York.

BANTAM & B colophon is a registered trademark of Penguin Random House LLC.

Published in the United Kingdom by Penguin, a division of Penguin Random House UK, as *Cuckoo*.

Hardback ISBN 978-0-593-87163-8
Ebook ISBN 978-0-593-87164-5

Printed in the United States of America on acid-free paper

randomhousebooks.com

2 4 6 8 7 5 3 1

First US Edition

Book design by Fritz Metsch

For Papi,
who taught me to chase my dreams

CLAIRE,
DARLING

I look down at her body, crumpled in an awkward heap, dark blood pooling beneath the head. I stare at the glistening burgundy puddle and try to make myself feel something—anything. Relief? Guilt? Regret? Fear? But strangely, and for the first time in a long time, I feel nothing at all. Does this make me a monster or is it how shock works?

She is completely still. I wonder if I should try to stem the bleeding, but even I can tell it's pointless. Her head is caved in on one side, dented almost, and she's foaming at the mouth. There is no undoing this.

Oh, God.

I step backward and stagger, losing my balance. I take in the scene. Tea spilled everywhere, a dead woman, and me, in the middle of it all.

PART ONE

ONE

September 19, 2025
Dear Diary,

I'm writing this on my way in to work. The tube is pretty rammed but I managed to grab a seat. Last night I was too busy to write, but it was a wonderful evening and I want to make sure to note down as much of it as I can so that I can look back on the memories. Our anniversary!

I picked up some celebratory prosecco on the way home, as well as all of Noah's favorite treats. Two juicy sirloin steaks from Sainsbury's, some potatoes, veg, and Jaffa Cakes for dessert. Obviously those were for Noah, he'll eat a whole packet in one sitting. The question is: Are they a cake or a biscuit? Noah says cake because of the spongy texture, and I'm inclined to agree. I managed to put together dinner for us, with some hand-cut chips roasted with garlic and rosemary. I didn't even overcook the steaks! Medium-rare, just how we both like it. I wanted it to be special, our first big milestone together.

Noah greeted me when I arrived home with a box of my favorite chocolates, which he'd wrapped in a ribbon—bless him. I'd made the right choices, too, because when he was helping me to unpack the shopping he brought his hand to his chest and exclaimed, "Steaks and Jaffa Cakes?" in dramatic delight. I slapped his hand away from the Jaffas playfully before he could spoil his supper. He slipped a hand around my back, kissed the base of my neck and said, "Happy first anniversary, my Claire."

I love when he says that. My Claire.

I spent all my energy focusing on him, on the dinner, on the night. I didn't want to spend one moment thinking about the other Thing that happened this time last year. I wanted it to be a wonderful night, to leave the past behind me where it belonged. Noah made it easy.

We spent the evening chatting away easily, always on the brink of flirtation. He put on some old-school romantic music while I cooked, Nat King Cole crooning about love and Noah occasionally stopping me to pop a chocolate bonbon into my mouth. Cliché, but it didn't feel that way. I know if I were watching I'd squeeze my eyes shut in a cringe, but I can't help behaving like this with him.

So he fussed about me while I seasoned and flustered over supper, sometimes pausing with a hand on the small of my back while he got us bubbly top-ups from out of the fridge, and I caught him up on how work has been going. I didn't want to speak about work particularly, but he asked. He's been so invested in it, which I suppose makes sense as he's the one who convinced me to apply for my new job.

I've been there for six months now, and I have him to thank for this role. I'd probably have just stayed put otherwise, but now I'm at a small boutique PR company and enjoying it so much. We laughed about the fact I'd been so worried about applying, going over the story again between sips of prosecco and sending joking eye-rolls at each other. He'd seen the job advert and printed it out, left it unsubtly on the kitchen table at my usual breakfast seat. I'd read it and pretended to forget about it, until a week later he'd raised it casually over dinner.

"Did you ever see that job ad I saved for you?"

I'd told him I just "wasn't sure it was the right role for me." He'd asked why, told me it sounded like the perfect next step for me, and that was when I realized I didn't really have an answer for him. It had sounded great, and he was so sincere in his belief I could get it that it made me give it due consideration. I'd been nervous to apply, of course. Mostly of the rejection if I didn't get it, but also of meeting a new team, having a new office . . . it all felt daunting and overwhelming. I didn't even have to say any of this, though: Noah knew. Somehow he always knows what I'm thinking and feeling. He spent the whole of that dinner convincing me I deserved a pay raise, and stroked my hair and told me I was brilliant, until it seeped in and I convinced myself to apply. And now here I am, six months in, probation officially passed!

So as I prepared our meal I told him about my newest client frustrations and the lunchtime gossip shared with Sukhi from my team. I'm not sure I'd go so far as to say we are friends, but I think we're getting there. We spend nearly every lunchtime together now, and occasionally talk about personal things outside of work. By the time I had caught him up on everything PR-related, dinner was steaming on two plates at the table, and he lit a candle and put it between us.

"To us." I held my glass up in the air and he mirrored the action with a smile that made me weak at the knees.

"To us."

After dinner, with a belly full of prosecco (okay, okay, and a glass of wine), my head was hazy as I made my way to the bedroom. I still have a bit of a headache now, truth be told. I'm obviously not used to drinking, but last night was a cause for celebration. Plus, this time of year, the things that happened the week I met Noah . . . well, it's an exception.

Noah insisted he'd do the washing-up as I'd cooked, and after the glasses of fizz I was too sleepy to protest. I was in bed, half-asleep and drowsy with alcohol, when I felt him slide in beside me. I'd been imagining us in five years, with a little baby, half him, half me. A loved, cared-for little baby who I would always put first, no matter what.

Noah's body was warm and firm against mine and I snuggled in deeper, smiling softly. We made love, of course. I fell asleep in the blissful throes of post-orgasm relaxation, and the last thing I remember was him saying, "Goodnight, my Claire," as I fell asleep in his arms. It was the perfect anniversary.

Claire

TWO

What are your plans for lunch?" Sukhi asks. She pops her head over the top of the partition around my work-station, blowing a strand of her thick raven-black hair away from her face.

I am standing at my desk with Photoshop on my laptop, a half-designed press release displayed on the screen. I'm feeling particularly short of creative inspiration today, so I was about to take a break and suggest a coffee to her.

Sukhi always has a cup of coffee and biscuits at eleven in the kitchenette—she calls it elevenses—and I now go along with her, pleased to have been invited to join the ritual. Her mug is kept on her desk instead of in the kitchen cabinet, for fear of someone stealing it. It proudly declares her to be #1 *Top Bitch* and is shaped to look like a poodle sitting on its hind legs.

In comfortable silence we walk around to the kitchenette. Sukhi places her mug on the side and then takes two digestive biscuits from the communal jar, slotting them into the giant mug's cookie slot, aka the poodle's mouth. In contrast I pull out the cleanest-looking branded mug from the cupboard and, after a quick wipe of the rim with a piece of kitchen towel, set about making the coffee for us while Sukhi munches on a third biscuit. Apparently if she eats it away from her desk without anybody seeing, it still only counts as having two.

"So, lunch?" she asks again. "Our usual?"

"I'm actually going to run over to Noah's office and drop him off his favorite," I tell Sukhi as I stir sugar into my coffee, leaning against the sink. "He's been really busy at work recently. I worry he isn't eating enough."

"Very generous," she says, dipping a biscuit into her coffee. "Any special occasion or just general girlfriendly concern?"

"It was our anniversary yesterday, actually—the eighteenth of September. One year!" I smile.

"Oh, God, is that what the balloon by the door is? Gave me a fright this morning," Sukhi laughs.

"Guilty," I admit, glancing at the giant pink heart balloon that I tied to the coatstand. "We celebrated last night with dinner. He's working straight through lunch today. Some big meeting or something. I want to see he doesn't starve," I explain.

"You guys make me sick," she jokes.

A flush of smugness warms my spine. It feels the tiniest bit toxic, a sharp mirroring of Mother and her loftiness, but I'm too busy basking in my happiness to reflect on that side of myself too deeply. It's okay to be happy, to feel content in myself. It doesn't make me like Mother.

It doesn't make me like Mother.

"Look at you, you're absolutely smitten!"

"Are you not, with your husband?" I ask, genuinely interested as I glance down at the jewel on my left ring finger.

"Well, I was at the start . . . It's different, we're childhood sweethearts. Not sure it's possible still to feel smitten after twenty years of farts and fights," she laughs.

I nod, understanding. "Yes, I suppose Noah and I did move quite quickly, but it feels as though I've known him forever. Though not too many fights—or farts—just yet!"

"Nice that there're still some things to look forward to." Sukhi grins, picking up her mug.

"How young were you then? When you met?" I ask as we head back to our desks. Sukhi gets to her chair and sits while I hover nearby.

"Thirteen when we met. Our parents forced us to hang out in the hope that when we were older, we'd marry." She laughs. "He was an annoying idiot at first, and I was pleased that I wasn't going to slot into that good-Punjabi-girl-marrying-right stereotype. But after a few years of occasional parent-organized meetings, we ended up actually getting along, and he asked me out properly when we were seventeen. My parents weren't super strict, so they let us go bowling together on our own. No cousins spying on us, as far as I'm aware. I guess it all started there, love amidst the bowling balls."

"So your parents won?" I grin.

"I like to think we're all winners." She winks.

I sit down as well, looking forward to lunch. I thought it would be nice to do a little surprise drop-off, something Noah would like. I haven't visited his work in ages, even though it's just around the corner, up Liverpool Street way. It's always wild to me that one moment I can be rambling down Brick Lane, vintage thrift stores and Spitalfields food market screaming hipster at me, then five minutes later be surrounded by suits and skyscrapers. I prefer my side of the area, working down from Liverpool Street station toward Aldgate. It's quieter, but a five-minute walk and I'm in the throes of Hipster-ville. So Noah is always nearby, which is nice to know, but I don't like to risk either of us feeling suffocated. This last year has been so lovely and perfect but I'm always worried that I'll somehow mess it all up, freak him out and push him away. That he'll wake up and realize he doesn't want me. I have this fear with most people I meet, this overwhelming sense that I'm unwanted and driving them away without meaning to. I'd like to say it's more complex than the cliché, but it's definitely Daddy Issues.

Mother never let me forget that.

"This is a bit messed up, isn't it?" Mother asked with a frown, holding up my homework sheet. I was eleven and had been asked to create a family tree for my history class.

I shrugged. "They said we had to start with our mums and dads and work our way back," I told her.

"Don't you ever call me 'Mum,' " she said with an overdramatic shudder. "It sounds common, darling. And we're not common, are we?"

I shook my head, even though I wasn't sure what being common meant. "No, Mother."

"Good. Well, I can tell you all about *my* history, no problem," she said with a big smile, lounging against the back of the sofa as though preparing to sit for a full-body oil study. "But when they ask about your father's side, you can tell them to sod off."

I shuffled my feet, a seed of anxiety planted in my belly. "I don't think I can tell the teacher that. I'll get in trouble."

"Well, you can't be the only child without both parents to ask, can you? What if he was dead? Or missing? It's not very sensitive to be asking kids about these things. If you ask me, this homework here"—she tapped the paper furiously—"is a load of shit."

I stood there gripping my pen and notebook, unsure what to say or do. "You can just tell me about your side?" I suggested, eager to move the conversation away from my mysterious father.

"Okay. Well, settle down, this could take a while," she said, clearly pleased to move the conversation back to herself. "And if they ask about your father, you'll have to tell them the cold, hard truth. Maybe they'll feel so bad for asking that they'll rethink this ridiculous homework task."

"What's the truth, Mother?"

"That he left us. Because of you, darling."

THREE

If I'm honest, another reason I don't go to visit Noah often during working hours is because his office makes me feel uncomfortable. The glass building towers over the others around it and is filled with slick City bankers, their thinning hair gelled back and their suits pristine. The women are even more intimidating—willowy, with professional blow-dries, clattering through the foyer in their Louboutin stilettos and wearing glossy slicks of red lipstick over their whitened teeth. I always feel out of place there, like a little maggot squirming its way into a beehive. My curves, the ones that Noah always compliments, suddenly feel too voluptuous, border-line offensive beside the crisp, tailored dresses of his colleagues. The light spattering of freckles that dusts the bridge of my nose feels overwhelmingly distracting compared to their flawless complex-ions. How can girl-next-door compete with Bond girl, ever? Of course, Noah always tells me that I'm ridiculous, that I'm perfect as I am and that I shouldn't compare myself to his boring colleagues, but it's hard to be a woman in today's world, constantly being told you're not beautiful or thin or rich enough.

"Can I come along with you at lunch? I slept terribly last night so I'm feeling a bit rotten this morning," Sukhi admits, popping her head back over the cubicle just before half-twelve. "A bit of fresh air and a takeout lunch will probably revive me."

I blink in surprise. I hadn't considered that she would want to join. I'm not sure how Noah will feel about this, but I must admit that a part of my soul glows at the idea of showing off my fiancé, flaunting his impressive office and glamorous co-workers.

"Sure," I tell her, before I can change my mind. "That would be nice."

Lunchtime comes quickly, and Sukhi accompanies me to the Caribbean stand round the corner. It's our go-to for Friday lunches, so no discussion is needed about what we're going to eat. It's nice building these quiet, unofficial traditions. They add comfort to my days and make me feel safe, somehow.

The food stall is painted bright yellow and the guys behind the counter are always cheerful, calling us "love" and dancing along to upbeat reggae as they work. Smoke spirals out from the pans behind them and the air smells sweet and spicy, full of flavor.

"Two portions of jerk chicken with roasted sweet potatoes, spicy rice, and a side of fried plantain, please," I tell the man behind the counter, raising my voice so it can be heard over their music speakers.

"From your admirer?" He winks in response, nodding at the balloon that I've brought along with me and is now looped around my wrist.

I flush. "Something like that."

Minutes later, two steaming boxes are dropped into my hands and I parcel them into a carrier bag, wrapping them carefully so they don't seep out of the polystyrene sides. The scent of the spices wafts out and it smells divine.

I smile to myself; Noah will be so happy.

As we walk, I'm concentrating on keeping the takeout bag as level as possible to avoid any smelly spillage. The balloon bobs around me annoyingly, and I have to keep swatting it away.

"So are you any closer to getting started with wedding planning?" Sukhi asks, her own bag swinging, carefree, beside her.

I sigh, glancing down at my beautiful sparkling ring again. "No. We're still working out our living arrangements and there's quite a lot happening at the moment for Noah at work, some big deal or something. We said we'd start looking at venues later in the year and go from there."

She nods. "Sounds sensible. Take your time with it and don't pile it on if you have other things going on that are stressful. If I could go back, I'd redo so much—we were so eager to get it done that we probably compromised on things we shouldn't have."

"Like what?" I ask, genuinely interested and keen to avoid making the same mistakes.

"Videographer, for one. We spent so much money on the photographer because my parents loved their style, so we scrimped on the videographer. One of my uncles volunteered to help out but turns out he just had a regular camera with a couple of lenses and a tripod," she tells me with a grin. "It ended up looking like a student's YouTube montage."

"That's awful!"

"Yeah, but we were young and just wanted to be married. Luckily for me, I had my own personal fleet of aunties filming all the key moments—I felt like an Indian Kardashian. But I'll tell you what you can skimp on—the flowers. Nobody remembers them anyway."

I nod, grateful for the insider information. "We're here," I tell her, putting an end to the wedding chat.

"Wow," Sukhi breathes as we approach the office building, which is guarded by two doormen who let us in through the rotating doors with polite smiles. I feel gratification wash over me at her reaction. Our own office building was once equally terrifying to me, a big block housing several companies. But after realizing most of these were start-ups run by entitled teenagers who wore cargo pants to work, the once-intimidating PR office quickly lost its shine for me. The carpets are tired, the desks are cheap gray metal with wires jumbled beneath them, though we do have a really nice meeting room with plush sofas and a glass coffee table for when client meetings happen. Noah's office, however, has definitely not lost its shine; the people filling its glassy walls are as sparkly today as they were on day one.

"What did you say Noah did again?"

Before I have a chance to reply, the receptionist at the gleaming metal desk beams at us artificially. "Good morning! How can I help you today?" she asks brightly.

I don't recognize her and realize she must be new. I smile back, keen to make a positive first impression. I wasn't a big fan of the old receptionist. Maggie, I think her name was. She was difficult, never liked me dropping in without an appointment and often refused to let me speak to Noah. Imagine! Not letting me speak to my own boyfriend. I complained to him about her a few times. In fact, we did bicker about it once or twice. He would defend her, which bothered me. I suppose I felt that he should always take my side in these things, out of loyalty. He, however, put business first, and wanted to keep a good relationship with her.

"She's only doing her job," he would say. Always a diplomat. I'd pout about it until he'd kiss my neck and tickle me and make me laugh, and then all the tension would ease out of us as though it had never existed. But he didn't ever mention Maggie leaving or a new receptionist starting. Odd.

"Hi." I smile at the Maggie replacement. "I just wanted to drop off a lunch for Noah Coors," I explain, raising the now-soggy bag with a flourish.

"And what company is he with?" she asks. For some reason, I can feel my heartbeat begin to accelerate. It's as though my body is trying to tell me something is wrong.

"Pulitzer Haas, but no need to interrupt him, I just wanted to drop it off," I explain. I suddenly feel mortified about the balloon that's flailing behind me. I really don't want to be any bother; I know how busy Noah can be and how high-pressured his job is. The last thing I want to do is embarrass him, turning up unannounced with a bloody pink balloon. I brush it behind me as though I can hide it, and feel my hair raising with the static. I don't have a hand free to smooth it down.

"Hold on two seconds," Not-Maggie says. Her voice is chirpy, but her smile is now wavering uncertainly, her perfectly plucked brows turning down into a confused frown.

Normally I would have walked away, desperate to avoid any confrontation, but Sukhi is quick off the mark. "Is there a problem?" she asks, stepping forward. I would never have the confidence to question someone as perfectly poised as this new receptionist, but Sukhi is nothing like me. In fact, watching her now as she looks down at the girl behind the desk, I can see that not a drop of self-consciousness permeates her bloodstream the way that it floods mine.

"It must be an error, just give me a moment." The receptionist smiles again with a tiny shake of her head.

"What's the error?" Sukhi asks with a frown. I'm already poised to leave, the forgotten lunch clutched in my hands.

"Well, it's just that I can't find any Noah Coors working for Pulitzer Haas," she admits, looking up at me warily.

That stops me in my tracks and I turn to face her fully. "That's . . . not possible," I tell her. "Check it again. Please," I add quickly, not wanting to come across as rude or demanding.

"I've checked three times now," she tells me.

"C-O-O-R-S?"

"Yes, Noah with an 'h,' Coors," she replies.

"Well, it must be a mistake," I say, slowly and clearly.

She blinks up at me. "How is it you know Mr. Coors again? Are you sure you have the right place?"

"She's his fiancée!" Sukhi exclaims incredulously.

I hold my hand up dumbly, my engagement ring glinting in the harsh office lights. I give it a little wave for good measure and the woman blanches.

"This is ridiculous, just call him and tell him to come downstairs," Sukhi says, turning to me.

"He doesn't really like me bothering him at work," I say, feeling nervous. I don't want to upset him, but my hand is already reaching for my handbag. I'm pulling the phone out of my purse when the receptionist leaps up from her seat. "Oh, Mr. Donahue!" She smiles, looking relieved. "Perhaps you could help us with something?" She beckons with her hand and an important-looking older man in a pristine pressed suit strides over.

"What's the problem, Sandra?"

"The system doesn't seem to be working. It's not pulling up someone who we know to work with you?" She glances at me for confirmation.

"Yes, Noah Coors at Pulitzer Haas? On the asset management team? I was just bringing him some lunch," I explain meekly, holding up the sad-looking package once more.

"Oh!" the man exclaims with a look of understanding, and my shoulders sag in relief. He clearly knows Noah. This whole debacle will be over in seconds and then I can get out of this building. People are now flooding in behind us, forming a queue to talk to the receptionist, and I can see curious glances thrown our way from workers returning with their Starbucks lunches and Marks & Spencer meal deals.

"Well, Noah doesn't work here anymore," the man explains.

The receptionist's mouth drops open like a guppy's and, behind me, Sukhi makes a tiny, gasping sound in her throat.

"What . . . what do you mean? He *does* work here, he comes here every day," I say, trying to keep my voice even and calm. I don't want to attract any more attention, potentially embarrass Noah in front of his colleagues.

"Afraid not," he replies, oblivious to the distress he is causing. "He hasn't worked here for a few months now."

I stagger backward, my ears ringing with shock. I drop the lunch on the floor and Sandra lunges forward, asking a doorman to bring me a glass of water. Sukhi has swooped in and is supporting me from behind. I can hear her saying *mistake* and *misunderstanding,* but the words are swimming in a messy tangle in my head as I try to make sense of what's happened. My fiancé wakes up every morning and goes to work, returning late in the evenings.

Only he hasn't been working here for months.

FOUR

September 18, 2024
Dear Diary,

I met a man today. This is probably the first time in a long while that I've written anything in this diary regarding someone other than myself, or Mother, which feels both strange and exciting. It's as though the universe is spinning around to try and make up for what it's put me through recently. This time last week I was a wreck, an emotional roller coaster, and now I'm writing about something as frivolous as a man. I'm sure I will look back on this and hate myself for my flippancy, but right now, I feel like a flattering distraction is exactly what I need to take me away from my current situation.

I was in Morrisons and immediately noticed him in the aisle with me because he was gorgeous.

"I'm sorry to bother you, it's just, I'm desperately searching for a lovely bottle of red, which I don't usually drink. You don't happen to have a recommendation or favorite, do you?" he said, almost nervously. He was obviously just out of work because he was wearing a suit in deep navy, which brought out the specks of blue in his eyes. His hand came up to his black tie, loosening it ever so slightly before he spoke to me.

I was flustered. I couldn't believe that out of everyone in that supermarket, I was the one he wanted to speak to. I actually turned to double-check he was looking at me, and could feel myself going red at the realization that we were the only two people in the aisle.

*I cleared my throat. "Is it for a special occasion? A date perhaps?"
My voice came out in an embarrassing squeak.*

*"No, no, a business thing. I need to present a client with something
nice . . . fancy, you know. Apparently the guy is a red man. I usually go
to the wine place near my office but they're shut for renovations."*

*I immediately felt a little bit self-conscious. He was obviously some
big, important City boy, but I just nodded. I knew the wine place he
meant. I'd gone in once, seen the prices, paled and left quickly before
anybody tried to offer me any assistance. Some of those bottles cost
hundreds.*

*"Perhaps this one?" I suggested meekly, holding up a bottle without
any idea what it was. I hoped it didn't taste like vinegar. I started
getting those intrusive thoughts I always get, about him trying it and
hating it and therefore hating me, but I tried to push them away using
the techniques I've learned from my mindfulness app.*

He peered at the label, then the price, and shrugged.

*"I'm sure it will do, it's only business after all, and courtesy of the
office credit card! You've saved my bacon with this, it must be my lucky
day." He smiled at me and I swear his teeth twinkled like in a cartoon.*

But actually it was my *lucky day. He turned to leave.*

*"There's a Chardonnay I quite like too," I added quickly, desperate
to prolong our conversation. "It's not quite as fancy as that one"—
I blushed—"but it's very light and dry." And I've even tried it, I
didn't say.*

*He looked at me with interest then, one eyebrow raised slightly. My
insides turned to jelly.*

*"Light and dry sounds good. Maybe I'll take one of those as well,
just for me." He smiled. "Is it your date-night go-to?" he asked.*

*I could feel him looking at me intently and knew I was blushing, my
cheeks doing their best to imitate a frying pan. I stared at my feet for a
moment, trying to calm myself. "No, no! No dates . . . no date-night
wines for me. I mean, I'm single." I trailed off and smiled at him,
embarrassed.*

"Are you now? That's interesting," he said, and his smile curved
into a wide, sparkling grin.

*We ended up chatting for ages in that aisle. When he asked if I'd like
to carry on the conversation over a coffee, I leaped at the chance. A tiny
part of me could hear my mother sneering in my head.* For God's sake,
Claire, darling, he's making a fool of you. Why would a man like
that want a girl like you?

*But I shook her voice away. She's gone, and I'm not going to let her
hurt me anymore.*

*So we went to Costa and had a great time. Conversation was easy
and low-pressure. We talked a little bit about what he did and what I
did, and he seemed genuinely interested. He worked in banking, which
obviously I don't know much about, but he didn't go into detail and I
feigned enough interest to keep the conversation going. It all felt fated,
as though after such a terrible week with everything that's happened
with Mother, I was owed this slice of happiness. I'll try to play it cool. I
know how these things usually go and have heard all the horror stories.
But I hope I'll see him again.*

Claire

FIVE

I'm sitting in the waiting area of this pretentious office block, shakily clutching a glass of water. Sukhi has her arms wrapped protectively around me, and even Mr. Donahue has paused his lunchtime excursion out of concern for my well-being. The new receptionist, Sandra, is crouching in front of me, holding some tissues. It takes me a while to realize they're for me, and that I'm crying.

"I'm sorry I can't help any more. I just know that he resigned back in February, to go on to a better role. He signed an NDA, we put him on gardening leave . . ." Mr. Donahue is saying.

Gardening leave? My eyes are flitting back and forth, my brows knotted together in frantic search of a reasonable explanation.

"Claire, did you really believe he was coming in every single day?" Sukhi asks me quietly.

"Of course I did! Where else would he be?" I snap, my voice shrill. I let my spine collapse, slumping into the seat, not wanting to draw any more attention to myself as I notice even strangers *outside* of the office are gawking in at me through the glass walls with open curiosity. I must really look a mess. The heat of shame pricks the surface of my skin like needles and I wipe the tissue over my puffy cheeks as Mother's voice rings through my head.

Claire, darling, don't you dare cry in public!

"Sorry," I tell Sukhi, ashamed of raising my voice, of losing my cool.

"Don't be silly," she tells me, patting my hand.

Mr. Donahue tells me, "I didn't even know he was getting married. You think you know someone . . ." He shakes his head sadly. "I have to rush now, I'm late for a meeting, but I hope you get . . . all of this sorted," he says with a vague flap of his wrinkled hand, before half running away from my shambolic state.

The receptionist discreetly slips away, returning behind her desk to deal with the lengthening queue while I sit, staring at a spot on the ground, my eyes glazed. Occasionally a tear drips off my wobbling chin and I feel wretched and wild, pathetic and exhausted, all at once.

"It makes no sense," I tell Sukhi quietly, my voice coming out thickly.

"Look, let's get ourselves together. I'm going to call the office, explain there's been a family emergency. Let's make sure you get home okay, then we'll get this sorted. You can't go back to the office today, not like this," she says, standing up with her phone out, already scrolling through her contacts for the office number. In that moment, I am immeasurably grateful for her friendship.

"Hi, yes, it's me, Sukhi," she starts, walking outside with her head low, her voice all business.

She'll make a wonderful, no-nonsense mother, I think sadly.

Sukhi really wants a baby. I know this because she mentions it regularly, fretting about her body clock and her endometriosis, which has made it difficult for her to conceive naturally. I'm hopeful for them. She's only thirty-four, which is still young in my mind. Plenty of time for her to have a baby. She has a brilliant doctor, to whom her husband is related, so she's getting the best possible advice to help them along. I always change the conversation quickly when she starts worrying about it, because I never know what to say to her when she recounts the stats and data about eggs and miscarriages. I try very hard to listen but then panic and this stresses me out, which is selfish, I know, because she's looking for comfort and camaraderie and I haven't been able to give her that.

If I'm honest, I've been having my own concerns about becoming pregnant. I'd love a little baby, but Noah has been quite reserved about it, overly practical as always. I raised it with him once, after a bit too much wine in a burst of boldness, and he gently reminded me that we were still young, that we should enjoy our time alone together and focus on our careers for a little longer before bringing a baby into the world.

"It's not a case of if, Claire, but when," he told me softly, instantly erasing any concerns I had and instead sending a lurch of excitement straight down into my womb.

He drew me into these exciting plans to travel the world before having children, and we've spent several evenings sharing fantasies and exchanging new destination ideas. Backpacking around Thailand, partying on the golden beaches of Brazil, sipping red wine in Californian vineyards. "You can't do these trips as freely with a child," he always tells me, sensibly. "Becoming a family will just have to wait a little while longer." And until today, traveling the world with my true love was a sacrifice I was willing to make. But that was before I found out my true love was a liar.

With Sukhi still outside on the phone, I take the moment of solitude as an opportunity to fish my own phone out of my bag.

I'm at your office. I came with lunch. Where are you?????????????? I text Noah.

Then I reconsider, remove a handful of question marks so I seem less crazed and hit send. I sit, clutching the phone so tightly in my hands that my fingertips begin to ache.

Sukhi comes back in and spots the phone in my grip immediately. "Have you heard from him?" she asks.

I shake my head. "I texted him," I mumble.

She frowns and opens her mouth as if to say something but seems to think better of it. "I ordered an Uber. Let's get you home," she tells me, gathering up my handbag. I notice her take the sodden tissues and, tactfully, the lunch that caused all of this confusion, and toss everything into a nearby bin.

"Come on, Claire." She ushers me out, giving the receptionist a brief nod as we leave through the revolving glass doors.

I want to fling something at them, so they'll shatter alongside the illusion of the perfect, honest fiancé I thought I had. Instead, I let go of the balloon, and don't look back as it drifts away from us.

SIX

When the Uber drops me off, I stand at the front door to our Clapham flat for a few minutes, unwilling to move past the threshold. My hand rests on the flaking gray paint, ready to push as I hold the key to the lock. But then I think of the note from Noah I woke up to this morning, carefully folded into a little paper bird on my nightstand.

Have a good day, love you x

I check my phone one more time. No new notifications. Panic is rising in my chest as I imagine him injured, hurt and unable to reach me. Is that why he's not replying?

But then I remember the receptionist's expression and Mr. Donahue's pity, and all the lies hit me again. He isn't hurt. I am.

I unlock the door quickly now and run up the stairs to our front door. We have a tiny studio flat in the grubby end of Clapham North; it's the attic apartment I was renting when we met, small but only temporary while Noah does up the house in leafy Dulwich that we're supposed to move in to later this year. I couldn't afford any better and I felt it was only right that I foot the bill for our temporary accommodation if Noah is funding the entire remodel of our future home. I want to contribute however I can to our future together, though my measly PR salary doesn't offer much scope. Noah's better with money than I am, has been saving for a deposit since university, so he was quick to put it down on our dream home and use the rest on the required renovations. At the time, it felt wildly romantic, but in this exact moment I panic that I have no financial or legal entitlement to that house and, if he is lying about his job, what else is he lying about?

"Noah? Noah!" I call as I enter, my eyes scanning the flat just in case he really is injured. I imagine him lying, trapped, beneath a piece of furniture, waiting for me to find him. But there's no reply, and no overturned pieces of furniture. Everything is exactly as I left it, minus Noah.

My breakfast bowl is still sitting in the sink, a jumper is thrown over the back of a chair. The flat is empty. I clench my fists, pivot and march back downstairs and outside, toward the high street.

Once I'm out of the gray-washed residential streets, I emerge at the central hub, brighter and bustling. Clapham is always busy, even if it's midweek. Young women in leggings carry yoga mats and laugh with their friends; dog-walkers head toward the common. Yummy mummies are lunching, babies in prams beside them; a few creative-looking guys in beanies are tapping away on their laptops in coffee-shop windows. My gaze flits from person to person, searching desperately for Noah's sandy hair. I stumble into his favorite coffee shop, a small independent run by a lovely Scottish couple.

"What can we get you?" the woman asks as soon as the entry bell rings.

"I'm actually looking for my boyfriend," I explain. "He loves coming here . . ." I trail off as I realize he's not at any of the tables.

She motions toward my phone with a flap of her hands. I realize it's because Noah is my wallpaper, and I loosen my grip on the phone enough to show her.

"Noah!" She nods. "He was in all the time." She glances up at me. "We've not seen him in a while though, sorry. I'd guessed he'd moved away. Hope you track him down." She smiles.

I force myself to smile back, leaving the cafe, my hands shaking with adrenaline.

I stand on the pavement, unsure of where to go next. I pull up Noah's number and press call, but it just rings out. He hasn't had an answerphone set up since I've known him, claiming he doesn't want work clogging up his inbox with messages. A flash of irritation runs through me as I send off another quick text.

Please, Noah. I just want to understand what's happened. I'm trying to find you.

Why would he hide a new job from me? If an NDA was involved, it must be a good move, to a competitor or something. I curse myself for not understanding what he does properly, for not knowing the ins and outs of his industry better. He'd always just wave it off as "semantics" when I tried to get more of an in-depth view of what his day-to-day looked like.

Lost for where to check next, I find myself wandering around Clapham Common, the sunlight fighting its way through the clouds and the smell of freshly cut grass in the air. My feet automatically power me forward as though they can't bear for me to be still. I'd rather be doing something than sitting at home losing my mind, trying to work out why my fiancé has been lying to me for the past few months. How did we go from such a perfect evening together last night . . . to this?

As I walk around the common, I notice a fitness class going on, and I remember that Noah went to it once in the summer. Without much else to try, I head over to the class. The man leading it is ripped, shouting out words of encouragement to everyone as he demonstrates some squat jumps. Feeling awkward about interrupting, I back off a little and end up sitting on a bench, watching and waiting for the session to wrap up.

I fidget, wringing my hands and tapping my feet as a light chill nips at my cheeks. One bench down from me, a man is swigging from a can of cider, and he keeps side-eyeing me as though I'm invading his personal space. He's wearing an oversized coat, an unruly beard covering the lower half of his face. He groans and grumbles to himself audibly. I self-consciously shift myself to face away from him and he begins muttering under his breath. I feel tense, alert, ready to run at the first sign of confrontation. He's getting louder and begins rocking slightly. I don't dare look over in case it spurs him on but manage to catch a little of what he's saying.

"Crazy bitch sitting next to me . . . sitting next to me here in my space. Bitch . . . Crazy bitch."

I'm just about to get up and find another spot when the sound of clapping reaches my ears and I look up to see the group giving themselves a round of applause, the trainer high-fiving them and telling them he'll see them next week. I get up from my bench and hurry over to him, all too eager to leave the bearded man behind.

"Hey!" The trainer smiles at me as I approach. "Looking to join in next time?"

"Oh! No, no, sorry. I mean, maybe. But that's not why I'm coming over. I was just wondering if you have ever trained my boyfriend. I think he did one of your classes last summer?" I hold up my phone and he frowns at the photo of Noah on the screen.

A kernel of hope blooms in the seconds in which he doesn't reply. Is he trying to remember the exact time he last saw Noah? Or maybe—

"I'm sorry, I don't recognize him . . . definitely not one of my regulars," he eventually says.

"Oh," I reply, my shoulders sagging. "Okay, thanks anyway." I turn to walk away.

"Mad Martin's Moves, look me up on Instagram, every Tuesday at three or Saturdays at eleven!" he yells after me.

I hurry away, embarrassed. What if Noah finds out I've been asking all around the common for him like some petty, jealous girlfriend? Perhaps the bearded man was right and I'm losing my mind.

SEVEN

September 22, 2024
Dear Diary,

The weirdest thing happened today. I bumped into Wine Aisle Guy. As in, literally physically bumped into him on the street. It's so wild when this happens in London—I mean, in a city of so many people, what are the statistical odds of walking into somebody you know? Fate seems to be working its magic once again. It's as though I'm living in some sort of rom-com. I actually burst out laughing at how ridiculous the situation was, and then he did as well, which I think broke any tension there could have been between us otherwise. "Are you stalking me or something?" I joked, and he laughed.

"Something like that."

He is still the most handsome man I've ever seen. You know when you meet someone for the first time and they're so gorgeous, but then you see them the second time and they look less good? I can't really explain it any other way, but they have lost that first-meeting sparkle? Well, it wasn't like that with Noah at all. If anything, he sparkled even more. So after this chance encounter in the street, we went to a nearby coffee shop. "Because it would be rude to walk into you in the street and not offer you coffee and cake in damages and compensation," he said, ignoring the fact that I was technically the one who walked into him.

We went to a place where he seemed to know the owners well. They were Scottish and had that easy banter you get between proprietors and *regulars, and I could feel them eyeing me with interest for turning up with him. Noah told me a little more about his family, I got his number, and we've been texting a lot since then.*

He's a great listener; I can't remember the last time anyone gave me so much space to talk and breathe. I know it sounds stupid as I only met the guy the other day but I really like talking to him. He makes me feel happier. I haven't felt like this in ages, it's as though I'm just waiting for reality to come and pop my bubble. I hope things continue to go as smoothly between us as they have so far. (Though, hopefully, with fewer surprise encounters. Knowing my luck, next time I run into him I'll be dressed in my old scraggly leggings . . .)

Claire

EIGHT

Back at home I'm pacing the tiny kitchen area, the walls blurring as I scurry back and forth and back and forth like a drugged lab rat. I'm dizzy with panic. Since my failed high street hunt I've tried calling Noah seven times now, and each time the phone rings out. I glance at the bottle of his favorite white wine I bought on my way home from Clapham Common, thinking we would sit down, talk everything through. I am angry, yes, but the wine is a sign that I want to work this out and listen to his side. The bottle now taunts me from the kitchen counter.

I don't drink very often. Never alone at home. I didn't go to university, so those formative years spent getting drunk and playing messy drinking games evaded me. Occasionally I'll have a glass of wine with Noah when he's had a hard day, or at work events, but Sukhi doesn't drink much either so usually I keep her company on softies. Deep down, drinking reminds me of Mother, of cleaning vomit from the carpet and the smell of bile.

But now my fingers are itching for something to do, and I find myself twisting off the bottle cap and pouring out a large glass, taking a gulp. It goes down easily, smooth and mellow. I swig more down, closing my eyes and letting the warmth hit my belly. I feel tears welling. I take another sip.

* * *

In what seems like no time at all, I've drunk half the bottle and decide to text Noah again. My concern about coming across as neurotic is long gone together with my sobriety.

Is this why Mother always argued with the men she dated?

WHERE ARE YOU NOAH? Call me, we need to talk, wtf is going on?

I hit send, and watch my words disappear into the cellular ether. A single tick blinks at me, mockingly, indicating that my message has been sent but not received. He's switched his phone off.

Rage builds in me and I storm over to the bed, ripping the drawer out of his bedside cabinet and searching through it feverishly for clues as to where he's been going every day, all day. My drunken forage turns up nothing of interest, nothing bizarre or odd or out of place. I move to the wardrobe, rifling through everything, pockets all probed. Nothing.

An hour later and the flat is a mess. I've torn the place upside down and can find no evidence of Noah being anything other than truthful. I sink into the dining chair and take another deep gulp of wine. The last drawer in the house to go unchecked is beneath my fingertips, a small side drawer in our kitchen table. I use it every day, so I know there is nothing of Noah's in there. But still, I decide to torture myself and open it.

NINE

October 5, 2024
Dear Diary,

Noah and I are still dating. He came over last night and I attempted to cook him dinner. I would love to be the type of woman who has a signature dish, who can rely on this one singular, phenomenal taste sensation on a plate for their first time treating someone to a meal. But I'm not. I don't think I ever saw Mother cook a meal for a man, so I'll blame it on her. When she used to go out and forget to feed me, I'd make myself a meal that was basically just mashed potato with cheese and bacon bits in it. God, I forgot about that. Delicious. But sadly, serving Noah a plate of cheesy fork-stabbed mash probably wouldn't be too impressive, and I no longer have the metabolism of thirteen-year-old Claire, so I went with spaghetti Bolognese.

Big shock, Noah is a great cook and ended up helping me as I went along. Not in an annoying, patronizing way. We just fell into sync quickly after he offered to help cut up the peppers and I found him sort of cooking alongside me. It was nice. I'd bought a bottle of wine to go with it as it was a special occasion, and we had a couple of glasses. I'm not used to drinking on weekdays and ended up getting quite tipsy from just the two little glasses, then I started telling him about the girl who bullied me in secondary school. How embarrassing is that?

I hadn't thought about Laura in years, but he'd asked about what I was like at school and it was as if all these memories were released. I didn't tell him the most embarrassing parts, of course; the nickname they made up for me or the chunks of time spent hiding in a stall in the girls' toilets while Laura and her little gang threw wet balls of toilet paper at the ceiling above me. But I gave him an overview, about how school was tough thanks to one girl in particular and her band of friends.

After we'd been talking for a while we put on a film. I must have fallen asleep because when I woke up it was the middle of the night and he'd turned the TV off and thrown a blanket over me before leaving. Beside me, he'd left this note made out of scrap paper that had been lying on my coffee table—he'd somehow folded it up into a little tortoise.

It was almost too beautiful to touch, until I saw the paper had been written on and obviously I had to unfold it to read the message.

Slow and steady wins the race, as it says in "The Tortoise and the Hare." You're beautiful and Laura probably peaked at school. You're my cute little tortoise.

I laughed out loud and texted him. He said it was origami, and that next time he was over he'd show me how to re-fold it back into shape.

Tell me this: Isn't that the sweetest thing you've ever heard?!

Claire

TEN

Inside the drawer are hundreds of paper animals, swans and turtles, butterflies and squirrels. Tiny, carefully folded pieces of paper, each carrying a message for me. They're the notes that Noah leaves for me, dotted around the flat at random.

You look beautiful!

I'd found that one beneath the bathroom mirror one morning, on a small origami bird.

Happy wife, happy life!

That one had been a tiny fox, placed on top of a box of chocolates I'd returned home to one day when I was on my period, shortly after our engagement.

I love you!

An origami rabbit I'd found left on my bedside table. So many messages of affection, of kindness and caring, all kept lovingly in this drawer.

Have an amazing day!

Good luck with your work presentation—you're a star!

Popped out for a pint, home soon—can't wait to cuddle!

Date night tomorrow? x

I stare at them, trying to work out how these beautiful little relationship receipts can come from the same man who lies about going to work every day. But I can't connect the two. There must be a rational explanation for why he hid the news about his job from me.

Perhaps he was having problems at work that he didn't want to worry me about. Maybe he'd even been fired and that was why he was on gardening leave. But then why would he not just reply to my calls and texts, let me know the reason why?

With a sigh, I scoop all the notes up and out of the drawer, dumping them onto the kitchen table.

Another piece of paper in there catches my eye. It's the ad for my job, which Noah had found and printed out for me, left unsubtly on the kitchen table all those months ago. I scrunch the ad up in my hands and throw it toward the bin, not checking if it meets its target.

Peering into the drawer to check it's totally empty, I see a little figurine stuck right at the back. I reach in and carefully prize it out, realizing that something must have spilled onto it at some point, because it's all tacky and sticky to the touch. It's a lizard made out of clay, all wonky and out of shape, with cracks in the surface and bits of fluff stuck to it.

I smile and put it by the sink so I'll remember to try and get it clean again later.

I was twelve years old when I made that silly little figurine. While Mother was going through a real Frida Kahlo phase, she decided that I had "artistic flair" and found me a private art tutor. It was one of the best things she ever did for me. I adored going to this bizarre, flamboyant woman's home once a week, ogling her collections of jewels and trinkets with amazement. Her name was Katya, and she was both wondrous and inspiring to my shy, preteen self.

"What bold use of lines, Claire! Bravo!" she exclaimed one day when I took a stab at acrylic paints for the first time, swooping my brush across the canvas with a newfound confidence nurtured by her encouragement.

"You have a fantastic eye, Claire. Many other students don't have this natural skill, it's something very special," she said another time, sipping on her lemon tea with a pleased smile.

These brief words of praise I held close to my heart. They warmed me from the inside out. Katya's home felt like a magical safe haven for me, a place where I could laugh and express myself, drink tea and play grown-ups with this amazing woman who taught me more about happiness than she did about art.

We'd have tea and biscuits and she'd show me how to mix water-colors, then teach me how to set up a still-life scene using a variety of her bizarre and curious artifacts. Ammonites and quartz crystal pendants, scratched old pocket-watches and paper flowers; Katya's home was full of creativity and imagination, innovation and origi-nality. "Fruit bowls are overdone and unwelcome here," she would announce with a smoker's laugh, waving around an African mask she'd sourced from a junk shop in Notting Hill before adding it carefully to our *mise-en-scène*.

Never one for convention, Katya had a pet lizard. It was a bearded dragon called Caitlyn, and I had initially been afraid of the strange, scaly creature. But after several weeks of having Caitlyn's beady little eyes watching me from her glass tank, I eventually came to find comfort in her presence.

I'd turned up to Katya's one day to find the lizard lounging lazily on the kitchen table, a mixing bowl of flour in front of her.

"Today, Claire, we are going to be trying our hand at the art of *sculpture*," Katya announced.

I eyed Caitlyn warily, but the lizard lay there peacefully, occa-sionally blinking but all in all looking as though she had absolutely no intention of moving anywhere at all.

"It's like mixing up a magical potion—all you need is a little salted flour and water . . . and poof!" Katya liberally splashed some water into the mixing bowl at that point. "Homemade clay!"

I watched in fascination as the flour turned into a sticky then smooth clay, which Katya kneaded on the table with quick, expert hands beside the very unimpressed lizard.

"I don't know what to make," I told her when she dropped a ball in front of me, several little picks and instruments laid out for me to use.

"Well, Caitlyn's not here on vacation, Claire! She's here to be your model and muse! Every sculptor needs a good muse, after all," she told me with a smile.

And so we spent that afternoon sitting at her kitchen table, rolling and kneading and poking and prodding at our clay until I had a very lumpy-looking rendition of a lizard, which Katya praised to the skies. Her sculpture, on the other hand, looked like something that a museum might display in the reptile section, though she assured me that mine was "an astounding use of technique for a first try."

The next week I returned to my Caitlyn sculpture, by then fully dried and ready to paint. I'd gone for bright pink with yellow spots and spikes, which Katya assured me was an "inspired decision." We laughed together, music playing, and she taught me how to stipple with a brush for texture, and to paint tiny scales using the edge of a brush for a realistic effect. It was wonderful.

The following week was the last time I saw Katya. Mother had driven me there as usual, but when we knocked on the door, there was no response. I stiffened, immediately concerned. Katya was always home. Mother sighed impatiently, knocking on the door several more times before tapping her toe histrionically.

"Let's wait in the car," she eventually suggested. The air around us had turned cold and brittle. Katya's car was not in the drive.

Five agonizingly slow minutes passed before we heard the crunch of tires on gravel and Katya's car turned in to her driveway. She had her window rolled down. Mother lowered hers to match.

"I'm so, so sorry! I was caught in traffic and—"

"You have wasted my time," Mother interrupted, her face dark with anger. "How dare you not be here on time for us when we are paying good money? You've let my daughter down!"

"I'm sorry, it won't happen again . . . the roads were so icy."

"Too right it won't happen again. We won't be coming back, you can be sure of that!" Mother shouted, spittle flying from her mouth as she rolled up her window and pulled away from Katya's house.

I turned to look back at Katya, clutching my painted lizard in my hands as we drove away from the one house where I'd felt at home.

I never did learn how to glaze my sculpture.

ELEVEN

realize I've thrown my phone across the room, where it now lies on the floor, mocking me. I stare back at it, thankful it hasn't cracked, urging it to ring, to vibrate with explanations from Noah. We will look back on this misunderstanding and laugh. We have to.

Suddenly, as though I've manifested it, my phone buzzes. I lunge myself across the room at an impossible speed, only to let out a frustrated huff of disappointment. It's Sukhi.

Have you heard from him? Can I call?

No. To both—I'm sorry, struggling a bit and not in the mood to speak, I fire back. I realize I haven't spent much time outside of work with Sukhi and feel a little overwhelmed by her reaching out so soon after my embarrassing debacle.

I stare at the screen and watch three dots appearing, and then disappearing, several times. She's obviously unsure how to reply. Can't say I blame her. What do you say to a woman who has found out that her fiancé has gone missing and doesn't work in the job she thought?

Eventually, a new message appears.

I found him on social media. I know where he works, Claire.

I press "Call Sukhi" immediately, and she answers halfway through the first ring.

"He doesn't have social media," I tell her.

It's narcissistic, don't you think? he had said to me when we first met. And I had agreed, embarrassed to admit I still had an old Facebook account active, which I used every now and again to see what old classmates were up to.

"Noah Coors, investment banker. He does, he's on Facebook, and I recognize him from the photo you have as your phone wallpaper," Sukhi tells me, her voice breathless and hurried.

"Hold on," I say, rummaging through my bag for my laptop. I hurriedly pull up Facebook, typing in Noah Coors. Three results. One is a young, spotty teenager, the other two are in America.

"I'm not seeing him," I say, trying to keep the irritation out of my voice.

"Look, I'm coming over now. Fateh's out watching football and I'm sitting here with things you need to see. I'll be half an hour," Sukhi tells me. Before I have a chance to respond, she's hung up. She must have my address from ordering me an Uber, because I've certainly never invited anyone from work over before. Usually I would panic, try to scrub every skirting board and tidy everything away into its "right place" before a guest arrived, but instead I slump down on the floor against the wall.

I pick up a pale yellow sofa cushion and hold it to my face. Then I smother myself with it and scream into its cotton surface. I shout like a feral thing until my throat is raw and stings. I remember the last time I behaved like this, then shake the memory away. I can't think of Mother now, my focus needs to be Noah.

The bell rings twenty minutes later and I stumble down the internal stairs and fumble to unlatch the door, pulling it open to reveal Sukhi. Her dark hair is scraped back into a ponytail, which somehow makes her green eyes look even bigger as they scan over me in concern. She throws herself around me in a hug and I stiffen in surprise.

Then she herds me back into the flat, her mouth set in a thin line of determination, a laptop peeking out of her tote bag.

She glances at my forlorn tear-soaked cushion when I let her in but doesn't comment.

"You live in a studio flat?" she asks, unable to keep the surprise from her voice.

"We have a renovation project in Dulwich, this is temporary," I explain, my voice coming out strangely monotone.

She makes an understanding noise and strides in as though she owns the place, ignoring the fact that I have quite clearly been throwing all my belongings around.

"Let me just . . . sorry, I had a bit of a tantrum . . ." I trail off lamely as I sweep all the love notes out of the way, clearing space for Sukhi to set her computer on the small, chipped table.

"It's not having a tantrum, Claire. You're just reacting to a stressful situation in the way that feels right for you. This is your home. If there's anywhere suitable for getting messy, it's the privacy of your own house."

I flush, touched by her kindness but equally embarrassed. "There was, at least, method to the madness. I was looking for clues," I admit, gesturing at the massacre of paper animals on the table.

"So I haven't been the only one playing detective," she says gently, a small smile on her lips.

"You're the only one who actually found something though," I tell her, sinking down in the chair beside her.

"Having a big family makes you good at online snooping," she tells me.

The laptop makes a busy whirring sound as it starts up, and I wonder if I should be offering her something to drink.

It feels strange, having someone else in my home. It's usually just Noah and me. I sit beside her, my eyes widening as she clicks on Noah Coors's Facebook page. And there he is. My beautiful, lying fiancé.

Pulling my phone up, I show her my own search results.

"He must have blocked you, so you couldn't find him," she tells me quietly, avoiding eye contact.

I don't respond. I'm mortified and can feel a red heat crawl up my face and down to my chest.

"I'm so sorry, Claire," she tells me.

I shake my head. "You have nothing to say sorry for," I say, and am shocked by the iciness of my tone. I've been blocked by my own fiancé.

"Do you want me to show you what I found?" she asks.

Part of me wants to say no, no, *no,* and return to my make-believe life with my honest, hardworking partner. Instead, I nod meekly.

She scrolls down and turns the laptop to face me. A post from February about Noah leaving Pulitzer Haas and starting his new job. He is now, according to this profile, working at Alliance & Gordon as investment director. Congratulations messages flood the comments section from friends I've never even heard of. My mouth is dry and I pick at my thumbnails until the skin around them stings.

"Are you okay, Claire?" Sukhi asks, placing a tentative hand on my back.

I want to shout at her that no, frankly, I'm not fucking okay.

Instead I snatch the laptop from her and begin scrolling down farther and farther, frantic for information.

I click on photos. There is Noah, partying with strangers in a bar I've never been to. Noah laughing, giving the finger to someone who has snapped a shot of him during a gym workout. Noah sitting in a room I don't recognize and watching a football game, his feet up on a stool and arm slung across the back of the sofa; a portrayal of total familiarity and ease with the surroundings that I, his future wife, have never seen before. On and on I scroll, gorging myself greedily on these photographs of his hidden double life while my brain screams in protest.

My blood runs cold as I pause at a photograph of him with his arm wrapped around a lithe blonde with dimples. I try to swallow, but it gets stuck in my throat. It's a photo he himself uploaded, and she's not tagged. Her skin is lightly golden, her straight hair thick and shiny, a gorgeous shade of honey blond that starlets would pay thousands for. Big blue doe eyes are rimmed with brown kohl, which emphasizes the darkness of her wispy, fluttering eyelashes. A pixie ski-jump nose, full rosebud lips and long, toned limbs complete the picture. Her arms are wrapped around Noah, one perfectly manicured hand resting on his waist.

I jump as Sukhi snaps the laptop shut. "Claire, don't torture yourself. Just wait until you've spoken to him. Looking at things like that will only make you reach the worst conclusions."

"What conclusions? Do you mean: Here is my boyfriend with his arm around a gorgeous blonde, while he's working a job he didn't tell me he had?" I force out, trying to ignore the tremor in my voice as the enormity of what I've seen begins to bear down on me.

"I mean, yes . . . but it might all have a reasonable explanation or not be as bad as it looks," Sukhi says.

I blink slowly, wanting so much to believe her. But I don't have to say it; we both know she's being over-optimistic about my situation.

"I brought wine," she announces, reaching into her bag.

"I don't really drink," I tell her, hoping she can't smell on my breath the wine I've already had.

"We don't have to drink it. I didn't want to turn up empty-handed and wasn't sure what else to bring that was appropriate," Sukhi admits.

"Do you think it will make me feel better?" I ask her.

She puts her hand down on top of mine and looks at me, properly. I fight every part of my body that wants to turn away, to stop her seeing the ugliness in me.

"No, I don't think it will make you feel better. I don't think it will fix anything. I don't think much other than your fiancé walking through the door right now will do that."

I swallow hard. "Would you like a glass with me?" I ask.

"Sure," she replies.

I head over to get two glasses from the cabinet and shakily pour the wine. I blink away flashbacks of Mother pouring herself mammoth-size glasses of wine before a night out.

This is different. I am in control. I am with a friend. And I am desperate to dull the ache of my situation.

"If ever there's a reason for having a drink and a friend round, it's probably now with Noah missing," Sukhi says, echoing my own thoughts.

I warm briefly at her use of the word *friend,* but my brain quickly spasms back round to the words *Noah missing* instead.

TWELVE

had a good friend once. Her name was Georgia and we were eight. She was an equally shy little girl and after a handful of summer lunchtimes spent hiding in the crafting room, our hour soundtracked by the screaming laughter and taunts of everybody else playing Tag outside, she spoke to me.

"You don't want to play Tag with the others?" she asked in a soft, whispery voice with a gentle lisp.

I looked through the window to the stretched smiles, the frantic chases and panting chests. I shook my head in response. "No."

"I'd like to play," she admitted. The first secret a schoolmate had shared with me.

"Why don't you?" I asked, curiosity overriding my usual shyness.

In response, she stuck her left leg out from beneath the table and lifted up her purple cotton trousers. My eyes widened. "Robot," I breathed.

She burst into delighted giggles and I recoiled immediately. She was laughing at me, making fun of me. I threw my hands over my face to hide my embarrassment, to hide myself. To my utter fascination, she leaned forward and her grubby paint-covered hands gently peeled mine off my face. "Don't be afraid. I'm not a robot, it's just a metal plate, see?" She tapped it with the end of her paintbrush. "I was born with a bad leg, but they're fixing it. For now, I can't run. I probably can't play Tag for a while yet," she told me.

"Oh," I replied lamely, unsure what else to say or how this entire interaction was making me feel.

At the end of that lunch break, she gave me her painting. It was a cat, labeled *TaBbY xxxxxx,* who she informed me was her cat, though he had run away. "If you see a cat that looks like that," she told me seriously, pointing at it with a jab of her finger, "pick him up and keep him, because he should come home. I miss him."

I had hurriedly crushed the picture into my bag, feeling oddly sheepish at having been gifted something so precious. Not just the painting, but her trust in my ability to help find and return the much-loved pet.

When I got home, I flattened Georgia's painting out on my bed, smoothing it carefully with my hands before hiding it at the bottom of one of my drawers. I still have that painting, in a shoebox under my bed. I don't think of her often, but I do think of that sunny afternoon.

My memories of her after that are painful ones. We were friends for a while, in the broadest sense of the word. Quiet lunches spent exchanging pictures while I listened to her stories, her secrets. Then one day: "Mummy said this morning that you can come over for tea after school, if you like," she said to me, casually, as though it was a frequent occurrence to be invited to someone else's home. "She said she can make pizza and chips," Georgia added with gusto.

"Pizza and chips?" I repeated warily.

"Pizza and chips," she confirmed solemnly with a nod. "You just need to ask the teacher if you can use the phone to get permission from your mummy. And get her to collect you from my house at seven?"

"I'll ask," I told her.

Of course, I had no intention of asking, of tainting my first outing with a friend with Mother's hysteria. Any outing I took had to be arranged at least two weeks in advance. She wouldn't have let me go any sooner, would have punished me for daring to ask, saying it wasn't part of our weekly routine . . . it was too last-minute . . . she would need time to scope out Georgia's family. But I didn't want to wait. I wanted to go and have pizza and chips immediately.

The way I saw it, I had three options: don't go, and lose the only friend I had; go, and be punished later; ask Mother, don't go and still be punished. To my eight-year-old brain, the choice was easy. And so I lied and told Georgia that Mother said it was fine, that I had borrowed the school phone to ask her. Georgia beamed and twined her arm through mine and chatted the whole way back to class about the games we could play together, the toys she was going to show me. I was so excited.

As home time crept closer, I started to feel extremely anxious. What if Mother arrived before Georgia's mummy? (She wouldn't, Mother was always late.) But then I started having other thoughts. What if Georgia's mummy adopted me? What if Georgia asked me to be her Best-Best Friend? I stood by the reception area holding clammy hands with Georgia, who proudly told the teacher on Going Home Duty: "Claire is coming over for tea tonight."

The teacher beamed at me as though I had won an Olympic medal. "That's lovely news! So nice to see you getting along with a friend," she said, turning to me. I blushed.

When Georgia's mummy arrived, she was not what I had expected. I had envisioned an angel, a sort of glowing savior who was going to whisk me away from my tragic life. In fact, she was the epitome of normal—a tired-looking lady with her hair in a messy bun atop her head, a puffy jacket trimmed with fur on the hood and trainers that my own mother would have called tatty. But she smiled warmly at me and told me, "You can call me Kate, love," and that little word of endearment was all I needed to warm to her.

"Sorry for such a last-minute invite. Georgia's cousin was coming over but she's feeling poorly and I didn't want the food to go to waste. I hope your mum didn't mind?" she asked me.

"No," I lied.

She held on to Georgia's hand, who held on to mine, and the

three of us walked the short distance to their house in this novel chain formation. Georgia chatted about our day at school and I marveled as Kate asked questions, engaging with her daughter and entertaining her in a way Mother never did with me. "And what about you, Claire? What was your favorite part of the day?" Kate asked me.

I chewed my lip, afraid of getting the answer wrong.

"Her favorite is English," Georgia supplied for me. "She has the best handwriting in the class and likes to read stories!"

"Well! That's lovely," said Kate. "Maybe you can teach Georgia to enjoy reading some stories rather than sitting in front of the telly all day!" But then she winked at her daughter, who giggled bashfully.

My cheeks turned pink and I looked to the ground quickly. Kate and Georgia were already off on another topic of conversation.

Georgia's house was a terraced home, the top floor with two bedrooms. We didn't go into Kate's room ("It's Mummy's private space," Georgia informed me seriously), but I had been so enraptured by Georgia's nest that I'd forgotten there was more of the house to see. Her room was painted purple, unicorn decal stickers plastered on the walls with reckless abandon so it looked as though they danced around us. She had a CD player, which seemed very grown-up, and a big desk for coloring in and homework. Her bed was laden with cuddly toys, and we ended up stringing some blankets into a makeshift fort. In the midst of a complicated and dramatic soap opera in which a stuffed teddy had cheated on a dolly with a toy giraffe, we were called down to tea.

Kate was bustling around, tidying bits away and sipping a cup of tea while Georgia and I discussed how the dolly would get revenge, when the doorbell rang. It wasn't a normal ring though: it was a frantic mash of the button, a continuous drilling sound accompanied by loud banging on the door. "Well! Someone's eager to see us," Kate joked, though her eyebrows were raised in annoyance. "Cor blimey, better find out who that is," she said, turning off the tap and wiping her hands on her jeans as she went through to the hallway.

I had fallen still, pizza half raised to my mouth.

"What's wrong?" Georgia whispered.

Mother's shrill voice reached me moments later. "You've *kid-napped* my daughter!" she shrieked.

"Now, now, wait a minute," I heard Kate say, her voice laced with authority.

"Let me *in,* before I call the police and have you arrested for kid-napping!"

I glanced at Georgia. Both of us were wide-eyed with fear.

"Calm down, calm down. Look, there's clearly been a misunder-standing. I told Georgia to invite Claire round for tea and thought you'd said yes—"

"I don't even know who the hell you are!" There was the sound of a small scuffle as Mother barged her way in, and I could hear her shoes clipping toward the kitchen. Georgia had dropped her cutlery and was standing by the table now while I sat there, still frozen.

"Claire! Claire, darling? *CLAIRE!*" Mother was sticking her head into every room and Kate had gone silent. When Mother ap-peared, she stopped short at the kitchen doorway, eyes quickly scan-ning the scene and taking it all in.

"Claire," she said quietly, eyes narrowing, "get your coat. We are going home. Right now."

I went to stand, pushing my chair out. I opened my mouth to apologize to Georgia, to Kate, but no sound came out.

"But we haven't finished our tea yet," Georgia argued, looking up at Mother.

I braced myself. Mother turned in slow motion, gaze ranging over Georgia slowly: her stained school shirt untucked from a creased skirt, her bare feet with chipped pink-painted toenails.

"*Excuse* me?" Mother's voice was quiet. She looked so tall beside Georgia, towering in her heels.

Kate moved to stand in front of her daughter. "The girls haven't finished their tea yet. Look, this is a misunderstanding. Let's just have a cuppa and a chat while they finish up and then Claire can go home. Gives you a night off making her supper," Kate tried again, desperation in her voice.

Mother turned to her with a sneer. "You call carbohydrates and frozen pizza *supper*?"

Kate blinked at her, fists clenched, and even as a child I could tell she was biting her tongue because Georgia and I were present.

"Claire, darling, get your things right now! We're leaving. I don't want you spending another moment in such squalor with this random woman and her poorly mannered cripple child," she added, throwing a significant glance at Georgia, who blanched.

"How dare you?" Kate exploded, a mother lioness rearing up to protect her cub. But Kate's claws were no match for Mother's, and I hurried up to Georgia's room and grabbed my coat and book bag while they exchanged heated words, Kate's furious and protective, Mother's cutting and cruel.

She marched me out of that house, with one hand gripping the back of my neck like a pincer, telling me how she had arrived at the school to find I wasn't there, how she had been terrified she had lost me, how they had told her I was at somebody else's house, and how I was a little liar—a dirty, filthy liar—just like my long-gone father, and that house and that woman were disgusting, and I would never, ever be allowed to play at a friend's house again . . . On and on and on she went, the whole way home, tainting what should have been one of my best days ever.

When I got back I realized she had raided my room, ripped up the pictures and notes Georgia had given me. All except for the one of the tabby cat, safely nestled away in my drawer. "You don't *need* any other friends, Claire. Nobody will ever understand you like I do. Nobody will ever love you unconditionally like I do. These so-called *friends* you meet at school will only tear you down in the end, whereas I will always be there for you. You will always have me, Claire, darling," she said in a falsely apologetic tone as she shoved my ripped-up treasures in the bin.

The next day at lunchtime I sat down at my usual table and Georgia glared at me, swiftly moving to sit elsewhere. She never spoke to me again after that.

But I did have a friend, once.

THIRTEEN

So now what?" Sukhi asks. We're in front of the television and the wine bottle is empty. Outside it is dark. Noah would usually be home by now, even if he had a late meeting. My brain already hurts, my eyes are blurred. I hate feeling I'm not in control of my own body. My reaction times are slow as I try to make sense of the scene we're watching.

I didn't ever drink as a teenager. Mornings spent holding back Mother's hair while she expelled bile into our toilet were more than enough to put me off binging. I would hold her hair for her, watching as she wiped her lipstick-smeared chin with her arm, spittle and vomit leaving a glistening snail trail across them. Eventually she would bat me away, and I would leave her to hobble into her darkened room from which she would not emerge until the afternoon.

On days like this she would waltz out as though the morning had never happened, exclaiming how well rested she felt and how desperately she had needed that luxurious lie-in. Most of the time, she'd end up going out again in the evening, and the cycle would repeat itself three or four days in a row until she would do a complete one-eighty, spending two weeks drinking nothing but overpriced diet juices and flirting with personal trainers at the gym. I only really drank water for most of my youth. "Fizzies rot your teeth," Mother would say disapprovingly whenever someone passed us, slurping out of a can.

"Full of sugar," I'd agree, while wondering what that bubbly candy-drink in a shiny red can might taste of.

Sukhi has put on some reality TV show. Despite staring at the screen, I haven't been watching it. I can't stop thinking about the fact that she's sitting in Noah's usual spot, that it's her body in place of his in my home. I shift uncomfortably, my eyes darting to the TV, and sigh.

"Still no response?" she asks, even though she knows he hasn't responded because my phone is on loud and has been lying between us, face-up, this entire night.

"No."

"Right."

"What would you do? If this were you?" I ask. I hear the slurring in my voice.

"Rip his balls off," she says with a small smile.

"What if he didn't turn up for you to rip his balls off?"

"Then I guess I'd probably go crazy trying to track him down," she admits.

"Sukhi! You're a genius." I scramble off the sofa and grab the laptop, returning to slump beside her with it balanced on my knees as I begin typing into Google.

Noah Coors, Alliance & Gordon

"I'll make us some fruit tea," Sukhi offers, heading for the kitchenette. I barely notice her slip past me as I scan through the results, reading an article from some boring economics website about Noah's new role and what it means for the company structure. There's nothing of any use at all here.

I head to the Alliance & Gordon website and quickly find his face on the investments personnel page, alongside his colleagues. I write out an email, directing it to his new work address.

"I don't think it's right to check work emails in the evenings," he told me once over dinner. It felt like a jab at me because I had been glancing at my phone. I immediately tucked it away in my pocket and gave a rueful smile.

"You don't have your work emails on your phone?" I asked.

"I do, but it's logged out unless I'm waiting for something in particular, otherwise I'd be unable to switch off and enjoy things like dinner with my girlfriend." He smiled at me teasingly.

At the time, I'd thought it was sweet, and made a mental log to check my phone less often when I was with him. Now, I'm irked by the fact there's yet another obstacle stopping me from contacting him.

At least I know for a fact that tomorrow morning at the latest, he'll read it. Assuming he still works there.

Noah, please call me as soon as you can. I need to know where you are. Worried sick. Please turn your phone on, or at least let me know where you're staying while we work all this out. I want to understand what's going on. Please. Claire.

No kisses, no exclamation marks. Trying to keep it calm and dignified. I hear footsteps and jolt out of my seat, eyes wide with anticipation, but it's just Sukhi returning with two steaming cups in her hands. I'd almost forgotten she was here, and the realization makes me glad that the wine is finished. I don't enjoy this hazy drunken feeling, where I'm sloppy and slow and unaware of who is in my home.

I force a smile. "Thanks."

"Any updates?"

"No. I've sent an email to his new work address but so far I've found nothing personal. Does he have any other social media?" If he's blocked me from Facebook, perhaps I'm blocked on everything else.

"I checked Instagram, but couldn't find anything, just Facebook," Sukhi says.

I type Noah Coors London into Google this time and am rewarded by the same investment websites and his secret Facebook page. My heart jumps when I find a Twitter account, but once I click onto it I realize it hasn't been updated since 2013. A long-haired, skinnier version of Noah in the profile photo is one I barely recognize, though the quirky smile is still there.

COME ON ARSENAL!!!!! was the last thing he posted. Memories of weekends spent in crowded pubs together hit me: Noah cheering and whooping for Arsenal; me sipping my wine slowly, trying not to jump in shock every time the room erupted into sudden roars and chants. I had never been interested in football, and only really went along to spend more time with Noah. I had loved watching him, so animated and passionate, eyes glued to the screen. Now I roll my eyes and close the window in frustration.

"What if we try calling him from your phone?" I ask, sitting up suddenly. "Maybe he'll pick up if the number isn't mine?"

"Oh! Good idea. Can't believe I didn't think of that," Sukhi admits.

I read out Noah's number and she types it in, setting it to loud-speaker mode.

I hold my breath as it rings and rings and rings.

"Noah Coors," comes his voice, short and abrupt.

Sukhi and I exchange glances, and I'm jumping up and down on the spot urging her to speak with manic silent encouragement.

"Er, yes, hello, Noah, my name is Sukhi—"

"How can I help you, Sukhi?" he cuts her off quickly, and I frown. It's unusual for him to be so blunt. This is a version of him that I don't recognize.

"I work with your fiancée, Claire."

There's a half-second pause before a dial tone kicks in. He's hung up.

We stare at each other for a moment in silent disbelief.

"He fucking hung up?" she says, her voice rising in anger.

I shrink back as she hits redial. It goes straight to voicemail.

"Bastard," she says.

"He's probably turned his phone off," I say quietly, stating the obvious to avoid having to address my emotions.

"God, Claire, I'm sorry but your fiancé is a dick. Who the fuck does he think he is, disappearing into his lies and then hanging up on us?"

"And why won't he take my calls? And why hasn't he come home tonight?" I add, taking another long sip from my tea.

"Or told you where he's staying," she mutters.

"Or who with," I say, my voice breaking.

There's a short pause while my last comment sinks in.

"Right, here's what's going to happen," Sukhi announces, rushing over to my kitchen cabinet and revealing an old box of chocolate biscuits I forgot I had. "We are going to put on *The Other Woman* and have our sleepy tea and biscuits in the company of Cameron Diaz at her man-hating best. Then you are going to pass out from tiredness in your bed so you don't have to stay up all night worrying about whether your shitty boyfriend turns up tonight or not. Tomorrow you will have such a terrible hangover that your physical health will override all your emotional distress and mentally you will be better equipped to handle the situation. Though hopefully the biscuits will help with any future hangovers. Ready?" she says, standing over me and brandishing the television remote and the packet of chocolate digestives with an authority I can't dispute.

"Ready, I suppose," I agree.

I don't know when I fall asleep, but it comes quickly and painlessly. I awake in the middle of the night to find that Sukhi has draped a blanket over me before leaving. I stumble into the bedroom where I pass out once more.

FOURTEEN

I wake in the morning, my mouth dry and my eyes puffy and sore. My lips are chapped, flaky bits of skin catching as I run my tongue across them. Sunlight streams in where the curtains went undrawn last night. I feel broken in every possible way. The emptiness of the bed beside me is an unwelcome reminder.

I am alone. Noah didn't come home. *Is this really the end of us?* I want to cry, and wait a beat for tears to come, but it seems I am drained now.

With great difficulty, I heave myself out of the oversized bed and bring a hand to my temple, which I briefly massage. The throbbing in my head is a result of the wine, the wine a medicine for the heartache.

When I enter the living area, I see that Sukhi cleared up most of the mess last night before she went. She has left a note on the table.

Call if you need me x

It's scribbled in a scratchy biro, rushed, a looped and slanted script scrawled onto the receipt from the wine she brought last night.

I stare at it for a long time before adding it to the drawer alongside all of the love notes from Noah. A scrap of authenticity amidst a cluster of lies.

My phone flashes. It's only Sukhi.

Hope you're okay this a.m. I'll cover you in the Tavistock meeting today.

It takes me a heartbeat to realize that it's Wednesday and I'm supposed to be at work. "Shit," I mumble.

Thanks. I need to call the office, I text her back.

I'm pouring a much-needed coffee into a mug when my phone rings and I rush to it, a wild scramble to hit "Accept Call," hoping and praying that it's Noah with some sort of explanation, an apology, to tell me he's coming home.

"Noah!" I exclaim down the phone as soon as I've hit answer.

"No, sorry, Claire, it's David."

My heart sinks. My boss. Right. "Oh," I reply.

"Sukhi has given me the top line on your situation and I wanted to call and let you know you're not expected to come in to work today, and I've set you up with some leave . . . if you want it. I just wanted to call and confirm that you're happy with this? If you are, we can chat again in a fortnight." David pauses and I still can't speak, my mind scrambling to catch up.

"You're not obligated to take it, of course," he continues. "But you have plenty of holiday to use up before the year is out and I thought it might be a good time to focus on yourself, rather than having work as an added stress?" His voice lilts interrogatively but we both know refusal is not really an option I can afford right now. Especially as I can barely speak to him without my head ringing from my hangover. And he's right—I've not taken annual leave since starting. I must have quite a backlog. What better time than when I find out my perfect life is a lie and that I need to learn how to become an investigator so I can trace my missing fiancé?

"Thank you, David. I'll take it," I manage to choke out.

"All right then, Claire. You take care now," he tells me, and the sympathy in his voice makes me want to cry.

Spoke to David, hope that's okay. Just said you were having some issues at home, no details. Sorry if I overstepped! From Sukhi.

No, it's fine, don't worry. I appreciate it, I didn't even think to call in, head is scrambled.

I bet. Hope you're not as hungover as me. Probably going to vomit on

Mark when he does his weekly budget spend presentation. This is why I don't drink!

I almost smile, setting my phone down. Part of me is mortified that David is now involved in my messy love-life drama, but part of me *is* relieved that I can take this time off to focus on what's important. With a jolt I realize once more, it's *midweek*. Noah must be at work.

With shaking hands, I look up the number for Gordon & Alliance Investments Team and press call.

"Gordon and Alliance, how may I help you?" a bored female voice answers.

"Hello, yes, I'm calling for Noah Coors, investment director, please?"

"May I ask who is calling?"

"His fiancée," I reply.

A short pause. "Let me dial up," she tells me, before an infuriating form of elevator music begins to play. I feel my fingers tighten in annoyance on the phone but am jolted out of my mental tantrum when she returns.

"I'm sorry, I'm unable to transfer you," she says. Her voice has gone cold and clipped.

I hold in a bellow of frustration. "I am his *fiancée* and I want to be transferred to him. It's important," I repeat through gritted teeth.

"His *fiancée* should have his direct dial and not have to call the front desk," she replies venomously.

"Look, I'm sorry, I'm upset. He didn't come home last night. God knows why. He didn't get in touch at all. And I don't have his direct dial because I didn't know he worked with you until twenty-four hours ago!" My voice breaks at the end of this and I hear a shocked inhalation of breath down the line. "Please," I try, my voice quieter, "I just want to make sure he's okay. Please."

Another short pause. "I cannot transfer you through to him today. I'm sorry, I really am. Can I help you with anything else?"

"But he *is* in? He's working in the office today?"

This time the pause is palpable, dragging out painfully. "I'm not at liberty to share that information with you."

I suck in a deep breath, think better of it and cut the call before I tell her exactly where she can shove her information.

I look down at my phone, shocked at my own anger, at my outburst.

I am wild and volatile, unable to control my emotions . . . I close my eyes and hold my breath as I slowly count to ten before opening them and exhaling. I am not this person. *I am not my mother.* I must stay calm, regain control. I must find Noah and work out what's happening. I'm so exhausted by being everyone's obedient little puppet. I'm sick of being Claire, darling. Mother was always in control of everything, I was constantly tiptoeing around her unpredictable outbursts. And, on reflection, Noah has always been in control as well. It was Noah who courted me. And Noah who has left me. Why am I always allowing people to do what they want? To hurt me. To toss me aside? To be in control of what I feel and who I am?

My heart is hammering in my chest and my fists are clenched, but it's not from anger anymore. It's determination. I am going to get to the bottom of this. I am going to get my fiancé back.

The Alliance & Gordon headquarters are, if anything, more impressive than Pulitzer Haas. They're in a different part of the City, toward Canary Wharf, which is an area I've rarely been to. I've also never had a reason before now to catch the DLR and I find myself amazed by the views of the Docklands financial district. I imagine I'm Katniss looking out at the Capitol in *The Hunger Games*—it's unlike any other part of London I've seen. All the buildings are sky-high, built from toughened glass and steel, and the rail line runs between them on a raised track so it feels like we're flying. Graceful suspension bridges and arches criss-cross between buildings. It feels like I have fallen into a futuristic, dystopian film.

Noah's new office is one of the many tall, looming structures faced with fancy mirrored panels. As before, doormen guard the

entry but I am not going to have a repetition of last time. I won't be
trying to get in this way; the gatekeeper will only turn me away
again. Fool me once, shame on you. Fool me twice, shame on me.
Instead, I go around the side of the building, where I can get a good
view of the front door but someone stepping outside would have to
crane around to spot me. There isn't a bench or anything, so I lean
back against a wall and wait. I check my watch—it's 11:30 A.M. I'm
not sure when he'll take his lunch, and I admit this is a gamble. He
could have meetings all day, or the building might have a canteen.
But I know Noah. I know he can't survive without a hit of coffee at
least three times a day, and free office filter coffee won't cut it. If he
doesn't leave for lunch, he'll leave for an artisan coffee.

Unless he has an assistant to do that for him now?

I chew on my lip. There are so many variables here, this could be
such a colossal waste of my time. But it feels better to be out doing
something rather than sitting at home, waiting for him to call. So I
wait.

And wait.

And wait.

And finally, *finally,* I see him step out. He's frowning at his phone,
and to my astonishment, he looks perfect. He's not disheveled, tired,
red-eyed, puffy-faced like I am. Instead, he looks fantastic, striding
along without a care in the world. Seeing him so content despite
knowing that I have been waiting at home for him, upset and confused, sends a bolt of outrage through me. I find myself imagining
that I am Sukhi, storming toward him with clenched fists and un-
leashing my indignation without a care for how it makes me look.
But I'm Claire, and I do care. I march determinedly over to him and
try to keep my face calm, even though my insides are quaking furiously in anticipation of conflict.

"Noah," I call, trying to sound casual. Several heads turn in my
direction, but the only one I care about is his. His eyes widen and he
steps back, arms raised in alarm.

"Noah, where were you last night? What's going on?" I ask, my voice low in an attempt not to call attention to us.

He's walking backward now, eyes darting from side to side.

"You need to go home," he tells me, his voice pleading.

"Home? You mean, the home you didn't return to last night?" Several people are listening now, their heads tilted curiously toward us, and I find myself wanting to give up and run away. But I don't. I watch as Noah's face turns pale.

"Stop waiting for me and stop fucking calling me!" he tells me.

I freeze, my chest tightening at the shock of being cursed at by him. "What?"

"Go home and just drop this," he says to me. His voice is low, he's obviously embarrassed by our audience, but beneath the pleading tone there's a hint of . . . anger. And the idea that *he* could dare be the one who is angry in this scenario snaps something within me, my control of myself and any fear of embarrassment torn away with it.

"*You're* angry at *me*?" I say, dumbfounded. "What have *I* done?" I am getting louder. "Oh, am I *embarrassing* you?" I say, hearing Mother's mocking tone in my voice, and Noah flinches. He's still walking backward.

"Go home and stop waiting for me," he finally hisses, before he turns and *runs,* like an actual child, away from me and back into his office. I go to follow him, but don't get very far. Both doormen are frowning at me and have stepped in front of the entry, blocking my way.

"Ma'am, we are going to have to ask you to leave. You are not allowed inside these premises."

"Noah!" I roar, holding out both arms and spinning away from them, seeing stars in front of my eyes as anger almost suffocates me.

Beside me, some teenagers are laughing, watching me. I think of Mother, of Sukhi, of their fierce bravery, and throw up my middle finger. They laugh even harder.

* * *

I am shaking the entire journey home, but one thought calms me. This is not over because I have walked away with new, confirmed information:

1. Noah works at Alliance & Gordon, and the Facebook page we found is definitely his.
2. Noah knows he has been caught out in his lies, and is afraid of something. Afraid of me finding out something else?
3. I am not able to confront him properly at his workplace and need to find a new way of speaking with him in person.
4. Noah seems to be trying to leave me, permanently. And before I uncovered all of these lies, everything was fine. So whatever it is he is trying to hide, it's big enough to leave me for. And I'm going to find out what it is.

FIFTEEN

October 30, 2024
Dear Diary,

*I'm not sure whether I've ever received a proper big bouquet of flowers
before, but I DEFINITELY have never received Hallowe'en flowers.
I didn't even realize it was a thing, but Noah continues to surprise me.*

*He sent them to my office, and they arrived first thing in the
morning. Big black and white roses with little orange pipe cleaner
spirals and black glittered paper bats in between. They were ridiculous
and over-the-top and I loved them.*

With them was a little note: Sorry about last night. And sorry we
can't dress up together. Next year!

*We've been spending more and more time together and I'd floated
the idea of us going to a Hallowe'en party dressed as Mario and Luigi.
I thought it would be so funny. But he's away all weekend for some
business trip apparently.*

*He's away quite a lot, which is annoying as we haven't been able to
spend much weekend time together. Mostly just the evenings after work.*

*And sometimes not even then, because he works so late. I don't really
understand his job properly. He tries to explain it but my eyes glaze
over and I can feel that none of what he's saying is sticking because it's
just full of figures and numbers and complicated phrases like
"investment portfolio" and "high-stake low-risk" and "top-line budget
versus net profit," which literally mean nothing to me. I just know that*

it's very full on, and that he sometimes needs to travel or work late nights.

"It's like being a lawyer, Claire. It's just one of the downsides to a shitty City job that pays really well."

I'd understood, but still felt rejected by his refusal even to consider going to a party with me. We'd ended up having a bit of an argument about it, and afterward I'd felt incredibly needy. I'd never considered myself a high-maintenance girl, but perhaps I require a little more quality time together and memory-building than I'd initially thought. Perhaps Noah is more of a take-it-slow guy, and the idea that I could potentially have made him feel claustrophobic or been too intense with that party suggestion sent a bolt of humiliation through me. I'd apologized for overreacting and told him that of course his work came before silly consumerist holidays, and he'd shrugged it off and said it wasn't a big deal. And then I guess he found these flowers! A lovely surprise. And he's right—there's always next year.

Claire

SIXTEEN

"What an arsehole." Sukhi has visited late after work again, and I'm filling her in on what happened when I went to the Alliance & Gordon offices. Her reaction is, I think, justified. I let the validation wash over me in a warm glow. It's like she said to me when she walked in on my messy flat: it's okay for me to react in the way I feel is right for me. In the same way that Noah always told me the emotions I feel aren't wrong or right, they're just ... me.

My truth.

Before, there was only ever Mother's way, Mother's truth.

What is Noah's truth?

I chew my lip. "He's not though. I mean, right now he's behaving like an arsehole, yes. But usually, he isn't. I think there's something deeper going on. Something weird."

Sukhi looks incredulous but holds her tongue, opting to pour herself a small glass of the grape juice she's brought over instead. "Was too hungover this morning to do it all again," she'd explained. And as promised over earlier texts, she also turned up with two large oven pizzas, which we've been picking at all night.

"And he hasn't called or made any contact since?" she asks.

I shake my head, chewing pensively on a slice of cold pizza.

"You're handling all this very well," she observes.

I shrug. "It's keep calm and carry on, or break down, cry, scream and fall into a pit of depression. Plus I did already tear my flat apart." I give her a small smile. "Honestly, though, I feel like while there are still so many unanswered questions, it's too early to fall into acceptance that we're really over."

Sukhi nods. "Spoken like a wise woman."

"I don't know if I'm wise or stupid, clinging on to the hope that there's a viable explanation for all of this."

"I think it's better to cling on to hope than to assume the worst and shut yourself off to any explanation before he's had a chance to say his piece," she says. "What's the next part of your plan?"

I sigh, putting my pizza slice down. "I really don't know. I could wait for him to reach out to me, but I don't think he deserves the luxury of time while I'm going crazy over here, wondering what's happening. But after what happened today, I feel like I can't go back to his workplace. I guess I'll keep internet stalking and hope for a breakthrough?"

"That is a shitty plan," Sukhi tells me.

"I know."

"Here, pass my laptop over, let's see if we can find out anything else," she says. I watch as she scrolls down his profile page. His most recent post was something banal, about football, but she goes through the people who "liked" his status diligently.

"This guy just looks like an arsehole," she comments, as we peruse the page of Jeremy Miller, a red-haired sleaze whose profile photo is him with two Hooters girls in a holiday shot.

"What about that girl? Who's she?" I ask, pointing to an Isabel Clarence who has liked Noah's status.

Sukhi duly heads to her profile and I relax when I see that Isabel is at least sixty, her page littered with updates about her grandchildren.

"Keep looking," I say, urging Sukhi back to Noah's page.

"What about this guy? You know him?" she asks, clicking onto a Blake Argent.

I frown. "I think I recognize the name . . ."

His profile photo pops up. He's a little chubby, with stubble and rather nice green eyes, but he isn't ringing any bells. "I don't think I recognize him," I admit.

She's about to click off his page when I grab her arm. "Stop! There! Scroll down!"

Sukhi scrolls down to Blake's most recent post, shared at 9 P.M. today. He tagged himself at a bar in West London, alongside four other names. One is Noah Coors.

First stop of the night? Completed it, mate. Second stop? Ballards. En route!

"Oh my God," Sukhi breathes.

I glance at the clock. It's 9:27 P.M.

"I'm going," I say, snapping the laptop shut. "I'm going to Ballards."

"Are you sure that's a good idea?" she asks, looking worried. "Right now?"

"I'm fine. And I'm going. If I leave now, I can be there inside an hour. I am going to confront my lying fiancé about his double life." My voice is coming out certain and strong, and Sukhi may mistake it for bravery, but I recognize it for what it is. A desperate need for answers. Hurt, confusion and a desire to understand what I've done to push Noah away like this. And between the cracks of all these emotions there's a slow, dangerous fury growing. I will not let him throw us away. We *will* fix this.

I have my trench coat on, my handbag already resting on my arm.

"I'm coming with you," Sukhi tells me.

"No, please, you don't have to," I start, but she cuts me off.

"You're not doing this alone. Come on, I'll get us a cab." She puts a supportive hand on the small of my back and it reminds me so much of Noah walking alongside me at bars, when he knows I feel out of place. I find myself walking next to her then waiting for the taxi outside, my heartbeat steady in my chest as I wait to confront Noah.

SEVENTEEN

You getting out anytime soon or what?"

The taxi driver has turned around to face us both, the stench of stale smoke wafting through his gappy teeth. He looks bored, as though this moment is an insignificant blip in his life, when for me it's *everything*.

Sukhi is gripping my hand.

"Give us a second," she snaps. For the hundredth time in the last thirty-six hours, I'm grateful for her being here, and let her know as much by giving her hand a little squeeze. I glance into the rearview mirror and can see my blue-shadowed eyes, patchy red blotches tainting my nose and cheeks, ugly and harsh against my pallor. I'm not looking my finest, I'll admit. A far cry from the woman Noah first met in the wine aisle. I take a shaky breath in and try to calm my mind for whatever is about to happen.

"Do you have a plan of action? Know what you're going to say?" Sukhi asks me gently.

I shake my head. "No plan."

"No plan is a good plan," she says with a small smile.

The city lights are reflecting on the windows, bouncing off Sukhi's bright eyes. I wrap my trench coat around myself a little tighter, hugging my stomach, and she reaches over and gently pats my hand.

I suddenly want to run back home, to crawl into bed and pretend the last day and a half never happened. I don't usually confront things. I don't storm recklessly into nightclubs with no plan. Even when I left Mother, I wasn't brave. I just stepped away and, when she didn't follow, carried on walking. But this time it's Noah stepping away, and I have to find some sort of strength within myself to force this confrontation. I want to run, but my mouth says, "Let's get this over with." I open the car door.

"Finally," the taxi driver mutters under his breath as we get out of the cab.

"No tip for him," Sukhi tries to joke with me, but it falls flat. Will I ever laugh again?

As though on cue, the sound of laughter erupts into the evening air as the door of the cab in front of us swings open and a trio of men floods out onto the pavement beside us, lighting cigarettes and speaking loudly about stupid, frivolous things that nobody cares about. Least of all me.

I step to the side to get away from them and Sukhi and I stand awkwardly in the queue for the club as I try to work out how to move, how to think, how to exist. The club is small and typically pretentious in that West London sort of way: potted plants dangling invitingly around the sleek exterior walls, gold sans-serif lettering spelling out the establishment name, matching vinyl pasted onto the condensation-fogged glass through which I can see bodies writhing against each other, hear the dull thrum of a beat.

"Got a light?" a guy asks me, his eyes glazed with alcohol. I flinch away from him instinctively, the smell of whisky fiery on his breath.

"No," Sukhi snaps, putting a protective arm around me and ushering me away from him like a geriatric patient.

What am I going to say when I get in there? Where do I even begin? What do I ask? Who is Noah in there with? The new work friends that he didn't deign to tell me about? The thin blonde? I take in another deep breath as my stomach clenches with nerves. We make it to the front of the queue quickly; for clubbers it's still relatively early. The bouncer raises his eyebrows at our jeans and trainers combo and for a moment I panic, thinking he may turn us away. But it's obviously a quiet night because he ushers us inside without a fuss.

As soon as we step in we get stamped on the wrist, a bouncer rifling through our handbags in search of weapons or drugs. After that we're waved through quickly and the stench in the air is a mix of alcohol and sweaty skin.

"I remember now why I never go clubbing," Sukhi says, her nose wrinkled.

It's dark, with hazy blue lighting tinting the room in a way that seems menacing. I'm squinting in search of Noah amidst the bodies contorting and curling around each other on the dance floor, limbs flailing.

I begin to feel extremely claustrophobic as people keep shoving past us to get down to the main dance area and Sukhi clings on tightly to my arm. "Let's get out of the entryway," she bellows into my ear, the music pounding over her voice.

I nod silently and let her lead me up toward a mezzanine overlooking the lower level. My eyes are frantically scanning the room, searching for my fiancé. My heart is thudding, the loud electronic music making it difficult for me to think. My senses are overwhelmed and I grip on to the railing tightly, conscious of how sticky my hands are.

"Maybe he's in the smoking area with someone?" I suggest, though the Noah I know doesn't smoke.

"Oh, God," Sukhi breathes. I follow her gaze and across the mezzanine, through the thick smog of a smoke machine, I see him. He's in a velvet-lined booth, and of *course* he's with the dimpled blond girl. She's thrown her head back, laughing at something he's saying. His eyes are twinkling, oblivious to anyone else in that bar, in his life. She leans forward and they hold hands over the table, his thumb circling her palm lazily, a gesture laden with affection. I don't dare blink. Beside me, I can feel Sukhi stiffen into a fighting stance, her fists clenched.

I see Noah gesture to the blonde's empty glass, already standing to get her another. She smiles at him gratefully, and then my fiancé bends down and kisses her, his hand around her neck. I cannot move.

It's not a Hollywood kiss, but somehow that's worse. It's familiar. It's sweet, warm and tender, automatic . . . a kiss they've clearly shared before.

"Bastard," Sukhi whispers under her breath. That word seems to snap me out of my paralysis and before I know what I'm doing, I'm marching toward him.

My claustrophobia has been replaced by determination as I shove and elbow my way through the crowd waiting to be served at the bar, my eyes quickly scanning countless suited City workers keen to quench their thirst. Frustrated, I head round to the side where the booths are. I see him, he's back placing two drinks on the table. *Quick work, Noah.* Sukhi is behind me, holding on to the back of my coat. I'm not sure whether it's so she doesn't lose me or so she can pull me back if necessary. I spot Blake, recognize him from the Facebook photo, but he's beyond the booth, flirting with a brunette woman, his hand grazing her hip as he leans in to hear her over the music. My gaze returns to my cheating boyfriend.

Noah's eyes widen as soon as he sees me. "Oh my God. What are you doing here?" I can barely hear him, but I can read his lips and his panicked body language. He did not expect to see me here.

He edges back in his seat. He has gone ghostly pale, eyes bulging out of his lying face.

Before I even have a chance to answer, Sukhi has leaped to my defense. "I think the better question is: What the fuck are *you* doing here?"

Noah's eyes widen a fraction and I almost feel sorry for him. Almost. Around us, people stop sipping through their straws to eye the show with interest, eyebrows raised, girls smirking and guys gawping.

"Excuse me? Who the hell are you?" the dimpled blonde pipes up, her words laced with indignation.

I'm about to tell her I'm his *fiancée* when Noah moves. It's subtle, a small movement, but the response it triggers from me is potent. He shifts so she is slightly behind him, his left arm coming down protectively in front of her.

He is protecting this woman from me. He is choosing this woman over me.

I want to slap Noah across the face. I want to rip the blonde's pretty little necklace off her dainty little throat. I want to flip the table over. I want to tackle them like a rhino running through plate glass, so that they're cut and bloody with tiny shards caught in their flesh, red specks decorating me. Of course, I don't do any of these things. But God, I really, really want to.

Sukhi must sense my shock and outrage because she mirrors the action, placing herself ever so subtly between me and my fiancé.

I tear my gaze from Noah and direct it toward the blonde. I notice that at the very front there is a single gray hair in her head, slightly thicker than the others and falling in front of her eye. It somehow makes her more beautiful, this tiny flaw proving to me that she is just as human as I am.

I rip my engagement ring off my finger and throw it at him, with all the force I can muster. It hits him on the shoulder, bouncing off into the depths of the club. Another bit of meaningless bling to decorate the tacky interior.

"It's *over*," I scream, my voice breaking into a distressed warble. I turn to rush out before I cry. I notice Sukhi beside me in my peripheral vision. She grabs a glass off the nearest table and chucks the contents at him, her aim perfect. "Sorry," she shrugs to the bewildered owner of the drink, which is now dripping off Noah's perfect golden hair. He is bright red. I glance quickly at the girl beside him in the booth, who has shrunk back, her eyes perfect wide circles, hand covering her mouth. "What the fuck?" she yells after us.

I turn back to face her. "What, you didn't know he was engaged?" I yell back.

"He's not engaged to you, you psychopath!"

At this, I see Noah put his hand on her waist, lean in and whisper something to her. He's trying to usher her away. He doesn't want her to know the truth.

"Walk away, Claire," an older girl told me, her disapproving glare fixed on Laura and her cronies as they cornered me in the hallway. I was thirteen at the time.

"Poor pathetic Claire needs defending, boo-hoo," my main tormentor, Laura, mimicked, making a show of wiping away tears from her face, balling her hands into fists. The girls she was with laughed. I tried to hold my head up tall and stay strong. I tried not to cry.

I went to walk away, to push through the small crowd that was forming, but she yanked my arm back, pulling me into the center again.

"Leave her alone, Laura," the older girl tried again, and I heard her voice crack as she tried to maintain some level of authority over the situation.

"Or what?" Laura sneered.

Her followers crossed their arms, eyebrows raised expectantly at my defender, waiting to see what would happen.

My heart was in my throat.

The girl shrugged, walked away.

Laura turned back to me, grinning. "Poor sad Claire, with her shitty cheap backpack and her greasy hair. Ewwww! I bet it smells," she screeched.

I saw red flames and tried to push through again, but some boys blocked my way, intent on the confrontation, and I was sent staggering back toward Laura.

I started to feel angry, trapped like a wild animal.

"Fuck off, Laura," I said.

"Oooh, Claire has grown a backbone," she jeered, turning to the crowd of spectators.

I stepped forward, fed up with being walked all over, ready for a confrontation.

"And I heard your mum's a filthy slag," she hissed.

I lunged at her.

I lose it then. Beside me, there's a tall bar table and some empty glasses left behind by a group. I swipe my arm recklessly over the top of it and a wineglass hurtles toward Noah and his mistress. He pushes her out of the way at the last minute, a scream erupting from her.

"What the hell!" someone shouts as the glass shatters against the wall, shards twinkling under the flashing blue lights.

Some of the men who were standing around start toward me, yanking me back and away. "That's enough," one of them is saying to me.

"Don't manhandle her!" Sukhi spits, wrenching me out of his grip.

A swarm of people have surrounded Noah and the blonde, a wall of bodies between us.

I don't wait to be thrown out or to see what will happen next.

I storm out, Sukhi hot on my heels.

I don't remember the journey home.

I leave her in the taxi and refuse to let her come in with me. I need to be alone. I get into the flat and the first thing I see is the picture on the wall of Noah and me in Barcelona, his arm around me on Las Ramblas, both of us beaming into the lens. I pick it up and hurl it across the room, crying out as I do so. It hits the wall and glass shatters everywhere. I'm thrown back to that moment in the club, directing the wineglass at them both. I'm sobbing in a heap on the floor. I feel Sukhi heave me up and drag me into bed. I hear her saying soothing things that I cannot fully make out or care about. She's come in anyway, followed me from the taxi. I want to be grateful for this friendship, but all I can think about is Noah, my Noah, kissing that beautiful blond girl.

His hand around her neck. My hands around her neck.

EIGHTEEN

When I wake in the morning, the bed is empty again. It shouldn't shock me, but it still sends a hollow pain through my chest. The memory of Noah kissing that blond woman last night flashes before me and I bring a hand to my heart because I can almost physically feel it breaking, the pain shooting through to my back.

I wring the bare space on my finger where, just yesterday, a golden band of love sat. It feels horribly empty now, the space gnawing away at my finger bone. I clench my fist shut. I can't believe he didn't come home. He chose *her*.

Staggering to the kitchen, I see that, once again, Sukhi has cleared up my mess, this time placing the photograph of Noah and me in the bin alongside the glass shards from the frame. I physically wince as the Claire smiling at me from the bin morphs into the blond woman, Noah's arm wrapped around her instead.

Who is this woman Noah has left me for, and why has he chosen her? I stumble over to the sink and forget a glass, drinking directly from the tap instead, desperate to give my body the bare minimum it needs to function so I can resume my social media investigation. Then I pour myself a coffee, quickly throw back a glass of water for my headache, and drag my laptop up to my seat at the table.

He chose her.

The familiar blue branding of Facebook lights up my screen and I ignore the "Log in" button and instead click the green "Create

new account" button. When it asks for my name, I type in **Emma
Smith**. A generic name. A name easily forgotten. With trembling
fingers, I search Noah's name and confirm that Sukhi was right.
There he is, profile photo grinning and accompanied by the spotty
teenage Noah Coors, and the two across the pond. He had blocked
my Claire Arundale profile. But Emma Smith can find him, and she
clicks onto his page. No new updates since last night. I'd like to
think it's because he's crying, lost without me, figuring out the best
way to get me back and rectify his lies. But then I imagine he and
the dimpled blonde from the photograph making passionate love
while I lie in my cold bed alone.

My hands clench.

I have an admission to make.

I was a virgin when I met Noah.

Boys had never taken an interest in me at school, and I was too
painfully shy ever to approach them myself. I had convinced myself
I was not worthy of male attention. The thought of sex, if I'm honest, made me feel sick. It brought up horrible memories from my
childhood, of my drunken mother sneaking different men into our
home after a night out. I would lie in bed and listen to them moan-
ing and grunting, the mattress protesting through the paper-thin
walls.

There was one particularly horrific incident when I was fifteen
years old. Mother had been out for the evening, and for once I hadn't
heard her come back home. She must have crept in at some point
after I'd fallen asleep, and she hadn't been alone. The man she had
brought back with her was so drunk that, after a toilet break, he'd
stumbled into my room instead of hers, climbing into my bed beside
me where he passed out.

The clammy heat from his body had made me so uncomfortable
that I'd woken up some time later. I'd frozen in confusion and fear,
a large hand holding on to my hip from behind. I remember my
heart seemed to stop for a second, before going into overdrive,
adrenaline driving me as I turned around and realized that I had

awoken to a hairy, naked body beside me, the reeking smell of Jack Daniel's wafting out of his open mouth. I felt his soft, flaccid cock pressing against my back.

I tried to scream, but it came out a strange, strangled sound, half gasp, half whimper. I scrambled away from him so quickly I fell out of bed. I landed hard and bruised my tailbone but continued crawling away from the bed until I was against the wall. I kept trying to scream but it came out in a wild, breathy croak. He awoke with a start, looking over at me in confusion.

"What the—"

"Get out!" I gasped, chest tight with panic.

He sat up groggily, blinking into the darkness and rubbing the back of his head.

My heart was thumping in my chest, adrenaline causing my legs to shake.

The commotion must have woken Mother because she rushed to my bedroom door in record time. I looked at her, terrified, desperate for some comfort. Instead, she had taken in the scene: me, clutching my bedtime T-shirt hemline, knees up against my wardrobe door, and him, naked and confused in my bed. She laughed then, throwing her head back as though the entire ordeal was one big joke. He sheepishly joined in after a moment of drunken confusion, while I sat there in silence, trembling. But when he got up and scurried out of my room, covering himself with one of my pillows, she paused before shutting the door. As she looked at me her eyes were hard, and I knew I was in for it.

As soon as I heard the door close behind him in the morning, I felt a change in the air. My body tensed, ready for an altercation, and sure enough I heard Mother's footsteps charging for my bedroom. I braced myself. She flung the door open, strode over to me quickly and slapped me across the face. It took me by surprise; I'd thought I was going to get a telling-off. She rarely hit me, but when she did I found it somehow easier to handle than her words. I gasped, bringing my hand to the hot sting of my cheek.

"You disgusting, jealous little slag!" she hissed. "To even *think* any man would be interested in you. You're pathetic, an embarrassment. No one will ever find you desirable . . . you're repulsive," she seethed, leaning in so close that her spittle flecked my eyes and I had to blink it away. "You will never be loved by anyone other than me," she said, and with such certainty that I felt it in my very core.

I had believed she was right. After all, I was nothing like her. Men fawned over her glamorous elfin features and buxom curves. Her extravagant costume jewelry and tippy-tap heels. Her quick wit and outgoing banter. She was nothing like me, so it stood to reason that no man would ever desire me.

Until Noah.

Noah had changed everything. When we'd made love for the first time it had been magical. There was nothing clichéd about it, no fireworks at the window, no flickering candle flames dancing across shadowed walls. Just me, him and the feeling that this was how my life was supposed to be. That this was *right*.

I look down at the profile photograph he's chosen. He stares back at me from the screen, and I imagine him with the blonde again. I re-imagine the night I lost my virginity to him, but instead of me with Noah, it's her. It's not my floral Brazilian briefs he's removing, it's a black lacy thong. It's not my gently sloping hips he grips with desire, it's her lithe, defined waistline. It's not my bouncy chestnut hair he runs his hands through, but her long blond tresses.

I feel sick.

I'm also conscious of my spiraling thoughts, that I'm leaping to conclusions, and that I have only seen one photo. So I begin trailing through all his recent photographs. Without being his friend, I'm limited to very few, and I've seen most of them yesterday with Sukhi, so I do what I have to do.

I find a photograph of some random woman on Twitter and set it as my profile photo. She's not pretty, but not ugly either. Un-memorable. I then begin adding random people from London as friends, to try and make my profile look legit. I fill in the "About Me" section with rubbish and write a few generic statuses so my page is full within half an hour. According to my bio, I'm a vegan caffeine addict who works in accounting and runs half marathons. Noah has a soft spot for animals and loves to run, so I'm hoping it will pique his interest enough to accept.

Then I take a deep breath and send my fiancé a friend request.

I know that it's unlikely he'll reply, so I force myself away from my laptop and, after checking my phone for the thousandth time for any call or text from him, I have another glass of water and wait for my friend request to be accepted.

NINETEEN

November 13, 2024
Dear Diary,

I honestly never thought this day would come, but it's happened. I lost my virginity. I mean, honestly, I was on the brink of being a thirty-year-old virgin. It feels embarrassing even writing it down, it's something that I should have been writing about a decade ago, gossiping about with school friends. Instead, I have nobody to tell and just feel relieved that it's finally happened, that the societal stigma of still being a virgin is wiped away, finally.

But anyway, it happened with Noah. He was round here recently. I told him about that time with the hairy guy and Mother—he always listens when I open up about my childhood, which is one of my favorite things about him—and he was really understanding. I still find that memory very difficult to talk about; my body reacts viscerally, even if my emotions are switched off to it. I still get tense and jumpy just thinking about it for too long, remembering how scared I was. Even thinking of Jack Daniel's makes me want to vomit. The spicy, honeyed musk. I hadn't spoken to anyone about it before, I still held a lot of shame over it, still felt as though perhaps some of it was my fault somehow. I know it sounds ridiculous, that I was only fifteen and the responsibility was on Mother to protect me, but those feelings of everything being my fault are embedded so deeply within my being that it's my instinctual reaction whenever I am upset about something.

Noah was really kind and helped me navigate the entire memory.

I spoke and cried and he held me. It made me feel so close to him. "I'm sorry you had to go through that, Claire," he murmured. And it was such a contrast to how Mother had been that I was caught in confusion, unsure if I even believed him. But after I'd relieved myself of that secret, I felt a weight lift off me. I stopped feeling like it was my fault, and I felt ready to become intimate. To trust that a man could want me. And so today it happened.

Noah did not push me, this was all my decision. I instigated it and I told him I was ready—because I was.

And it was perfect. In hindsight, I'm glad I waited this long. I don't think I could have found a better guy. He was very gentle and understanding and kept checking in to make sure that I was okay the whole time. It was a bit uncomfortable at the start, as I knew it would be, but we found a rhythm eventually and it started to feel much better.

Initially I'd been self-conscious. I know he must have so much more experience than me, have seen so many bodies, and I began to worry about how mine compared to the others. But his eyes had hooded over and his hands had roamed gently and I could tell in that moment that he was definitely not thinking about anybody other than me. I'd felt empowered, and attractive, and wanted.

I'm quite relieved, to be honest—the longer I stayed a virgin, the bigger a deal it felt. I didn't think I'd ever meet a man who would understand my fears around intimacy and be so patient with me. Before now, I couldn't even be in a bed with a man without being reminded of that revolting, fleshy body I'd woken to find beside me. I feel like a new woman, as clichéd as it sounds, and I do believe that it's less to do with the sex and all to do with the closure I got from speaking about that particular trauma. I have Noah to thank for both.

Claire

TWENTY

I t takes barely any time for him to accept.

I have thirty-five more "friends" than I did when I last checked Facebook, and scroll through the random faces hurriedly until I breathe a sigh of relief when I spot the one I have been looking for. Noah.

I immediately click onto his page and am pleased to discover that my hunch was correct—now that I am "friends" with him, I have access to many more posts than before.

I start on Noah's page. He hasn't updated it since last night, but I go through all his photos until I find another one he uploaded of himself with the beautiful, dimpled blonde. It looks like it was taken on the same night as the first picture I saw, judging by their outfits. Other photographs from this night out show a flurry of faces I don't recognize.

I click onto the photo of Noah and the blonde and see that while he hasn't tagged her, someone has mentioned her in a comment below, giving me access to her full name.

Lilah Andersson looking fab as always! Xxx

My nose wrinkles and I click onto her page, ready to absorb her life into my brain. Born in Sweden, one year younger than me. Of course she's Swedish—with her beautiful honeyed skin, golden-blond hair, sparkling blue-green eyes. Her mother was a model according to a photo of Lilah and an older, very similar-looking woman tagged as Maja Andersson with the caption Hot Mamma model mum ☺ A quick scan of Maja's page and I can see the resemblance instantly. Lilah has inherited those sickeningly sweet dimples framing her full lips, and that pert little upturned nose. For a split second, an invasive thought enters my mind. *Why couldn't I have inherited more of my mother's looks?*

I shake the thought away, then see myself in the reflection of my laptop screen, a distorted shadow grimacing. How could I ever compete with literal model genes?

I switch on the webcam on my laptop and begin an excruciating process of self-inspection. It feels like I'm torturing myself, my face blinking back from the camera with, beside it, Lilah's photograph still visible. My eyes flit quickly from myself to the photograph, drowning myself in comparisons. My flesh looks pale and pillowy, hers is toned and tan. My lips, shapeless and boring. Hers are juicy, topped by a perfect cupid's bow. My carefully groomed eyebrows suddenly seem outdated, hers naturally bushy and perfectly framing her eyes. How did Noah ever find me desirable in comparison? The more I look at both of us side by side, the more my body morphs into something grotesque. Have I been deluded all along? I've always been told I was pretty, in a quiet, bookish sort of way. Was that just everyone's way of saying that, in fact, I'm repulsive?

Because Lilah . . . she's a goddess. The Male Fantasy personified. I continue reading, reading, reading, scrolling through Lilah's page and drinking in her life like it's an elixir.

She went to an all-girls school until she moved to the UK, and she now works at an international fashion retailer as a content director, whatever that means. She has a master's in marketing from Exeter University. She's a keen kickboxer. She loves animals. She drinks green smoothies. She goes to hot yoga (gross). She smokes menthol cigarettes when she's drunk. She edits all her photos to look like they were taken on an 8mm film camera. She goes to a spa for a facial once a month, and drinks white wine spritzers. She goes home often to visit her parents and her sister. She dabbles in watercolor painting.

And she has been dating my fiancé since before I even met him.

TWENTY-ONE

I am the other woman. Not perfect Lilah.

But why? Why would Noah even have entertained the thought of being with me when he's had her all along? And why take it as far as proposing to me? My mind is spinning with possible storylines for the situation. Maybe it's an abusive relationship and he's been trying to leave her for years, tempted away by my meekness? But it didn't look that way at the club. I rub the space on my ring finger as though a genie might appear and give me all the answers, but nothing comes. I wish I hadn't thrown that ring at him. It seems too final, as though I had made the decision I was cutting him and our engagement off when really I want to work this out. I want him to come home. I want everything to be fixed.

I pull out a notebook from one of the kitchen drawers and begin scrawling on it, trying to get my thoughts out on paper. I write down the date of the upload of the first photograph of Noah and Lilah together, I write down the date we met, I write down our engagement day, I write down the day he supposedly left Pulitzer Haas; I write and I write and I write until I've covered two sides of paper with random dates, random names.

I look down at my manic jottings and slam the notebook shut, shocked by my own ignorance, my desperate search for answers now permanently recorded in ink for anyone to see.

But then something I've written catches my attention.

Feeling a rush of determination, I leave the flat. I know one place

Noah *always* goes, and it's worth swinging by to see if he might be there now.

The smell of hot air and stale sweat hits me as I step into the gym. I feel distinctly out of my comfort zone, hard bodies brushing past me with a confidence that tells me they're frequent gym-goers.

"Can I help you?" the young girl behind the counter offers. "Are you looking to join?"

"No, actually, I just wanted to check if my boyfriend had been here this week at all?"

A guy behind me barks out a laugh and I feel my cheeks grow warm.

"I'm not checking up that he's exercising or anything," I explain quickly. "But he's been lying to me about where he is and I'm trying to piece it all together," I say, lowering my voice and holding steady eye contact.

"Oh! I see," the girl replies, and her eyes flit from side to side as she chews on her lip. "Look, I'm not supposed to do this, it's against policy to share customer information, but between you and me, I know what it's like to be cheated on," she confides under her breath.

I bristle. "Nobody said he's *cheating*. It's probably nothing. He's probably got a good explanation," I tell her, flushed with embarrassment, the shock of seeing his kiss with Lilah hitting me once more.

"Sure," she replies, and I can tell she thinks I'm a naive little loser.

I sigh. "There has to be an explanation for where he goes when he's missing, right? One that doesn't include a full-blown affair?"

Am I speaking to her or myself?

"What's his name?" she asks me, obviously not wanting to give me her honest opinion on my situation. I wonder who hurt her, if she has mended from a similar pain as the one I am feeling right now.

"Noah Coors."

She gives me a tiny nod and types it into her computer. "I'm sorry, I can't give out customer information." She speaks loudly, I assume for the benefit of the other people in the reception area. "Is there anything else I can help you with?" she asks. She's frowning at the screen, then lowers her voice again. "He must have transferred. Same gym, different part of the city. He's registered at the Lime-house branch now," she tells me.

I scrunch my nose. Limehouse? Then I realize that it's right next to his new office.

"You've been so helpful. Thank you, thank you so much," I tell her, putting my hands together prayer-style.

"I hope you work it all out," she tells me. "Or kick his ass to the curb," she adds with a smile.

The gym at Limehouse is identical to the Clapham one, the same musty smell of dried sweat and condensation dripping off the glass panels that divide the workout space from the reception area. It makes me feel dirty just breathing the air.

"Can I help?" the guy at reception asks me. He's young, barely out of his teenage years, and lean.

"Yes, I'm looking for my boyfriend. He's registered at this gym and I think he comes here a lot?" I hold my phone up.

"Yeah, I recognize him. He comes either early morning or pretty late, right?"

"Yes," I reply, even though I don't know when my boyfriend goes to the gym because I don't even know where he lives.

"So . . . what do you want from me?" the guy asks.

I realize for the hundredth time today that I really have absolutely no idea what I'm doing, or what I hoped to gain from leaving the house. I was just so desperate not to be at home, to be doing *something* to try and fix my relationship, that I came out in search of answers.

"I guess just . . . Does he come alone?" I eventually settle for.

The kid shrugs. "He signed up with one of our personal trainers and so he has pretty regular sessions, which he does alone."

"Okay."

"You want me to tell him something next time he checks in? I can leave a note on our system?" he offers.

I give a tiny smile. "No, I think he's got the messages. It was more just for me to know that he's coming, working out, staying healthy, you know?"

The boy stares at me when I say this. "Er, right. Do you want to join? We do joint PT sessions for couples?" he asks.

"No. I'm good. Thanks," I tell him.

As I turn to leave, outside the gym I see a flash of golden hair above the groups of lunchtime workers.

"Noah," I say out loud, rushing out of the gym reception. "Noah?" I call again, pushing through the crowds. He's walking away from me, a takeout coffee in one hand, a phone I don't recognize in the other.

"Noah!" I call louder, several heads turning my way before returning, uninterested, to their lunches.

He's walking toward a small park, and I'm weaving between people on the crowded pavement before finally grabbing his arm and spinning him around, my heart in my throat and my chest bursting with adrenaline.

But it's not him. It's another tall City boy, frowning at me.

"Oh, God. Sorry, I thought you were someone else . . . sorry, sorry!" I tell him, backing away. He's already returned to his phone call, heading for a nearby bench, and I hear him say, "I dunno, some weird girl," to the person on the phone before wiping my presence from his mind.

TWENTY-TWO

Back at home I'm hot with embarrassment at my escapades at the gym, at grabbing that stranger like a thirsty desert-dweller reaching for a mirage. I cradle the glass of white wine I've poured myself to help me relax. The bottle is put away in the fridge, out of sight. I'm nervous of picking up a habit I didn't think I'd ever develop, a dependency on alcohol that mirrors Mother's too closely for my liking. So I'm just being cautious, keeping an eye on it. Earlier when I took my first cool sip, I could almost feel her next to me, breathing down my neck and demanding I pour her a glass too.

I distracted myself from Noah briefly with memories of Mother, but eventually my mind cruelly flitted back to him: how he discarded me on the phone with no care for who I was, for how I was . . . and then again, at his office. The cruelty, the demand that I go home without him. Is that how easy it was for him to leave me?

I was once invited to a birthday party. A seventh birthday party for a boy in my tutor group; I can't even remember his name. The entire class had been invited, and I had definitely been included out of duty rather than desire. My mother found the invitation crumpled at the bottom of my schoolbag and insisted we go, set on the idea that not turning up would reflect badly on her. She cared a lot about what others thought of her.

"I don't want to go, Mother," I told her weakly when she brandished the invitation in my face.

"Why not, Claire? It's a *party*, for God's sake. It'll be fun, there will be cake!"

I didn't know how to answer, how to explain the crushing anxiety of socializing in an unknown setting. I was only seven, after all. So I clasped my hands together pleadingly, hoping she would somehow sense my worries and smooth them all away.

"They'll think us rude if we don't go. You don't want to be the weird one, the only one to miss out," she said instead, emphasizing the word *weird* with a wrinkle of her nose. "Do you?" She peered at me as though interested in my response, but I felt the threat behind her words.

"No, Mother," I responded dutifully, avoiding eye contact.

In the car on the way there I wrung my hands until they hurt, worrying about what would happen once we arrived. Would I be left out? Made fun of, perhaps? What would I say? Who would I speak to? At best it would end up with me standing awkwardly on the fringes, unsure how to behave or join in. At worst, I would be made the center of attention and mocked mercilessly. By the time we pulled into the driveway, three sad balloons bobbing against the gates, I was in such a state of panic that I refused to get out of the car though Mother was standing outside. I shook my head feverishly, clutching white-knuckled on to my seatbelt.

"Come on, Claire, darling, don't be ridiculous." Mother laughed shrilly, rolling her eyes at other parents who gave her sympathetic smiles as they dropped off their rosy-cheeked cherubs. But nobody came over to us or tried to convince me to join in. The other children rushed past me, clutching gift-wrapped parcels, not a second glance thrown my way as I clung to the seat in fearful desperation.

Eventually, much to my embarrassment, I began to cry, and I saw my mother's eyes harden. "Okay, love. If you're not up to it, we can head back home," she announced loudly, making sure that the other parents were witness to her show of sympathy. But when she got back into the car, she reached over and pinched my thigh, hard. I bit my lip to stop myself from crying out—I knew it would only make her more angry. As soon as the car had pulled away from the driveway, she launched into a terrific rage, shouting that she would never drive me anywhere again, that I had wasted her afternoon, that I was a useless, boring child.

I sat twisting my hands in my lap on the journey home. Part of me was relieved that soon I would be home, back in my bedroom alone. The other part of me was terrified about Mother's neurotic meltdown, that she might feel pinching my thigh wasn't enough to satisfy her fury. I began skimming through ideas to protect myself. Was hiding the safest option? And if so, where? The garden shed, perhaps? But then if she were to find me hiding from her, surely it would only fuel her anger.

Realization dawned that I was the child and she was my mother, and I would have to endure whatever punishment she doled out to me because there was no escaping it. When we arrived I scrambled straight for my bedroom. To my great surprise she did not follow me, remaining in the kitchen instead. I didn't dare move in case she heard me and came through to continue her attack, so I sat on my bed, listening. My senses felt heightened, every step she took followed by a quick mental assessment of how far away she was from me, what direction she was moving in. I heard the clanging of pots and pans, the hiss of a boiling kettle as she began to cook dinner. This was shortly followed by the scraping of cutlery on a plate as she ate dinner, alone. I waited for her to call me to join her, but she never did, so I remained where I was, rooted to my mattress. I did not get dinner that night.

The next morning, I tiptoed into the kitchen where she was cleaning up after her breakfast. "Good morning, Mother," I said quietly. She did not turn, did not react in any way. She simply continued scrubbing her plate as though I hadn't spoken.

"May I . . . may I have some cereal, please?" I asked, my stomach sore with hunger.

Again, she didn't respond, though I noticed her fingers tighten on the sponge. She did not want me to exist in that moment.

Very slowly, I began to move around the kitchen, serving myself cereal. When she turned, I flinched, waiting for her to tell me off. She glared at me for a moment, then stormed out of the kitchen and into her bedroom. I ate my cereal quickly, then had a second bowl. I washed it up myself, not wanting to give her any further reason to be upset with me, then retreated back to my lair.

She did not speak to me for ten days.

My punishment was finally over on the eleventh when she began speaking to me again as though nothing had ever happened. Bewildered, and desperate for her affection, I played along as though the last week and a half had never happened. Inside, I was reeling, confused and on edge. One error could send me into that terrible, lonely limbo once more. A ghost in her life. I had learned to feed myself, aged seven, but I never did go to another classmate's birthday party. In fact, I'm not sure I was ever invited to one. I may not have known what a birthday cake tasted like, but I knew what hunger tasted like, what being ignored for days on end in my own home tasted like.

Poison.

Memories wash over me freely, Mother blurring into Noah. Frustrated, I click back onto Lilah's page. I scroll up and down and down and up again until I have every photograph memorized. Every outfit detail studied, every important name and date learned by heart. Every image of her with Noah is engraved on my mind. The timeline of just how long they have been together has shocked me, a catalogue of photos chronicling a long record of deception.

The snap of them together in secondary school; Noah in his preppy uniform blazer, tie askew, and Lilah laughing beside him, her checked skirt hitched up shorter so it skims her golden thighs. The shot of them abroad in Toulouse, at a famous wine bar; her in a gorgeous little black dress with matching peep-toe heels, and Noah in shirt and smart trousers. Her wineglass bears a perfect imprint of her red lips. A picture of them on some sort of country walk, and even without makeup, grinning at the camera as she hoists herself up some rambling hillside, she is perfection. She's wearing leggings that amplify her pert little backside, a sports bra that shares a sliver of flat midriff, a backpack slung over her shoulders as she grins at the camera, holds a water bottle in her hand. Ahead of her is Noah, who is not looking at the camera but at Lilah, with pride and admiration on his face. I glare at the photo as though I'm there with them. I imagine grabbing Lilah and throwing her all the way down the hill, watching her roll, roll, roll away from Noah and me.

When I'm satisfied that I have drunk in all that Facebook has to offer on Lilah, I switch to LinkedIn, scouring through her connections and network. I quickly source her company name and google the offices. Not too far from mine, in a fancier West London borough. I slot that knowledge away for later. I'm interrupted by my rumbling stomach. I glance at the clock and realize it's lunchtime and all I have consumed so far today has been half a coffee and that glass of wine. I groan, frustrated to have to pause my investigations. I realize I look a state; I was in such a rush to get to the gym that I left the house in my comfies—an old oversized T-shirt with a band logo on it and some seriously bobbly cotton joggers. But driven by hunger, I throw my coat over the top, shove my feet into the pair of trainers that are beside the door, and head out.

I thought the lack of food would make me wobbly on my feet, but the brief blast of fresh air is taking the ache in my head away and I find I feel fine despite the alcohol melding into my bloodstream. I pop into the nearest corner shop, which is about forty steps from my front door. The man behind the till barely looks up at me, and I shuffle to the freezer at the back and grab an oven meal that I can throw in to cook without any effort, along with another bottle of wine.

I pause on my way back to the till and turn abruptly, the tails of my coat flying out behind me dramatically. I return the wine, swapping it for a new jar of coffee, and then choose some milk with the furthest away best-before date. I won't turn to drink like Mother did to cope. I have to keep a clear head if I want to work out everything with Noah. I don't want him to come home and find me drunk on the floor, a sorry mess of a woman.

I plonk all my goods down by the till carelessly and the assistant scans them through without interest, without judgment and without a care in the world. The lucky bastard. He probably sits and scans all day long, so involved in his own boring life that he doesn't even think to concern himself with his customers, with the bedraggled woman in front of him buying a frozen lasagna on a Thursday afternoon.

"Cheers," I say, as soon as the payment has gone through, not waiting for a bag and hooking the foiled meal in the crook of my arm, wielding the coffee in one hand, the milk in the other as I march out of the shop and back home. As soon as I'm back in my flat I boil the kettle, getting impatient and ending up pouring half-heated water from the kettle into a mug with coffee and milk, before returning to Facebook, this time perusing all of Lilah's friends' and family's pages.

There's one sister, Olivia, who seems to split her time between London and Stockholm. She lacks much of the shine and sparkle that Lilah has, her page a boring blend of competition reposts and avocado-on-toast snaps. She doesn't seem to use it much, and certainly does not record any details on Lilah, so I quickly move on.

Lilah's friends are all similar to her, the sort of women that I would feel self-conscious to be seated next to at a restaurant. They are slim and glamorous, successful and *fun*. They *reek* of fun. Their profiles are littered with pleasurable trips to get manicures together, amusing inside jokes that nobody else understands, cliquey day-trips to Instagram-hot-spot cafes and nights out at karaoke bars. It's all so relentlessly jolly.

By the time my meal is sitting congealed on a plate next to me, I'm on Instagram, where Lilah's mother, Maja, has posted a photo of herself in a beautiful London townhouse, its cream carpets perfectly hoovered behind her, the giveaway lines highlighted by the

crystal chandelier that lights up the room she's in. I don't know anyone whose mother is on Instagram. I find myself wondering if
Mother would have been on it and decide she would have loved it. I
can imagine her feed now, filled with selfies and over-exaggerating
the edits, perfecting herself and her image to influencer levels. I
wonder how much of Maja's images tell the true story.

In this photo, she is sitting on a cream sofa, ankles neatly crossed
like she's royalty, one arm around Lilah, both of them smiling. For
the second time I find myself noticing how closely Lilah resembles
her mother, though Maja's face has a few more lines around the eyes
and mouth. Her hair is a shade or two lighter as it whitens with age.
She looks so elegant though, even has pearls around her neck.

I think of my own mother as she was in her last days, her yel-
lowed teeth, dyed by decades of Marlboros, the smudged black kohl
that always lined her eyes, her tacky high-street heels and forever-
laddered tights.

I look back at the photograph of Lilah and Maja. There's a glass
coffee table in front of them with sparkling gold peg legs, a bouquet
of peonies in a ceramic vase. I wonder if they are from Noah.

I read the caption. **Visiting my beautiful girl in London.**

I look at the location. Tagged—Chelsea, London, UK. I can almost hear Sukhi's voice and what I know she'll say when I tell her
next time we speak: *Of course Lilah lives in Chelsea. We should have
made a list of the most affluent, pretentious, perfect London boroughs
and just guessed.*

I save the photo into a file I've created on my desktop called "The
Double Life" and then continue trawling through Maja's feed.
Eventually I go back far enough that I find one of her with Lilah in
the same pearly cream room—but it's empty, moving boxes scat-
tered everywhere, and Lilah and her mother are holding up glasses
of champagne to the camera.

Caption: **Moving day! And a gift from her mama . . . You can take the
girl out of Sweden, but you can't take Sweden out of the girl! ;)**

I swipe to the next photograph in the carousel and it's a book called *A Hygge Home: Tips for Scandinavian Coziness Wherever You Are in the World.*

I roll my eyes and flit back to the photo of them with the boxes and champagne. Behind them is a large, beautiful window, the type with fancy cornicing around its arched frame. I zoom in as far as it will allow me, and I can see the river. They are in Chelsea, somewhere along the riverbank.

I swallow a mouthful of food and it goes down slow as tar. That house must have cost a fortune.

I squint at the photograph, pixelated from where I've zoomed in so far to see the river, but I can just about make out a road sign and some of the letters.

Feeling like a detective on a true-crime show, I open a new tab and start working my way around Google Maps, starting in Chelsea and searching for a street near the river with the same length of lettering as the pixelated road sign in the photograph. I soon find what I'm looking for. St. Margaret's Avenue. The *St.* and *Av* make it quick to find easily, and I can just about make out the blurry *M* for Margaret. I google the road name and feel slightly nauseous as the first result records the average house price for that street. It's more than I could ever hope to earn in a lifetime in PR.

With a bitter stab of the mousepad, I switch to street view and immediately recognize the view from Lilah's window.

Before I know what I'm doing, I'm closing the door behind me, my coat wrapped around me. It's a forty-minute walk from my house in Clapham to St. Margaret's Avenue in Chelsea, and I could do with some more fresh air.

TWENTY-THREE

gaze around in awe. After arguing with myself and questioning my sanity for the entire walk to Chelsea, I have made it. Just when I had almost convinced myself to turn back, I'd spotted the road I was looking for ahead of me and knew I had to see the house itself. Lilah's house.

The street is gorgeous. It's a postcard version of London, the sort of street I've walked past without a second thought a hundred times; but being here now just a stone's throw away from the Thames and knowing someone who lives on the street, knowing that *Noah* has spent time here, is making me see it in a whole new light. I don't want to be, but I'm impressed. Even more than impressed, I'm jealous. I can feel envy slowly filling me to the brim with every new luxurious detail I take in.

All the homes have beautiful, intricately patterned encaustic tiles leading up to porticoed facades, fancy French shutters hiding away beautiful cream-painted lounges and open-plan spaces, which flow outside onto terraces and patios bordered by lush green planting. Cherry trees line the pristine pavement—there isn't a takeout box or littered flier to be seen. I'm not at all surprised to spot two teenage girls doing an impromptu photoshoot outside one of the houses, giggling as they assess their poses together, heads craning over a phone.

So this is how the other half lives. This is how the other *woman* lives.

I am thankful for the teenage girls' background presence—without them, I would feel painfully out of place, waiting for someone to storm out of their front door and tell me to leave, that I don't belong.

I nod politely to a woman who walks past me, striding confidently in a pair of red-soled shoes as a little fluffy dog in a leather jacket struts beside her, eyeing me suspiciously when we cross paths.

Range Rovers and Porsches sparkle in driveways, and I'm eyeing them all up enviously when a sight stops me in my tracks. It's Noah's car. His shining black BMW is parked in a driveway, his CooR5 license plate mocking me. My chin wobbles, but I purse my lips together and continue stepping forward, edging closer to the property.

It's beautiful. Ivy crawls up the white stucco exterior while wisteria in flower hangs artfully around the soft butter-yellow front door. A gleaming 48 is painted onto the transom above: 48 St. Margaret's Avenue.

I see a flash of movement at the window and duck down, dropping behind Noah's car. My heart is beating so hard. After what feels like an eternity, I dare to peer carefully over the bonnet and see a ginger cat on the windowsill inside Lilah's house, watching me intently through the glass, its tail flickering behind it. I breathe out with relief and even have a little laugh at my own silliness. Look at me, creeping behind a car for fear of a cat.

Then the realization that Noah now shares a cat with this woman, a living being that he cares for and loves alongside her, hits me. The ginger cat glares at me, as though taunting me. *I see you,* it's thinking. *And I am in here, living in this house with your fiancé and Perfect Lilah while you are out there, squirming around like a garden slug.*

I stare back at the cat. I imagine it curled up in Noah's lap, Lilah beside him, stroking its ginger head absentmindedly while they watch TV together. I imagine it jumping onto their king-size bed in the mornings, rubbing against them for attention as they laugh together, naked. I imagine Noah coming here after work, Lilah texting him and asking him to feed the cat.

He may as well have a child with her. The very thought makes my blood run cold, but I shake my head resolutely. *It's just a cat.* There was no sign of a child on any of the Facebook pages I trawled through. It must just be the cat. Which is irritating in itself because I know for a fact that Noah is a dog person. He's always wanted a German shepherd, so this cat must be a Lilah Thing, something she's forced on him and which he resents her for. Yes, that must be it. It's Lilah's cat.

I stick my tongue out at the animal childishly, and it eyes me nonchalantly.

I'm still half-crouched beside Noah's car. I desperately want to see into the house, but the lights are off and so all I can see are reflections bouncing off the glass from the last of the September sun rays. I need to get closer, but I'm afraid, and the parked car means that Noah is probably inside. I don't think I can handle seeing him right now. Especially not here, in *her* territory.

The sudden realization of where I am jolts me, and I physically reel backward into one of the cherry trees.

I grasp at the trunk and edge slowly around it, so that if someone were to look out of the window of number 48, I would be mostly hidden. I stand with my back against the trunk, my eyes shut, breathing in and out slowly and trying to calm myself. *What am I doing here?* What did I hope to accomplish by coming? Do I feel better for finding out that Lilah lives in a stunning townhouse with a stupid cat and my cheating boyfriend's car parked outside?

Do I hell.

Without looking back, I rush down the street, head hanging, bound for my lonely studio apartment.

TWENTY-FOUR

Back at home I stalk up and down the kitchen area like a restless caged animal. Sukhi has tried to call twice but I can't speak to her, to anyone. My fists are clenched and my eyes keep involuntarily darting to my laptop, which I have turned off and stuffed beneath the sofa in an attempt to dampen my urge to scroll up and down Lilah's Facebook page, endlessly comparing myself to her.

As though that's even possible, with her perfect body and perfect personality and perfect life. *Why* did I go to that house? It's only exacerbated my self-torturing imagination, setting a scene for this long-standing affair that I can see even more clearly in my head now. The front door where they stumble in together after a few too many drinks at the local gastropub, Lilah giggling as she trips and Noah catching her before she falls. The front of the house where she'll pose for her Instagram photos before an event, Noah proudly leaning against his car to snap a picture. So many scenarios that before I could tell myself were just self-torture. Now there is at least an element of truth to them.

Despite my good intentions earlier, seeing the beautiful house Noah is living in has sent me spiraling down a hole of self-pity and I fish the rest of the bottle of white out of the fridge. I pour it lazily into the nearest receptacle but realize too late that I've poured it into Noah's lettered mug. I stop drinking, shove the mug away and swig from the bottle instead—the mug was just slowing me down, anyway—but find it empty. I grab my keys and purse and head out to stock up. It's going to be a long week. I'm just stepping into the corner shop when my phone vibrates. I hastily unlock it, but it's only Sukhi.

In Clapham, fancy a drink?

I squint at the message, dithering. I look at the wine shelves with a new sense of longing, then back down at my phone. I think of Georgia, and with a sigh, I find myself replying, **Sure. The Falcon?**

See you in ten.

"God, Claire, are you all right?" Sukhi asks, wide-eyed. It's only then I realize that while she is in post-work drinks attire, her blazer stripped off but smart-casual day-dress and brogue combo intact, I am still in a mucky tracksuit, which I can't remember putting on. I'm not even sure if I have used deodorant. I pull a face at her in response.

"Jesus, stay here, I'll get you a drink . . . Do you want a Coke?" she asks, her brows furrowing slightly.

"Wine, please," I tell her, without looking up.

She ushers me into the seat beside hers before half-running up to the bar. I lean on the sticky pub table, wondering how long I need to be here before I can make an excuse and leave, go home to research more about Lilah.

Sukhi quickly returns, a small glass of white in one hand, a grimy glass of water in the other. "I figured if I can't convince you to have a soft drink, I can at least try to keep you from being sick later," she tells me solemnly, pushing the glass of water in front of me. I don't tell her how much I've already been drinking since I last saw her. Instead, I hold up the water to her gratefully and toast, "To cheating fucking liars!"

She grins at my swearing, then holds up her own glass of Coke. "Fuck toasting him. To *friends,*" she says pointedly, and the word lights me up from the inside out. *Friend.*

"So, how have you been today?" she asks, sipping her drink.

I frown, trying to work out how to share my feelings—and what

I've done—without sounding like a psychopath. "A bit all over the place," I settle for, before draining the water and switching to the wine.

"I mean, obviously. Who can blame you? I'd be a wreck," she tells me.

Sukhi *gets* me. Sukhi *understands* me. It's okay for me to feel like crap, the love of my life has been living a secret double life. It's okay for me to be wearing stinky old trackies out in public. If anyone deserves a breakdown, it's me. "And I *am* a wreck," I confide, taking a slightly bigger gulp of wine before continuing. "I just keep thinking about that girl and comparing myself to her, you know? Like, why me? Why is he doing this to me?"

"Oh, hun," Sukhi says, nodding along sympathetically. "You mustn't think about the other woman, you'll drive yourself into a dark place and make yourself feel so shit comparing yourself to other people. It's not her that's the issue anyway, it's *him*. He's the one who lied, who betrayed your trust."

Betrayed my trust? "I hadn't thought of it like that," I mumble into my glass.

"It's easy to get so caught up in thoughts about the other woman because you have no history with her. It's easy to be angry at her. But the real betrayal is from your partner: He is the one you should be directing all your negativity toward," Sukhi says.

I'm frowning, drinking to avoid having to answer right away.

"I know it hurts to think of him wronging you, but that's what's happened. He's not been stolen away from you, he's turned his back on you. Don't get it twisted. And remember, it's *his* loss."

"But why?" I half wail, my glass now drained. Sukhi's glass of Coke is still nearly full, so I glance quickly at the bar and hope she doesn't notice.

She does. "I don't think you should drink any more today, Claire," she says gently.

I ignore her. "Why would he do this to me? I thought he loved me," I say, and my eyes are now openly streaming. Some guys must be staring because Sukhi glares over my shoulder and shouts, "Take a picture, why don't you?" and throws up a finger.

I hear a couple of jeers and then she rolls her eyes, turning her attention back to me. I refuse to look behind me, not wanting to see anyone drawing amusement from my pain. The cruelty of strangers feels too much to bear, on top of everything else.

"Some guys are just shits," Sukhi tells me, and it takes me a moment to realize she's speaking about Noah and not the guys behind me.

"But Noah isn't like that," I argue. "He's *perfect.*" I drop my head into my hands in dismay.

"Nobody's perfect, Claire."

But he was. He *is.* He has cherished and protected me. He's taught me how to believe that Mother, the school bullies . . . they were all wrong. That I matter, and my feelings matter. It's the same way Sukhi makes me feel: safe and appreciated. I wonder if I would have been friends with her at school. I think, sadly, probably not.

"Hairy Clairy, Hairy Clairy!" Laura was singing in a stupid high-pitched whine, her rabble of mean girls flicking bits of torn paper at me as I walked down the school corridor, holding my backpack up as though it could shield me from their words. Their cruel cackles echoed in my ears. The paper might not have hit its target, but their viciousness did.

"Do you have as much hair down below as you do on your arms, Hairy Clairy?" one of Laura's hounds asked, glancing quickly to her pack leader for approval. Laura smiled her crooked smirk, and the girl's grin widened.

"Nobody would know, she's such a virgin," Laura replied with an exaggerated grimace, miming wiping tears from her eyes.

"Little Hairy Virgin Clairy!" one of the pack shrieked. At this new nickname, they burst into such loud laughter I felt like my ear-drums might split. My face was burning hot and at this point I just wanted to get away, to escape it. So I said goodbye to any pride I had left, and ran. I tore down the hall and they chased after me, singing, "Little Hairy Virgin Clairy!" until they couldn't run anymore for laughing so hard. I managed to hold my tears in all the way home, but as soon as I was through the front door they came, streaming down my face, and I collapsed on the floor, clutching my backpack and sobbing.

"Claire, darling, is that you?" Mother warbled from her bedroom. I quickly patted my eyes dry, stood up and tried to straighten myself out, but she was already sticking her head round the door and peering at me with curiosity. "Are you crying, Claire?" she asked. Her voice was gentle, and for a moment I thought I saw the side of her that so rarely came out, the kind and nurturing side.

"What happened, sweetheart?" she drawled, coming into the room properly and draping herself over an armchair, peering at me with her head tilted as though I were a fascinating TV drama she couldn't look away from.

"Nothing, Mother. Just some girls at school, it's no big deal." I tried to brush it off, swung my bag back onto my shoulder so I could lock myself in my room and forget, but I could see the glint in her eye, the love of drama emanating from her as she leaned toward me.

"What girls? What did they say? Shall I go to the school, talk to the head?" she demanded loudly, embracing her role as the heroic mother, the pained guardian of a bullied young schoolgirl.

The thought of Mother at the school causing drama in front of Laura and her friends made me want to drown in a hole of shame. "No! Mother, no, please. It was nothing serious, just some teasing!"

"Well, if it's just some teasing, why are you so upset? What were they teasing you about?"

I stayed silent, staring at my shoes.

"Claire, darling, what were they teasing you about?" she repeated, but her voice had dropped lower, her pretense of being a worried mother gone. Her mask slipped and she reverted to her usual self, the one that expected to receive whatever she asked for.

"They made up a song," I mumbled, knowing she wouldn't drop this until I told her everything.

"A song. A song about what?" she asked, and I felt that she'd almost lost interest, eyes on her nails, which she was now examining carefully.

"They . . . they were calling me a hairy virgin," I admitted, the words like salt on my tongue. I was flushing so furiously I thought I might have a fever, sick with mortification.

I waited for a moment, too afraid to look up, and then Mother burst into peals of loud, heartless laughter, ringing in my ears as cruelly as Laura's cackles had earlier.

By the time Sukhi drops me at my front door, I'm swaying. It takes me two tries before I get the key into the lock, and I give her a thumbs-up as I wobble through the doorway. She waves at me and the taxi pulls away, taking her back to her own un-messy life.

I stumble into the flat and any resolve I had earlier in the day cracks. I fish my laptop out from its pathetic hiding place, booting it up and heading straight for Noah's page as my first port of call.

One new update. A new status, posted this afternoon.

Looking at growing the family . . .

My heart judders to a painful halt.

Beneath is a photo of a litter of puppies, and he has tagged Lilah. My vision goes hazy for a moment, the wine now tasting like acid on my tongue. Does he have no shame? What *family*? *I* am his family. His family is *me,* here in this apartment that's filled with memories and a year's worth of commitment.

A second account is tagged and I click onto it. It appears to belong to a dog breeder, as it takes me through to a page called Rosie's Rottweilers. I can see their most recent post was advertising the latest litter of pups—this must be the photo Noah shared—but note that they aren't ready to go to new homes for months.

I roll my eyes, scrolling back up the page. "Months!" I slur angrily at the screen.

Rosie's Rottweilers are premium breeders and trainers of ped-
igree Rottweiler guard dogs. Our dogs are trained by fully li-
censed security personnel from birth to be sound defense dogs
for the family. We are particularly popular with celebrity clients and high-value clientele. Please email with any training
or pup requirements. N.B. Prices start at $10,000.

I blink. *Ten grand?* Noah is spending *ten grand* on a dog? It's not
even a German shepherd! Is this a joke? Why would he do this?
There are so many dogs that need homes in rescue centers—why
would anybody fork out that kind of money for a pet?

I close Facebook and head to Google, searching for Rosie's Rottweilers. I find the official website and start reading up. It looks like
these dogs are bred for people with a lot of money who need to feel
safe or have their mansions and treasure troves protected. I shiver at
an example video, which shows a huge bear-like dog they claim is
only nine months old biting someone. On command, he closes his
jaws around the man's carefully padded arm. He shakes at it violently, ripping at the protective layer so forcefully that the man is
sent stumbling forward, struggling to hold his position. Finally, the
trainer calls the dog to stop, and it instantly releases its hold, saliva
dripping from its jaws.

I wonder if they've been burgled recently.

I think of that lovely house, nestled on that fancy street, where
my fiancé's double life exists along with all the secrets he's hiding.

I wonder what in that house it is worth paying ten grand to
protect.

TWENTY-FIVE

November 17, 2024
Dear Diary,

I can't believe I'm even writing this, but Noah has asked me to move in with him. It caught me totally off guard. I was out doing my weekly shop at Tesco and he put his arm around my back as I pushed the trolley and said, "How do you feel about us moving in together?"

I stopped the trolley and stared at him. "What, like, permanently?"

He grinned. "I wouldn't move in with the intention of moving out again, if that's what you mean."

I smiled nervously. "You want to live with me?"

"I mean, it makes sense, doesn't it? We spend every day together, we're here doing the weekly shop together to buy all the dinners we're going to eat together. It doesn't really make much sense paying for two separate locations, now does it?"

I broke into a beaming smile. "We'll move into your place?" I squealed. Noah has a gorgeous apartment in Balham.

"Well, actually, I was thinking of selling that and using the money to buy us somewhere new, so we could start afresh."

I got butterflies then. "You . . . want to buy us a house?*"*

"I mean, not a castle or anything but yes, somewhere that suits us both. Mine feels a bit of a bachelor pad, and it's clear my bachelor days are over," he said, grinning.

I threw my arms around him and said yes, of course. "I can't wait to house-hunt! Do you want to stay in Balham?"

He shrugged. "Do you *want* to be in Balham?"

I twisted a strand of my chestnut hair around one finger. "I've always loved Dulwich," I admitted, thinking of the gorgeous park where there are often horses from the nearby riding school.

"Dulwich it is," he declared, and I squealed and wrapped myself around him in excitement.

Before meeting Noah, I honestly never imagined myself living with anyone again. Mother always used to say that nobody would put up with me the way she did, and it kind of stuck with me. I envisioned any relationship I had being wrecked once we moved in together, the closeness turning suffocating as they noticed all my faults and flaws. I like to think I'm a clean and tidy person (growing up with a woman who would scream at me if I left my shoes by the door does that to you), but the fear runs deeper than that. It's a strange, innate feeling that they would be able to see my soul, how broken and fucked up I am on the inside, how worthless all through. And then they would hate living with me because my grossness would surely begin to seep into their own life, driving them away from me.

I haven't shared these feelings with Noah. I know he would tell me I was being ridiculous, and it feels too much to admit to him. I think saying it out loud would make me seem so self-hating that nobody would even believe me; it would seem as though I was only saying it to chase compliments. So I've kept it to myself and decided that it's worth the risk to move in with him. I feel strongly enough that we can make it work, because he's so understanding and forgiving of my flaws.

If I'm honest, I'm nervous in general about moving in with a man, and all the surface-level parts of me he might notice and hate as well.

But I know I must try. I'd do anything to be with Noah. Within days he sent me a link to a gorgeous house in Dulwich, but it needed work.

"We're paying for the space, really. We couldn't afford a house this size otherwise. We'll need to renovate it," he warned me. But we agreed it would be perfect, a fresh start for both of us. I've said that while it's being done, he can stay at mine. It might not be ideal, what with it *being such a tiny, rubbishy studio flat, but he seemed up for it. Said it would be nice and cozy. Which is sort of romantic if you think about it. I love how he always knows what I'm insecure about and picks up on it and twists it into something positive. I'm just so lucky to have him in my life.*

He'll be joining me this weekend, and I feel like I have loads to prepare. I want him to feel welcome, so I went to the supermarket to get some of his favorite foods and when I was there I saw these cute alphabet mugs, so I bought one with a C for Claire and one with an N for Noah, so when he opens the cupboard he'll know that it's not just my flat anymore, that someone else lives here and it's just as much his space as it is mine. I hope he likes it. I hope he likes me. I hope he likes me as much as I like him. I can't imagine him doing anything to put me off him, but I'm dreading all the little things I may do to put him off. Like accidentally leaving leg hairs in the bath after I shave, or listening to Taylor Swift loudly on a Sunday morning. Or just being myself. But I guess this is part of being in an adult, cohabiting relationship. I'm still learning to navigate this world, and it's daunting and rewarding all at once.

Claire

TWENTY-SIX

'm unsure if it's the alcohol, the adrenaline or the cloak of darkness that makes 48 St. Margaret's Avenue look so different by moonlight. Everything seems hazier, dreamlike and, if possible, even more perfect than before. I emerge from my hiding place behind a tree opposite their home, and next thing I know I've rushed across the street, squatting beside Noah's goddamn car again, still parked in front of Lilah's house. Without even realizing what I'm doing until it's already happening, I take out my front door key and drag it hard down the side of his precious BMW before I slink closer to the property. It makes a satisfying high-pitched scratching sound that sets the hairs on the back of my neck prickling. *Enjoy that, Noah.*

The front room is lit, emitting a warm, flickering glow through the window. The plantation blinds are shut but they've been yanked closed halfheartedly and I can probably peer in through the slats if I get close enough. Part of me thinks, *What the hell are you doing here, Claire? This is ridiculous, go home.* But then I think of the Rottweiler website and a raging curiosity takes over, a desperation to know what's going on behind that yellow door, to reveal whatever sick, dark secret it is that Lilah's guarding. Something is not right. Normal Average Joe couples do not spend ten grand on a protective security dog if they don't have something mega-valuable to guard. I don't think it's something as normal as a safe either. Perhaps it's not about their money, but where that money's coming from? I don't really know much about Lilah's father, but I'm sure no model makes enough to set their daughter up like this in London unless they're Cindy Crawford.

I slowly edge right into the strip of shrubbery beneath the front window, shuffling awkwardly until I'm squatting beneath their windowsill planter, holding my breath. What for? I don't know. In case someone comes and suddenly pulls aside the shutters and then opens the window and randomly leans right out and finds me? I convince myself I'm being overly cautious, but the wine has made me woozy. A sudden loud noise could be the end of my investigative mission. I have to keep it together. Better to be over-cautious than caught out.

I'm listening, my fingers splayed out in the dirt in front of me to help keep me balanced, and I can hear the low, monotonous buzz of a television. Slowly, so slowly that it feels almost comical, I begin to rise until my hands are gripping on to the window ledge and I'm peering over the flowers and through the slats, hunched over in the darkness. I inhale sharply as I see him, leaning back casually on that luxurious cream sofa from the photos, her body tucked in beside him and her head resting on his chest as they watch a gardening show together. Noah doesn't *garden.* This is wrong, all *wrong.* This isn't what he likes. She's changed him. He would never spend his free time watching something as dull as a gardening show. I'm grinding my teeth and leaning so close to the glass that my nose is almost pressing against it.

They aren't moving, aside from his thumb, which I notice lazily tracing circles on her shoulder. Apart from that, I could almost pretend that I'm looking at a photograph, another snapshot posted to her showy Facebook album. I glare at her, daring her to see me. Then I shake off this poisonous hatred and remind myself to focus on the setting, what clues I can find as to why Noah left me for this horrible, awful woman. Any hints as to what they need an attack dog for. Noah's well off, but this is another level of wealth. Of course, I don't know what his new job is paying him, but even with a much higher salary, a house like this would be pushing it. Plus, all the decor is clearly hers. This screams old family money. For a split second, the question of whether that's why he's with her crosses my mind, but I shrug it off immediately. He has money. He is not the type of man to rely on anyone else for finances, so no. This is just a happy coincidence for him, I'm sure.

Beneath the TV (which is now going into detail on *seed types,* for God's sake) is a gorgeous marble mantelpiece. There are framed pictures displayed along the top of it. I squint, trying to force the images into something sharper, the effects of the wine blurring the edges a little too much. I can make out one of Lilah with two other beautiful blond girls—cousins, perhaps?—and two featuring herself and Noah, his arms around her in both. I inhale slowly through my nose, allowing myself a second to close my eyes as I do so, breathing deeply and trying to quiet my brain like my mindfulness app taught me. I count to five, then to ten as I let the breath go. Once I'm done, I feel better. Lighter, more in control, and more sober somehow too.

The lounge adjoins a dining-room area, divided from it by glazed double doors, which are standing open. Lilah's handbag is visible on the table and of course it's a beautiful black Prada bag, which probably cost an arm and a leg.

I feel myself childishly roll my eyes at her predictability.

God, I hate her. I feel hatred literally bubbling beneath my flesh as I watch her draped over my boyfriend as though he is hers. I snap back into focus though when Noah says something to her, then stands and leaves the room. He must be going to the toilet. I watch her for a moment, as she replaces the warm, muscular body of my boyfriend with a sofa cushion, still in the same curled-up position, her head resting on the plumped velvet pillow. She's wearing pajamas and of course, they're fucking silk. Cream silk trousers, trimmed with lace, a matching top and Ugg slippers on the floor beside her. Her golden-blond hair is wrapped up in a messy bun that would require an entire team of hairstylists to replicate on my own head.

Her skin is glowing and her lashes are dark, even though it looks like she's not wearing any makeup. I'm just about to assess her bone structure in more detail when, beside me, the front door flies open. My whole body freezes in shock and anticipation, my heart in my mouth and the wine frightened out of my bloodstream. Moments later the ginger cat sashays onto the front path, where it stretches lazily before peering over at me with interest. The door has shut again. Noah was letting it out. My body sags with relief. I wasn't seen, but it was all a bit too close for comfort.

I slowly edge backward, away from the house, and away from my cheating fiancé.

I spend the night tossing and turning. By 5 A.M. I can't take it anymore. I want to message my only friend, but obviously Sukhi will be asleep. So I put on a film, try to take my mind off things. It doesn't work. I'm overwhelmed with thoughts and emotions after my trip to St. Margaret's Avenue and too hyper to sleep although I'm exhausted.

Around 9 A.M. on Friday morning I become aware of sunlight streaming through my windows. I must have dozed off for a few hours. The TV is playing something random, the film long over.

On the coffee table, my phone blinks at me with a notification. Lilah has uploaded a new photo.

TWENTY-SEVEN

November 30, 2024
Dear Diary,

We spent the day visiting one of the Christmas markets on the South Bank. It was cold, but we wrapped up properly and had a lovely day out. Noah likes the hot apple cider but I went for a hot chocolate, and we wandered around looking at all the stalls and Christmassy knickknacks together. There was a small stall with beautiful handmade pieces, jeweled rings and carefully carved pendants, which I stood poring over.

"Do you want something?" Noah asked.

I whipped my hand back, ashamed for wasting the stallholder's time. "No, no. Just looking," I laughed. "Pretty though, aren't they?" I said, peering at one of the rings. It had little birds carved into the gold band, a sparkly stone of some sort set in the middle.

"Yes, unique," he agreed, taking a glance over my shoulder.

"Come on, let's go ice-skating," I suggested, pulling him along.

I was awful. Like Bambi on ice, all the gear and no idea. I ended up clinging on to the railing most of the way around. Noah was better— but not by much.

"Not a skater boy back in the day then?" I asked.

"You can talk! Trash talk from the sidelines. How about letting go of the railing?" he teased back.

I watched him stiffly drive himself forward, legs straight and body tense. We were both terrible, but at least neither of us fell!

Claire

TWENTY-EIGHT

may have turned on notifications under my Emma Smith Facebook and Instagram accounts, to alert me whenever Noah or Lilah update their profiles so I can keep track of their relationship. I'm not proud of it, it makes me feel seedy and desperate, but surely I'm owed some sort of explanation, which Noah is clearly not going to give me.

I need to understand what I did wrong, why he left. Clearly, he has been with Lilah since they were children, so maybe he's just staying with her out of some sort of misguided loyalty? Or a fear of change? I mean, if he had been happy with her, truly happy, why would he have asked me out? Why would he have created this beautiful life with me, put a ring on my finger, if he was content with her? I can't help but be hopeful about the fact that her left hand is clearly bare. So he must like me more. There's something she must be holding over him, keeping him with her against his will. I just need to find out what it is. You may think you'd behave differently, but when push comes to shove, if you found yourself in a situation as bizarre as this, I don't doubt you would be doing the same.

I open the notification and pull up the photograph. It shows a gigantic bouquet of flowers that must have cost a small fortune. For a moment I feel a stab of panic—is she engaged? *Pregnant?* But no, my heartrate slows right down as I take in her caption. **Lovely surprise from clients.** Then I take in the setting and realize, of course, it's a work thing. The background isn't a home environment, I can see strip lighting that indicates an office, and the desk that the bouquet is showcased on isn't the sort of designer shabby-chic piece that would fit in at pristine number 48. She's clearly at work.

Perhaps there are secrets that could be extracted from studying her office. I haven't even considered it so far, but if Lilah wants to store something she can use to blackmail Noah into staying with her, it would make sense that she'd conceal it somewhere he didn't have access to. I flit back to LinkedIn where I type in her full name and click through to the company page. She works for Sparxx, a luxury womenswear brand that I've heard of but haven't ever shopped at. It's a bit overpriced and housewifey for me, a lot of pastel cashmere jumpers and beige cigarette trousers. Beneath the "About" section the company head-office address is listed in Notting Hill. It's not *too* far from my own offices. From home, it's a bit farther than I'd want to travel and I don't usually head that far west but I have the whole day off. Maybe I can do a bit of window shopping while I'm there. I tell myself that it makes sense, that I'll just have a little nosy around the area. I work out the best route to take.

I get dressed in one of my staple work outfits: pale blue shirt, gray trousers with boots and my long camel coat. Then I throw on a pair of sunglasses and put a black scarf into my handbag before I make my way to the Underground station. It's not that I want a *disguise* per se, but I don't want to draw attention to myself. Lilah might be walking around the area and recognize me from the altercation at the club.

Another thought strikes me—how much does she know about *me*? What has Noah told her to explain the incident where a stranger threw a ring at him in a club? Maybe she thinks it was just a one-night stand, or maybe he managed to keep it from her entirely. I mean, why would she stay with someone who had been cheating on her for over a year? Does she have no respect for herself? And all this time Noah has been with me, where did Lilah think he was? The whole way to the Underground station I wonder what is *really* happening behind the closed door of number 48.

TWENTY-NINE

When I exit at Notting Hill Gate tube station the sun is streaming down. It's busy, heaving with people looking to soak up the sunshine and enjoy the boutique shopping, so I step back into the doorway of a bank to catch my breath and still my thoughts. I'm pondering Lilah's reason for staying with Noah despite my very public outburst at the club. There are so many questions and loose ends that my mind can't get past. I feel like I need a notebook, spider diagrams and a full-on thriller-movie-style pinboard with red strings linking facts and evidence, to help me work out what the hell happened and what Noah is thinking.

Tourists heave in waves in front of me, all moving in the same direction toward Portobello Market. I slot into the swarm, letting them carry me along with them as I follow the little blue Google Maps trail. Usually, I'd feel flustered by the sheer volume of people, but today I hold on tightly to my purse and phone and focus on reaching my destination.

When I reach Lilah's office, I need to double-check I have the right address. I'm just surprised; it's such a fancy company but this is a small office, based above a random restaurant. There's no signage at all until you get to the front door and then the company logo is stuck on the buzzer for Floor 3. I hop from foot to foot, unsure of what to do now that I'm here. I decide to go into the restaurant beneath the office and try to be rational about things, work out why I'm here and what I hope to gain.

I'm relieved to discover that it's not a typical overpriced Notting Hill restaurant, more like a small traditional cafe, and because it's only 11 A.M. it's still quiet before the lunchtime rush. A little bell rings as I push the door open and a chirpy-looking girl greets me. "Eating in or taking out?" she asks brightly.

"Eating in. Can I take that window seat?" I ask, nodding over at a high table that looks out onto the street.

"Sure, no problem! When you're ready to order, just come on over to the till."

I settle myself down, gazing out and wondering if this is the same view Lilah has all day from her desk. Stores and independent boutiques line the street at ground level while flats above them have huge, beautiful windows looking out and down onto the busy scene. The housefronts are painted in pastel colors, creamy pinks and soft blues making everything seem part of a cheerful stage set. Small pop-up stalls selling bohemian jewelry and leather pouches and wallets line the pavements. Everything seems too picturesque for this to be London.

I end up ordering a club sandwich and a cappuccino, and take my time with them as I go over possible courses of action now I'm here. I'd envisioned a huge office that I could slip into unannounced, something similar to Noah's, but it's clear this isn't the case at all.

I finish my sandwich, running a finger over the crumbs and popping them into my mouth. I am about to call it quits and head back home when I give a jolt of surprise. There in front of me is Lilah. And she's coming into the cafe.

I slide lower in my seat, bringing my head down and quickly whipping my scarf up and around so it's covering half my face. The waitress chooses that exact moment to come over to me and I curse in my head, hoping it doesn't direct attention over to me as the bell rings, signaling Lilah's entry. "All done here? Are you ready to pay the bill?"

I nod quickly, not saying anything in case my voice is recognizable from the scene at the club. Lilah is so far oblivious, over at the counter where she's holding a phone away from her ear while she orders a large flat white, to go. I need to keep my head down until she leaves. The waitress is yapping on at me, but I'm not listening, nodding halfheartedly and holding out my contactless card. As we wait for the machine to print the receipts, I risk a glance up. Lilah's back is to me but that Prada bag is slung over one shoulder and she's wearing a perfectly tailored duck-egg blue suit with cream court heels, the leather supple and expensive-looking.

"Yes, I'm so sorry, please tell Hannah I'm going to be fifteen minutes late to our lunch meeting. We had a staff call that overran but I'm on my way over now. I'll be there as soon as possible," Lilah is saying into her phone as her coffee is handed to her. Her voice is breathy and feminine, with the slightest hint of an accent. "I'm on my way to the station right now. If she can hold the reservation I'll be there as soon as I can." She turns directly toward me and I quickly look down, staring into the dregs of my coffee. I sit totally unmoving, too scared even to breathe, waiting for her to stop, stare, say to me, *Oh my God, you're the girl from the club!*

But nothing happens. I breathe a sigh of relief and slide off my stool, thanking the waitress absentmindedly as Lilah leaves the cafe and I watch her, still on her phone, heading off toward the Underground station.

She'll be gone for an hour if it's a lunch meeting. Minimum. That's more than enough time for me to pop into her office and have a quick look around. This is an opportunity that's been gifted to me by the gods, I'm sure of it. I can be in and out in twenty minutes, tops.

THIRTY

My finger shakes slightly as I ring the buzzer labeled "Floor 3."

"Hello, Sparxx?" a voice answers.

"Hi, yes, my name is Hannah. I'm afraid I've had a bit of a mix-up with Lilah. We were meant to be having lunch but got confused about where we were meeting . . . Anyway, she's on her way back to meet me now but told me to come up and wait in the office?"

What feels like an hour passes and my heart hammers in my chest with anticipation. My palms are sweaty and I'm trying to work out how fast I can run away when the door makes a clicking sound. "Okay, come on up," the voice replies, sounding bored.

My shoulders sag in relief and I wipe a line of sweat from my upper lip. By the time I've traipsed up to the third floor, the sweat is back. I pull at my coat. You'd think a company charging £300 for a jumper could get a lift installed. Once I'm on the third floor, a big glass wall with the Sparxx logo on it shows me the office in its entirety. It's very small and it looks like there's nobody around except the receptionist, who is flicking through a magazine.

"Hi," she says without looking up. "You said Lilah is already heading back to meet you, so I don't need to call her?"

I step in past the glass wall. "Yes . . . no, don't worry!" I force a laugh, nerves making my voice break. I swallow. "She messaged as she was getting back on the Underground, she won't be long." I give her my most convincing smile, but the girl is already back to looking at her magazine. "Well, you can just take a seat here or head through and wait in her office." She points to a small box room with three desks in it.

"Okay," I say nonchalantly, heading over to the office. My timing is perfect—everyone is out for lunch. I check on the girl at the front desk one more time. She's inspecting a horoscope website intently now, the magazine forgotten on her lap. Easily distracted. Good. I close the door quietly behind me.

I quickly scan the three desks in the room. The first has a picture of two kids in a photograph frame, so I instantly discount it. The next displays a birthday card that loudly declares: "Harriet is 30!" That leaves only one desk. And, sure enough, that huge bouquet is atop it, with a "Thank You" card. I hurry over. I take a little peek at the card and it confirms what I already thought.

Dear Lilah, thank you for all your hard work with us on the Instagram campaign and for your patience. The pictures are perfect! Can't wait to work with you again. Bella xxxxx

I roll my eyes in the way that Sukhi would, closing the card and slotting it back in between the leaves of the bouquet. The desk itself is boring on the outside, much neater than the other two with fancy-looking stationery and paper-organizer trays decorating the surface. I should have known—of course she's mega-organized.

I sit down experimentally in her cushioned desk chair. I can smell the faint residue of a sickly-sweet floral perfume. Nothing like the spicy citrus one I wear that Noah loves. *Loved.* I try to get on to her computer, wiggling the mouse, but of course it's password-protected and I don't have the time or the knowledge to hack that, so I move swiftly on to the drawers, my ears listening out for footsteps approaching the door the entire time.

The first drawer is filled with loads of correspondence and "vision board" files, whatever they are, plus magazine clippings. I turn to the second, which seems to be more personal. She's stashed a spare deodorant, a lipstick and a hairbrush in here. I look at the name at the bottom of the lipstick and can barely contain my laughter. *Bunny*

Boiler. I pick at the hairs on the brush with interest. A little part of her that I can just snap. I pull a strand off the bristles, tying it around my finger until the tip starts to redden, and then give a sharp tug. I get a sick burst of pleasure from the sight of her hair ripping in half, fluttering sadly to the ground. I place the brush, minus that single strand, back in the drawer and return to my sleuthing.

I rifle quickly through the papers, and most of them are boring and work-related but then I stop on something that catches my eye. It's a copy of her employment contract. It seems a bit weird to have a copy of this in your drawer at work, but I'm also interested to know her hours and salary. I take it out carefully, making a note of what it was wedged between so I can put it back in its rightful place. I scan over the information, mostly stuff I already know, her job title, name, address, and try to swallow down a lump of jealousy when I reach her salary. Needless to say, it makes my annual pay look like loose change. Still not enough to warrant a house on St. Margaret's Avenue, so I suppose I can confirm my family money theory.

I mindlessly flick through a couple more pages and stop dead when I notice something that makes my blood run cold. On page six, she has taken a highlighter and circled around the maternity leave section.

My brain leaps into overdrive, immediately jumping to conclusions while simultaneously trying to stay calm and rational. But she's written something as well, beside it. In loopy cursive handwriting, which I have to squint to make out: "Secondment 2025."

Secondment? But what does that mean? Is she trying to use maternity leave as a secondment? Or take back-to-back leave? Is she planning ahead? She can't be pregnant—I saw her drinking in a bloody club just the other day! My mind is going 500 miles per hour when something else in the drawer catches my eye, something I must have shuffled out of place when pulling out the contract. I carefully slot that back where it was and lift the pile of papers to reach the edge of a photograph peeking out from the bottom. I scrabble for it, hearing movement on the other side of the wall, heading closer. I don't have much time. I snatch at the photograph and when I see the image on it, I think I may vomit.

Brown eyes, chestnut hair and a small mouth stare back at me.

Lilah has a photograph of me in her desk drawer.

THIRTY-ONE

jerk backward in the chair, slamming the desk drawer shut just as a figure appears in the room.

Oh my God.

It's not Lilah.

I feel like I may collapse with relief. My mouth goes slack and I'm slick with sweat after my discovery. *Why does Lilah have my photo in her office drawer? Why is she circling the maternity section of her contract?!*

"Oh! Hi. Can I help you?" the girl asks. She's approaching the next desk, the one with the birthday card on it, dropping a handbag and removing her coat.

"No, thank you, I'm fine. I had a meeting but it's just been canceled," I explain, holding my phone up randomly.

"Right," she murmurs. I notice she's looking at me curiously, narrowing her eyes as though she might recognize me. The hairs on the back of my neck stand to attention. I don't know why, but something inside my head is screaming, *Leave now, hurry, leave now!*

"Okay, well, better be going," I say, rushing out without allowing myself to fall into conversation, keeping my head down as I go. The receptionist with the magazine looks up and starts to say something to me, but I'm already past her and flying down the entry stairwell, fingertips skimming the banister in case I trip in my hurry. I bolt out of the front door. Before I know it, I'm running as fast as I can away from that building, the glossy picture of myself still in my possession, my shy smile crinkled where I clutch the photograph in one of my fists.

My legs are aching and my lungs burning before I allow myself to stop. I'm taking deep, gulping breaths, doubled over beside a bench.

"Are you okay?" A concerned woman approaches me and I wave her off with a flap of my hand and a few nods. She backs away looking bewildered. I don't know if it's the long sprint or the panic swelling in my chest that has caused this, but it's a good few minutes before I shakily seat myself on the bench and feel my breathing start to slow. I look down at the crumpled photo in my hand and feel so many emotions that it's blinding, my vision literally spotted with rage, fear, panic, jealousy and desire.

I squeeze my fist shut around the photograph again and order an Uber to take me home. I'm silent the entire journey.

When I get home, I sit down at the table and look at the picture one more time. It's my face, front-on, and it's been cropped so that almost all you can see is a passport-photo-size headshot of me, grinning stupidly. I squint hard at it, though, thinking I recognize the background. There's crystal-blue sea and in the faraway distance, beside my right ear, I can make out the tiny, shadowed shape of a boat. I frown.

I quickly log in to my Facebook account—the real one, not the sock-puppet account—and start trawling through my photo albums. And there it is. Me, on holiday in Spain, uploaded about two years ago. In the original photograph you can see my whole outfit: I'm wearing ill-fitting cargo shorts and a plain white vest top, my pale skin bleeding into the white cotton in an ugly, touristy way. I'm on my own. I had asked someone walking past to take the photograph for me.

I'm embarrassed by it now. I barely recognize the girl in the picture. The milky skin that Noah always kisses softly looks sickly under the harsh Spanish sunlight. My comfortable beachwear is hideous. I'm embarrassed that I uploaded this to Facebook for everyone to see, so blind to my own former self. Embarrassed that I was so alone before Noah that I had to go on breaks solo, because I had nobody to ask, nobody to invite who would say yes.

I feel moisture on my hands. I'm crying. When did that start? I close my laptop and pour myself a glass of wine, but I don't drink it because soon I'm sobbing so loudly and savagely that I'm sure my neighbors will call the police. I curl up into a ball on the sofa and I cry and scream until the cushion is sodden and my face is so red and blotchy that I barely recognize myself in the mirror. I wail like I'm in mourning and, in a way, I am. I'm humiliated, I'm lonely, I'm angry. I'm mourning my life with Noah, because without him, I'm back to being that sad, pathetic girl in the photograph.

The photograph that Lilah somehow had and stashed away in her office drawer.

I sniff, pulling myself together as the cogs in my brain begin to work, my rational side squaring up to spar against my emotional side. *How did Lilah have that photograph?*

It was uploaded two years ago, which was before Noah and I started dating. So did she find it then, or did she find it later? And why *that* photo?

Did she know about him dating me from the start? Was *she* stalking *me*? A shiver runs down my spine at the thought.

Eventually I retreat to my bed, wine undrunk, and climb underneath the covers, closing my eyes so I can concentrate. I try to clear my mind so that I'm focused and rational, hoping some sort of explanation will come to me, one that doesn't make me afraid of Lilah, or worse yet—afraid of Noah.

It's clear the only place Lilah could have found the photograph is my Facebook account. That's my fault for uploading it and having loose privacy settings. So the key questions to answer are: Why was she looking me up, when was she looking me up, and why did she go to the lengths of keeping a printout of the photo in her office?

The only reason she could have for searching for me on Facebook would be to do with Noah. We have no mutual friends, no prior relationship. Either she found out about us somehow and wanted to see who I was, or he told her about us—though that would make no sense. Unless she saw a text or something from me and researched my name?

But that doesn't explain why she printed the photo out and kept it at work. I'm frowning, my eyes still closed, as I try to pick apart all the puzzle pieces. But after a few more hours of lying there and going over reason after possible reason, one thing is clear. The only way I'll ever get an answer will be to have a conversation with her and tackle this head-on.

I think back to the last time I confronted someone and feel a pit yawning in my stomach.

It was around a decade ago, and I was eighteen. I had been saving the wages from my weekend job in a newsagent's for two years, hoarding every penny away like a magpie. That corner shop had been my salvation, my retreat away from home, and I had taken every shift going, covered every sick colleague, done every late shift. It kept me out of the house, it kept me busy, *and* they paid me.

After psyching myself up for days, I was cooking dinner. My mother sat waiting expectantly at the table. Then I took a deep breath and told her I was going to move out.

I felt the sudden stillness in the room. My shoulders tensed as I continued chopping a carrot, desperately trying to avoid looking at her despite feeling her stare burning into my back.

Then the silence was shattered by her brittle laughter. "Oh, Claire, darling, you almost had me there for a moment! You are a funny one, aren't you!" she crooned.

I kept chopping the carrot, too afraid to turn around and face her. "Mother, I'm so sorry but I'm not joking. I'm serious. I found a little flat and I'm eighteen and think it's about time I got out of your hair."

"Nonsense! What are you on about? You don't have any money,

you can't afford to move out!" She laughed again, but this time I could hear the doubt behind it, her voice wavering ever so slightly.

"I've been saving, Mother. From the shop."

"Saving?" She spat out the word like it was arsenic. "Well, then it's mine! You owe me for raising you for eighteen years. Don't you think? Do you think it's fair that you've been saving all this money while I spend mine feeding you?"

I felt my body tense. No. *No*. She couldn't do that, take my money. It was my only chance of escape.

"Mother, I've already spoken with the estate agent and paid the deposit, I'm sorry," I told her, trying to keep my voice calm and level. The silence in the room that followed this announcement lasted a beat too long.

"You ungrateful bitch!" Mother suddenly screamed, standing up. She snatched a glass from the table and hurled it at me. I ducked and flinched as it shattered everywhere.

"You ungrateful, spoiled brat! How *dare* you decide a thing like this and not tell me? And save all that money behind my back without even considering paying toward the bills here, your upkeep?" She started toward me and I curled into myself, backing up against the sink. My eyes flicked toward the discarded knife lying on the chopping board. I should have kept it in my hand, shouldn't have left it within her reach. A whip of a glance and yet she saw it, followed my gaze to the blade.

Her whole attitude shifted in the blink of an eye. "Oh my GOD, Claire! You think I would hurt you? I would *never* hurt you, not the way you're hurting me! I *love* you. I bore you, didn't I? My first child, my only child!" She began crying, wailing hysterically as she sank back into the nearest chair, bringing a shaking hand to her forehead in a show of despair.

I stood there, still as a statue, unsure how to deal with her when she got like this.

"How could you do this to me? How could you do this to your poor mother? I love you so much, Claire, darling, you know I do.

Nobody will ever love you as much as I do! Why would you do this to me when all I've ever done is love and care for you?"

I bristled slightly at her words, but remained still, trying not to show any sort of reaction. That was what she fed on—reaction.

She continued, "I have no husband, no other family, and you're abandoning me, leaving me here entirely alone?" She wept and sniffed dramatically.

What came out of Mother's mouth and her actions rarely aligned. Moving very cautiously, I slid the knife behind me. I didn't trust her not to reach for it, to sink it into my side before she even realized what she'd done. She was too unpredictable. "Mother, I'm not abandoning you, I'm not going far. I'll still see you all the time—"

"You think I'd want to see you? After you've left me like this? *Betrayed* me like this?" she spat at me, crocodile tears instantly vanishing. She stood up again and stalked toward me as I backed up once more against the sink. I could feel the edge pressing into my lower spine. She gripped my wrists, pinning me there, and I was surprised at her strength. I wondered if I would have purplish-blue bracelets in the morning, reflecting the pressure from her fingertips. Then I gasped in surprise as she spat in my face. I was unable to wipe it away, her claws still gripping on to me, and felt it slide slowly down my cheek. I held eye contact, refused to turn my face away. I hoped she could see the hatred burning behind my eyes.

"You will never survive without me, Claire, darling. Nobody will ever pay attention to you, or care for you the way I have. You'll just carry on your whole life being invisible. If not me, what reason would anybody ever have to notice you? To think of you?" she hissed, toe to toe with me. She was so close I could feel her breath on my face, her narrowed eyes boring into me.

"Claire, darling. Listen carefully while I tell you something very important," she said, her voice low and dangerous. "If you leave me, if you move out and abandon me, you will live to regret it."

I left that evening.

THIRTY-TWO

'm standing outside number 48 St. Margaret's Avenue, shaking like a leaf. I cannot believe what I am about to do. It's Saturday morning, and while Noah's car is still outside the house, I also know that every Saturday morning, without fail, he goes out on a run. Not a short run either, Noah is a very fit and healthy individual. No, he will run for at least an hour, usually topping twelve kilometers. I assume that staying over at Lilah's house hasn't changed this.

But I've obviously timed myself to arrive extra early, watching to make sure I see him leave before I make my move. And sure enough, come 9 A.M. the door swings open and there he is, looking as gorgeous as ever. He's wearing tracksuit bottoms and an old T-shirt and has his earbuds in. I've squatted behind a tree on the opposite side of the road and faked tying a shoelace, watching him as he fiddles with his Fitbit.

But then, instead of kicking off his run, he does something strange. He looks back at the house, as though checking for something, and heads over to his car. He unlocks and opens the boot. From where I'm peering around the tree, I can see him removing an old gym bag and rummaging around in its pockets. Then he pulls out a phone. But it's not *his* phone. No, his phone is sitting on his shoulder, strapped there by one of those fancy running belts. This phone is an odd little brick, like the burner kind a drug dealer would use. My heart thuds in my chest as I watch him slide it into his trackie bottoms. While his back is turned as he sorts out the bag and the boot, I hurry away from the house. At the end of the road, I crouch down behind a tree and wait, holding my breath.

Sure enough, a few minutes later Noah appears. He's frowning at the burner phone then he presses it to his ear, still walking. He's coming toward me and I worry that if I look up at him, he'll feel my gaze and spot me, so I keep my head down, tucking myself into the smallest space I can. I hear his voice saying: "Hey . . . Yeah, I know, I'm sorry . . . I know, I'll make it up to you . . . Yeah. I know. Mmm . . ."

My stomach is in my mouth. *Who is he speaking to?*

"Listen, I need to wrap some stuff up first," he's saying, and I'm crawling along to try and keep up with him without being seen. My stomach is in knots.

"I know, I know, but I . . ." And then he's too far away, across the street from me, and there's no way I can follow him any longer without being seen. I let out a huff of frustration, collapsing back onto the ground with my back resting against a wall to compute what I've just learned.

Noah has a burner phone, which he is hiding from Lilah, and which he hid from me too. He is using it to speak to at least one person, though I have no idea who that person is. So there's Lilah, there's this new layer to Noah's double life and there's me. None of this is making any sense, none of it is slotting together. How does he have the fucking *time*?

I peer back over the wall tentatively and see him in the distance. He must have finished the phone call because his hands are now empty and he's jogging away confidently until he turns off toward the riverfront and I can no longer see him.

It takes a lot of strength to restrain myself from shouting after him, demanding to know who he was speaking to, begging him to take me back. But no, today isn't about Noah. It's about Lilah. I wait five minutes in case he has forgotten something and comes back early, but after that has passed I feel brave enough to head back to her yellow front door. I've been standing outside it in a panic for at least three minutes now. I don't know what I'm most afraid of: whether it's hearing what she has to say about Noah, finding out why she had my picture in her drawer, or why she was circling maternity rights information. Whatever it is, there's something gripping me by the throat, stopping me from knocking.

So I close my eyes and take deep breaths.

I had been living alone for seven months when I first started getting the phone calls from Mother. Contrary to what I had promised her, I had not made the slightest effort to visit her since moving out. Initially, guilt had kicked in and I had thrown her a bone in the form of a couple of brief emails, informing her of my safety and asking if she was well. I received pages and pages in response, short *novels,* all varying in storyline. In some, she was depressed, unable to get out of bed without her darling daughter, her reason for living, beside her at home. In others, she was having the time of her life, she had three new boyfriends and was partying in ways she could never have imagined had I still been living at home with her, because I had always been a block on her true potential. And in some she said she was glad I was gone because she had never truly loved me. I had been a negative presence in her life and she hoped that I realized now just how much I needed her, how much I owed her, because it should be obvious to me that without her I was nothing.

So I'd stopped emailing.

And then, three months later, the call came.

I remember experiencing that same gripping sensation around my throat at the sight of her name on the screen. It restricted my breathing, made me pause with my hand over the "Accept" button. Until finally, curiosity won out.

"Claire?" Her voice, sounding very cold and clear.

"Hi, Mother," I replied, trying not to sound as wary as I felt.

"Well, it's just a quick call," she began, sounding sharp and snappy in comparison to her usual dramatics. "I want to let you know I have cancer. Stage 4, incurable, in my lungs. No point even trying chemo and, to be honest, it's not worth the hassle. If I'm going to die, I'm doing it with a full head of hair, thank you very much. So anyway, now you know," she said, breezily. "Goodbye, Claire, darling." And with that, she hung up.

I stared at the phone in my hands for a long time, unsure what to do. Was this another game? A trick? Mother loved tricks; she loved to do anything that would capture my attention and send me running back to her. I quickly weighed up the pros and cons of calling her back, and decided I had to. A huge part of me believed this was just another lie, another ruse to get me rushing to her bedside with flowers and an apology. But I knew I couldn't live with myself if that turned out to be wrong.

So I called back, and she let me run through to voicemail. So I left one. And a text message. And I emailed. They were all roughly the same in content: I asked how long she had left, whether I could come and visit, how she was feeling. I told her how sorry I was, as I knew was expected of me. After a week I'd had no reply to any of them, so I sent a huge bouquet of her favorite flowers to the house, still too afraid to visit unannounced. Too wary of what I would find there. I was afraid of seeing her weak and frail, sickly and dying, proof that I had left her alone, sick and helpless. I was equally afraid to find her strong and healthy, playing out another lie so she could mess with my emotions as though I were a puppet with no feelings of my own. I was afraid of being pushed away in my own mother's dying moments. I was afraid of every other possible scenario when it came to her.

When I received no response to my gestures, I became angry. She was punishing me. This evil, lying woman did not have cancer. I was convinced of it. This was exactly the type of thing Mother would do to command attention, to force me to come back. She had once told the school she had sprained her ankle and kept me home for a week, running around her like a servant, bringing her food and wine in bed and plumping pillows behind her back. I had caught her in the middle of the night going to the bathroom, striding confidently along without so much as a twinge in her ankle, but had pretended not to see anything and continued doting on her for three more days after that.

She was doing the same thing again, but this time a more extreme scenario, because my defying her and leaving home was an extreme measure, so she had to punish me for it in equal measure. Yes, this was all a ruse, I told myself.

Except it wasn't.

THIRTY-THREE

September 11, 2025
Dear Diary,

The anniversary of Mother's death has hit me harder than I thought it would. I feel like there's no right way to mourn. I feel like I should be crying hysterically, but nothing comes. And then I feel guilt-ridden and awful. How terrible a person must I be, not to miss Mother at all? She wasn't perfect, but she tried her best, didn't she?

I didn't even tell Noah about the anniversary, I still didn't want to address it, didn't want her to taint this new life that I have with memories of her. But I guess somehow he found out about it—I have no clue how. And so in the morning, he had a bouquet of flowers ready and he told me he was taking me to the church where she is buried to lay them down.

Honestly, I got a bit upset. I felt it was invasive. He doesn't understand my relationship with her or the conflicted feelings I still have about her, and I didn't want to spend the whole day thinking about her when for so much of my childhood I was forced to put her first. I wanted to put Claire first today, to put Mother on the back burner of my mind. Just spend a normal, boring day with my fiancé.

Noah told me he thought this attitude was unhealthy, that I needed to process her death properly. And even if I didn't feel genuinely mournful, we could lay the flowers together and then leave and get lunch somewhere. I kicked up a fuss, said I didn't want to go and that he had no business pressuring me into it. He conceded this was true and apologized. I sat on the bed sulking for about ten minutes before I told him he was probably right, I should go and make my peace and that I appreciated his thoughtfulness.

He drove me to the church where I'd told him she was buried, a ramshackle field of gravestones outside a crumbling church isolated amidst endless residential southeast London streets. I hadn't visited the grave since her funeral, and as we walked past all the others with flowers and messages laid on them, I felt a fresh stab of guilt.

When we got to the gravestone, we stood in silence and I stared down at it, reading the words again and again and again.

Trina Arundale
1971–2024
Loving mother, friend and angel

I didn't choose those words. The guys at the funeral parlor did. I'd decided I couldn't care less what the tombstone said. But as I read it over and over and thought about how her remains were somewhere underneath, rotting away and feeding the earth, I began to sob.

I hunched over, wailing, the flowers beside me and Noah silently rubbing my back.

He waited in silence until I was finished, then took my hand and held it all the way back to the car.

When we got in, he'd told me he was proud of me.

I'm still not sure if I was crying from rage or sadness.

Claire

THIRTY-FOUR

The time for being afraid is over. I can't continue living in this limbo of guesses and half-truths. At the very least, it will give me the push I need to get over Noah and move on. Even though that thought makes my mouth tremble. I draw a deep breath and knock, hard, three times on the butter-colored door.

I hear light footsteps approaching and Lilah opens it. As soon as she sees me, her eyes widen and she tries to close the door in my face, but I step forward and jam my foot inside the frame.

"Lilah—"

"You need to go," she tells me shakily. "I'll call the police!"

So she knows who I am.

"Please, Lilah. I just want to speak to you," I tell her, trying to keep my voice calm and even.

I see her hesitate, but her knuckles are still white as she grips the edge of the door, and I try to make myself look as unthreatening as possible while she peers at me through the sliver of space, her beautiful eyes large and wide as a doe's.

"I just want to talk. I—I'm struggling to understand. To process what's happened," I explain.

"I can't let you in," she tells me quietly, eyes darting frantically.

"That's okay. We can talk out here?" I try. But I see her eyes flick to a neighbor opposite who is pruning a rosebush by the pavement, and I know a part of her doesn't want an audience to this conversation where she will have to admit to stealing my fiancé.

"Look, I really do just want to talk. Maybe we can have a cup of tea or something?" I try again. My voice is gentle, soft and reasonable, the tone I've used at petting zoos when trying to convince the lambs to come close enough for me to stroke them. I'm desperate for answers, need to understand why Noah has done this to me. It's worth humbling myself to act this way.

I can see her wavering, but eventually she must feel sorry for me because she lowers her head and opens the door so I can come in. I step in slowly, afraid of startling her, and rub my shoes on her door-mat politely.

"Let me go and switch the kettle on," she says. "You can sit down."

"Thank you." I nod, and perch myself awkwardly on the edge of the giant cream sofa where I saw them snuggle up together a few nights ago. I rub my hands up and down my legs, and my heart is beating unnaturally quickly as my whole body anticipates the pain that is sure to follow this conversation. The house smells of her. Sickly and floral. There aren't many signs of Noah around: a pair of shoes that I spotted beside the door, his coat on the rack. Everything is tidied away in its place. Carefully selected, neutral-colored trea-sures are out on display, decorating the shelves and alcoves. There is no room for mess in this woman's life.

A minute or two passes, and I can hear Lilah running the tap and taking mugs out. Something feels wrong, but I don't know what. It's as though my senses are on high alert, every sound ampli-fied, and my entire body has tensed, waiting for the danger to show itself. *Run,* my instincts think. *Stay,* the other part of me demands. *Stay and put an end to all this. Find out the truth. Find out what they're hiding.*

"Do you take cream or sugar?" she calls out.

I roll my eyes. Of *course* she serves her tea with cream and not semi-skimmed milk like the rest of the British population. I imag-ine snorting with laughter over this later with Sukhi and feel a burst of strength, sitting up a little taller.

"Just sugar, please, one spoon," I reply, shifting in my seat and wringing my hands together in my lap.

Lilah appears shortly afterward, two mugs in her hands. I notice she places mine on the coffee table in front of me rather than handing it to me.

"Thank you," I force out. I take the steaming cup and cradle it in both hands, happy to have something to hold to stop me fidgeting.

Lilah is looking at everything in the room except me, eyes darting here, there and everywhere. I notice she has also brought her mobile phone through, and it's sitting beside her on the armrest of the chair she's sunk into. She was beautiful in her pictures, but up close in real life, she's breathtaking. She looks airbrushed, for God's sake. I feel a stab of envy. Of course Noah would prefer a woman like this. Any man would. How can I even blame him for falling for her? I feel a flush of heat creep up my neck and my face redden with embarrassment that I ever thought I could compete with a woman like this.

"Why me?" I ask quietly, trying not to let my voice break.

"Excuse me?" she asks, looking directly at me for the first time.

"Why me? Why have you done this to me?"

"Look, Claire, I don't know what you think has happened, but I haven't—"

"You stole my fiancé!" I cut in, and can't help raising my voice. Lilah shrinks back into her chair.

"I—"

"He was all I had! Look at you, Lilah. *Look at yourself.*" I bristle, momentarily shocked by how much like Mother I sound, but I continue. "Look at all you have!" I take one hand off my coffee cup to gesture around me. "You are beautiful, you have this gorgeous house, you have money, a loving family. Noah was *all* I had, and you took him." My eyes have teared up now and I feel rage boiling inside me at the injustice of everything.

"Look, Claire, it's not like that. I know it seems unfair, but that's not what's happening."

"So what *is* happening?" I snap.

"It's . . . hard to explain," she says feebly.

"This is bullshit," I mutter under my breath.

I feel a sudden need to hurt her, to hurt her like she's hurt me. "Do you know about his burner phone?" I ask.

She draws in her breath sharply. "Burner phone?"

"Yes. The one he keeps in his car boot."

I watch with morbid fascination as Lilah closes her eyes for a moment, as though exhausted, and her eyebrows furrow in what looks like sadness before springing back into their usual perfect arch.

"I do. I thought he'd got rid of it."

Part of me is confused she knows about his secret. It makes my grand reveal much less grand, and significantly less satisfying. I wanted Lilah to feel the same shock and betrayal I felt days ago when I found out about her.

"It's none of your business, it's something I'll speak with him about. If he has another burner phone then I know what he's using it for and . . . well. We'll have to deal with it, I suppose."

I watch as her face crumples, noticing that it doesn't seem to detract from her beauty at all. I thought seeing her in pain would make me feel better but find that it doesn't. Not at all. Lilah may be feeling shit about herself, but it doesn't change all that's happened. It doesn't bring Noah home or erase all his lies and deceptions.

She gathers herself quickly, to her credit.

"I'm sorry. For telling you that." I don't know why I'm apologizing, but there's something about the familiarity of betrayal that makes me feel sorry for her. We've both been duped by the same man, after all.

She shrugs.

"What is it for?" I ask.

She opens her mouth, as though to answer, then shuts it again.

Her lips thin into a hard line and the seconds tick by audibly, the grandfather clock in the corner of the room highlighting the silence that drags out.

"You came to my office," she says, breaking the silence with a change of subject. She sounds very confident.

I look up at her. There's no point in denying it, she clearly knows. I shrug. "I wanted to see if I could find any evidence about why Noah left me."

She closes her eyes for a moment, her nostrils flared, as though trying to remain calm. Which irks me, because if either of us should be struggling to remain calm right now, it should be me. The forgotten fiancée. Not the thieving lover.

"And did you?" she asks instead, which surprises me.

"Yes, actually. I did." I reach into my pocket and pull out the photograph of me, hold it up to her triumphantly. I watch her shoulders tense.

"Care to explain this?" I ask, tossing it onto the coffee table.

"I printed it out to share with the others at the office," she mumbles.

"Well, that much is obvious. Why?" I ask.

I watch her fight with herself to find the correct answer, but eventually she sets her shoulders back and stares me dead in the eye. "So they knew not to let you in."

I snort. "Why would you do that? It was the first and only time I ever visited. I didn't know your name until the other day! And when did you get that photograph of me?"

"When you first met Noah," she admits. Her tone has shifted and something about it seems off. The hairs on the back of my neck stand up and I feel newly apprehensive about this situation, about where this conversation is headed. I came in feeling confident, set to find answers, but I suddenly feel like I want to get out of here, like I'm being left with more questions than before.

Beside her, her phone flashes repeatedly. Someone is messaging her in quick succession. Her eyes flit to it quickly, then she reaches out and turns it onto its screen so I can't see it anymore. I bristle.

* * *

I was fifteen. I quickly snapped my laptop shut the moment Mother entered my room so she couldn't see the screen. Usually, I could sense her presence, hear her footsteps. But I'd been immersed in what I was reading and hadn't noticed her approach.

"Dinner is ready," she said, keeping her eyes fixed on me. "What were you looking at, Claire, darling?" she asked, taking a step closer.

"Nothing," I replied quickly. Too quickly.

"All right then. Well, go wash your hands and sit down to eat," she said, standing very still. I hesitated, not wanting to leave the laptop. That momentary hesitation was all it took. She leaped toward it with alarming speed, snatching it from my bed and rushing through to the kitchen, where she flipped it open to find my internet window shining up at her. I rushed after her, gabbling that it was a school project, excuses flowing out of my mouth like bile.

She had a hand to her chest as though I had driven the breath from her body.

"Claire? What is this?" She turned the laptop so the screen was facing me. The webpage I'd been looking at was revealed. **LEGAL PARENTAL EMANCIPATION FOR MINORS.**

"It's for a school project, Mother. That's all."

"Your school is teaching you how to *divorce* your parents?" she said, her voice very quiet.

"Yes," I replied.

"You are a liar, Claire," she said.

"No, Mother. I swear," I started, even though I could hear the lies on my lips and they tasted of poison.

"Don't you love me? Don't you know how much *I* love *you*?"

I barely had a chance to process what was happening before she had raised my laptop and lobbed it at me full-force. I took a step back, but not fast enough. It landed against my shinbone with a hard crack, the screen fractured, and my leg gave way beneath me. I scrabbled backward like a crab to the safety of my bedroom, tears streaming down my face and the cut on my leg leaving droplets of blood on the kitchen floor. She didn't follow me. I cradled my bruised and bloodied shin and wept quietly, listening to her loud sobs and wails through my bedroom door.

"So you knew? You knew this whole time that he had started seeing me? What was this, some sort of sick couple's game? Did he ever love me?" I sob. I'm openly crying now, but I can't stop now that I've started. "Was this some messed-up, twisted game to see how pathetic a woman he could entice? Did you both choose me together? What the fuck is this, Lilah?"

She flinches and glances at her phone, which somehow enrages me even more.

"No, Claire, please, it wasn't like that . . ." she starts, but I'm too angry to listen anymore. The sound of my name on her lips makes me feel sick. *Claire, darling, please,* Mother said as I packed my bags to leave her forever.

"And what about the contract in your office desk?" I ask.

Lilah pales. "What?"

"Why were you circling the maternity provisions? Are you having a fucking baby with my fiancé?" I shout.

"No! No, I'm not pregnant," Lilah says hurriedly. She's reaching for her phone now, one hand on it.

"So why were you circling maternity entitlement?"

I have stood up from the sofa now, still gripping my drink. She is crying now. She looks like a fucking portrait, an angel shedding tears for her loved ones, her lips trembling daintily. Nothing like me, the furious, red and blotchy beast before her. "*Why were you circling maternity entitlement?*" I roar again.

"We're trying! We're trying for a baby!" she gasps through her fetching sobs.

And then everything goes hazy as every atom of me blooms into dark, festering wrath.

THIRTY-FIVE

Before I know what I'm doing, my hand is stretched out and I've flung the cup of boiling tea toward Lilah's face. She shrieks and lurches backward, but I've stepped forward and have pulled her up and out of her chair with surprising ease. She's small and light.

"You fucking bitch!" I scream.

"God, please, Claire, you don't understand . . ." she starts, whimpering as she tries to wipe the tea from her eyes so she can see me. "I can't explain this situation properly," she gasps.

I can't explain why he left us, darling. Other than it was because of you. Because he didn't want you, I hear Mother saying in my head, speaking about my father.

"I would love my baby. I would want and hold and care for my baby," I tell her. "You already have the world. You don't deserve to have his baby too."

"Please, Claire," she tries again, her voice barely above a whisper. Snot has begun to seep from her nostrils.

I'm disgusted by her, repulsed by this entire ugly situation. I don't want to touch her, to have her become this strange in-between object that both Noah and I have touched, one with love and the other with hatred. And so I push her away, desperate to leave this house, and am stilled by the sound of a loud crack. I realize she has hit her head on the edge of the marble mantelpiece.

"Lilah?" I whisper.

I look down at her body, crumpled in an awkward heap, dark

blood pooling beneath the head. I stare at the glistening burgundy puddle and try to make myself feel something—anything. Relief? Guilt? Regret? Fear? But strangely, and for the first time in a long time, I feel nothing at all. Does this make me a monster or is it how shock works?

Lilah is completely still. I wonder if I should try to stem the bleeding, but even I can tell it's pointless. Her head is caved in on one side, dented almost, and she's foaming at the mouth. There is no undoing this.

Oh, God.

I step backward and stagger, losing my balance. I take in the scene. Tea spilled everywhere, a dead woman, and me, in the middle of it all.

My brain starts going into overdrive. The neighbor across the street definitely saw me coming into the house. Fuck. *Fuck.*

And then Lilah's phone vibrates and I look down to see a message from Noah.

Why the fuck did you let her into the house, Lilah?! I'm on my way home now.

And that's when I hear the police sirens.

THIRTY-SIX

February 3, 2025
Dear Diary,

I'M ENGAGED!
   I AM MARRYING NOAH COORS!
   I AM GOING TO BE MRS. COORS!
   I cannot believe it. I can't stop shaking and crying, this is the happiest day of my life. Noah proposed. Even in writing it looks bizarre, as though it's somebody else's news and not mine. He totally took me by surprise—I truly didn't think he'd be ready for this anytime soon. After all, we've not been together long in the grand scheme of things. But I got home from work and he had a romantic song playing, one of those old Etta James ones, and he had lit candles everywhere. Candles on literally every surface, it was a huge fire hazard but so stunning. Streaming from the ceiling were dozens and dozens of white paper birds—a flight of doves hanging at different levels, drifting above us with their wings carefully folded to replicate birds in flight. He'd made a romantic dinner too, and I walked through the door stunned by the sight of the origami doves and candles and freaking out about what the hell was going on. I think my heart stopped beating in my chest in apprehension.

   And then he got down on one knee and proposed. And it was with the ring we had seen together, the ring from the Christmas market, with birds engraved onto the band. I couldn't believe it, could barely even take in what was happening when he spoke.

"Claire, I know it's early days but when you know, you know. I don't want to wait. I want to be your husband and build a life with you. You're the love of my life. Will you marry me?"

Of course, I started sobbing hysterically and screaming "yes" right away, before he could change his mind or take it back. I could barely even eat because I was so excited, but he had gone to such an effort and made a lovely spread—a charcuterie board with the wine I had recommended to him when we met and some cheese we fell in love with in Venice and grapes and meats and fancy crusty rolls from that pricey Borough Market stall I love so much.

He told me he wanted to love me forever, that he'd gone back to the market and picked up the ring and had been saving it while he worked out the proposal scene. I was overwhelmed by his thoughtfulness. I didn't need a big flashy diamond, and he knew it. He knew what I'd want would be something thoughtful, something lovingly picked out just for me, that rested on a beautiful joint memory.

A part of me felt sad I didn't have anyone to call to share the exciting news with—but that feeling was fleeting. I don't need anybody else, not now that I have Noah. I'm so happy . . . So happy that a tiny part of me worries it's too good to be true, if it will all come crashing down soon. But that's just me being a natural pessimist. I deserve this happiness. I deserve Noah.

Claire

PART TWO

8 MONTHS LATER

THIRTY-SEVEN

May 15, 2026
Dear Sukhi,

I'm sorry it's taken me so long to reply to your last letter—thank you for
sending it. Hearing from you is one of the few things I look forward to,
and news about life on the outside helps to keep me grounded. I'm sorry
I reply so scarcely—sometimes I am just so ashamed of the situation
you're in, having to write to someone in prison, that I can't bring myself
to make the trip to the postal box. But I appreciate your letters and keep
every one of them, even when I don't reply. How is everyone at the
office? Is my media coverage still terrible? I'm almost afraid for when I
come out, of what I'll find waiting for me. The things they'll be saying
about me . . . I doubt I'd have managed to stay off social media this
long if it weren't for . . . well, being in prison!

I have a new cellmate. My last one was released on Monday, the
new one is called Ella. She's maybe a bit older than me. I was wary of
her at first, she asked me what the fuck I was looking at on day one, but
we've found ourselves an easier rhythm now. I have no interest in
making my time here even more miserable by not getting on with my
cellmate. It's awkward enough having to go to the toilet in front of a
stranger without having someone giving you evil eyes while you go.
She's in for battery on a night out. I asked her why she's being kept on
remand and she just said "previous charges." I didn't ask about those—
I'm not sure I want to know. We mostly keep to ourselves, but it's nice
to have the company. For the few days between my old cellmate leaving

and Ella arriving I was left with nothing but my thoughts. They've been spiraling again.

I have a headache almost constantly and would die for an ibuprofen. Unfortunately, the prison isn't very keen to hand out pills to prisoners, so I'm having to massage my temples all the time to try and keep it at bay. Anyway, please do keep writing to me. The closer we get to the trial date, the more nervous I am. I don't know if I'm more scared of being found guilty of murder and rotting away in here forever, or of being released and having to face reality after all that's happened. It feels like there's no winning situation for me.

Claire

THIRTY-EIGHT

Grosvenor, my legal-aid barrister, flicks a speck of lint from my blazer, her caramel-colored eyes narrowing critically as she sweeps them over me. She frowns pensively. I've dressed as smartly as I can, in a discreet knee-length black dress, paired with the flat shoes she told me to wear so that I would look meek and small. I've pulled my hair into an unassuming low ponytail. Grosvenor is wearing a dress similar to mine but which I can tell is more expensive by the tailoring. It's fashionable, which doesn't surprise me. She must only be in her mid-to-late thirties. She has topped it with a blazer, mid-height block heels and her trademark sleek straight hair. It falls to her shoulders like a protective sheet. Her makeup is very pared back, with a nude lip against her ghostly white skin, and she looks ready for business.

"Right, today's not going to be easy, okay?" she tells me sternly, gripping both my shoulders. I nod back at her. I'm emotionally spent, utterly exhausted, yet my body feels coiled with tension. Now my fate is squarely in the hands of other people, ones I can't control or persuade.

Everyone can be persuaded to do what we want eventually, darling, Mother would say, waggling her eyebrows knowingly. But I'm Claire, and I have never had the sway over others that she had.

"They're going to come for you, hard. But we know what they're gonna say," Grosvenor tells me.

"We do?" I venture.

"We do. And I have counter-arguments ready for all their probable lines of attack. So don't get stressed, don't get emotional and don't react, okay? That is really important. Whatever is said, do *not* react. The last thing we need is some journalist getting a photograph of you looking angry and plastering it all over the *Daily Fail Online*. We can discuss everything in private afterward, okay?"

This rundown is making me even more nervous, and this time when I nod it's shakier. I shouldn't have looked at the social media folders yesterday—it's set me on edge. I think if Grosvenor had been in the room she wouldn't have let me, but she'd popped out to the toilet and I politely asked her young and nervous-looking junior counsel, who obliged me. These are folders Grosvenor keeps in her files tracking all social media posts on relevant people's pages since The Accident. I've been living in this bizarre limbo for the last eight months, my only understanding of the outside world coming from her. But seeing the social media posts printed out on paper has given me the horrible wake-up call that I badly need. It had made me realize the severity of what happened, and the possible repercussions I'm facing.

NOAH COORS

01:43

Will I ever feel okay again?

12 comments 56 likes

NOAH COORS

13:35

Went to do food shop and they had Lilah's favorite chocolates—the ones they only bring out at Easter. Bought them for her out of habit. Still missing her so much.

8 comments 48 likes

NOAH COORS

04:12

Can't sleep. Can't switch my brain off. Wish I'd been home to save her. Wish I'd never gone on that run.

28 comments 32 likes

NOAH COORS

08:19

Why???????

2 comments 8 likes

I'd been starved of information about what had been going on with Noah since the terrible accident—desperate to know how all the people involved were doing. But his page made for painful reading. I felt a hollow sensation in my belly with every status I read— alongside a stab of pain at all the things I'd hoped he'd written but hadn't. No words of endurance or acceptance. Not a mention of my name. It was clear from the printouts of his mournful late-night posts that he basically just had a public breakdown over the loss of his perfect girlfriend, followed by an extended lapse of silence about anything or anybody else.

Grosvenor has my social media pages carefully paper-clipped together as well, of course. Both the Claire account and my dummy Emma account, though obviously both of these have been silent for the past eight months.

Lilah's page, unlike Noah's, was loud as a marching band. It had been filled with messages of love and grief every day since the news broke, pictures and old stories shared on her feed like it was a blooming scrapbook.

FELICITY NEWARK

16:34

Remember this day last year? Was so funny. Can't believe no more days like this to come. Miss you so much you gorgeous angel. Love you always xxxxxxxxx

KEVIN MARKWELL

09:10

RIP xxxxxxxxxxxxx Miss u x

17:08

Can't stop thinking about you tonight. I miss you so much. Can't believe we'll never have another night out together again. You were too good for this world, Lilah. Love you. xx

KIM LEE

19:12

Still thinking of you. I'm sorry I wasn't there enough at the end. Hope you're shining up there, angel girl xxxx

She didn't have as many comments before she died. It's as though people are using her Facebook page as a diary to share their own emotions and feelings of guilt. Guilt over not having seen her for so long, guilt for not picking up her last call, guilt about canceling their last dinner meeting . . . all I see on her page is guilty people looking for a way to lessen their own heavy burdens.

But not me. With Grosvenor's help, I've gone over what happened that awful day at 48 St. Margaret's Avenue countless times and am convinced that I am not guilty of anything other than giving way to my emotions. I should have stayed calm and cool. But I didn't, I lost it, triggered by the idea of Noah having the baby he'd denied me with another woman. And it led to this terrible accidental death. And honestly, thank God that Noah called the police from his run, because they came right away. If they hadn't, I would have had to pull myself together and try to deal with her injury myself, while sorting out an ambulance and all the rest. It's as though Noah was there to lend a hand without even knowing he was doing so.

Grosvenor disagrees. "It should have been you who made the call. That would have helped our case immeasurably. It would have looked like you were doing everything in your power to get help," she said.

"But I didn't have time to get help, I barely had enough time to register she'd fallen," I argued.

"It is what it is, we can't circle around if-onlys. We have to work with the facts."

I huffed in annoyance, exhausted by arguing with her. We've argued a lot, which gives me hope that we have a fighting chance at trial because Grosvenor is *good* at arguing. We argued about why I didn't make the call for an ambulance when Lilah hit her head. We argued when I had to admit I had pushed her. I'd omitted to share that originally, too afraid, aware of just how guilty it made me look.

"You don't think you could have cut me some slack and told me this at the beginning? Now we need to go through this again from the start." Grosvenor's voice dripped icy irritation.

"Sorry," I mumbled, shuffling my feet under the table.

"You honestly didn't think we would find out eventually?"

I shriveled in my seat. "She must bruise like a peach; I really didn't push hard. It wasn't meant to hurt her—I wanted to keep her away from me!"

"Self-defense?" Grosvenor asked.

"I didn't say that," I muttered. "I was angry about the baby. I couldn't bear to look at her and wanted to get out of her perfect house—I didn't push hard."

"It doesn't matter how hard you pushed her, Claire. The fact of the matter is you pushed a woman, causing her to crack her head on a mantelpiece and die. If not for that push, she would still be here. You think the prosecution are going to wave this murder charge away and say, 'No big deal, it wasn't a *hard* push?'"

I began to cry.

"I hope those are tears of regret," was all Grosvenor said with a sigh. For a moment, I thought she meant regret about lying to her.

It took a minute before I realized she meant regret for pushing Lilah.

We've even argued about Mother. I still don't understand why she is involved in any way in this case, why this is something I should examine with Grosvenor. She calls it a mitigating factor, but I've told her I don't need stupid pitiful excuses about my rough childhood because I *didn't mean to kill Lilah.*

Grosvenor disagrees. She really does like to cover all bases.

"Did your mother ever hit you?" she asked me one day.

I frowned. "Sometimes."

"Often?"

A shrug. "I can't remember."

"Can you try?"

"I don't understand what Mother has to do with this case," I argued once more.

"Please, Claire. Can you just do what I'm asking?"

"Where is my necklace?"

I was sixteen, and Mother stood at my bedroom door, leaning against the frame with her arms crossed. She'd asked the question casually, in a tone that suggested she couldn't care less, but I could see a glint of that hateful darkness behind her eyes and my heart sank at the realization that yet another argument was in store.

"What necklace?" I dared ask.

"You know what necklace." Her lips pursed.

I sucked in my cheeks, unsure what to do next, and my fingers twitched in anticipation of an attack. If I asked again, she'd get angrier. If I stayed quiet, she'd start to prod me. I licked my cracked lips.

"The necklace that David bought me," she continued when I couldn't decide what to do.

My brain started flitting through her roster of men, trying to recall which one was David and if I even knew about any necklace he'd given her.

"It was gold, and had little butterflies dangling from it," she went on.

I looked to the ground. I'd never seen a butterfly necklace.

"Why are you still sitting there? Help me search for it," she ordered.

"In my room?" I asked.

"Yes. I've looked everywhere else and can't find it, so it must be in your room."

"It's not," I assured her. That was the wrong thing to say.

"You stole it, didn't you?" She was seething, taking a step into my room. Instinctively, I shrank back, as though with that step she'd crossed an invisible barrier and now that she was in my personal space, I was more vulnerable than before.

"I didn't, Mother," I said, knowing it would do no good.

"You're a filthy little liar, I know you took it! It was so beautiful you nicked it!" she yelled. Another step toward me.

"Mother, I really don't know which necklace you're talking about," I pleaded.

"*Liar!*" she shrieked. "It would never look right on your chubby little rugby-player neck. You were jealous of how it looked on me, so you took it, didn't you?"

I raised a hand self-consciously to my neck and mentally added it to my list of physical features to be embarrassed about. *Maybe I should get some scarves,* I thought to myself.

"I did not take your necklace," I tried again. "Why would I when you would see it on me if I wore it?" I reasoned.

There was no point—Mother couldn't be reasoned with. Not when she was like this.

"Well, then, you took it to hide away from me, to upset me. You were jealous that a man could like me enough to give me something so lovely and special, when you've never even had a boyfriend, let alone a gift from one! So you took it, and you hid it, didn't you?" she ranted on, growing more hysterical. Then she began flinging my things everywhere, rooting rapidly through my own pathetic costume jewelry collection before flinging the stand across the room and rifling through my desk drawers, sending things flying as I begged her to stop.

I ran and grabbed her arm at one point, in a moment of madness, trying to prevent her from turning all my desk drawers out onto the floor. She hissed like a cat, spun around and smacked me on the side of my face, with her fist closed. It was the first time she'd punched rather than slapped me.

I barely even registered the pain before she spun back around again and continued her search for the necklace.

Once my room had been turned upside down, with no sign of her precious necklace, she stalked out, wagging a warning finger at me. "When I find that necklace, Claire, darling, you're in for it. Do you hear me, you thieving little cow?"

"Yes, Mother."

A week or so later, she found it. I don't know where, but it was around her neck one morning at breakfast and she looked at me, smirking over her mug of coffee, as though daring me to make a comment. My bruises were a dirty yellow by then. I said, "Good morning, Mother," and sat down, keeping my eyes averted from those golden butterflies and wishing the chain would tighten around her long, slim throat.

Grosvenor wanted an answer. I couldn't avoid it. If I closed my eyes tightly, I could see myself at several different stages of my life. Age six, crying in my bedroom, scribbling in a teddy-bear journal "I hate Mummy," my right cheek hot and pink. Fast-forward and I'm fifteen, staring into the mirror to study my swollen upper lip, holding an ice cube to it. "I remember her hitting me several times," I said eventually, with a frown. "I remember the moments that followed more clearly than the violence itself."

Grosvenor nodded, her face betraying no emotion. She's good at hiding them. Good at remaining distant from me while peeling apart my soul and forcing me to relive traumas and horrors that go far beyond the death of Lilah.

"This is going to be a rough ride, Claire," she warned me.

I waited for *darling* to follow, but it never came.

THIRTY-NINE

That's Rick Dodgson for the prosecution," Grosvenor whispers, nodding over at a short, stocky man with shiny skin. Strange blotches frame his hairline under the curled white wig, and he scratches absentmindedly at a rash on his neck while speaking with one of his team. He has the same sharp, predatory gaze as Grosvenor.

We are standing in a sad, scuffed corridor in the Old Bailey, waiting for our assigned courtroom to empty out so the trial can begin. I keep fidgeting, unable to stand still, tugging at the hem of my dress. I'm conscious that while it was once quite flattering on me, now it hangs loose, due to my recent weight loss, leaving me looking lank and frumpy.

A thought crosses my mind. "Will we see Noah today?" I ask Grosvenor, wincing at how pathetically hopeful my voice sounds.

"No, Claire. He has been called as a witness so is unable to be present in open court until he has given his evidence. Those are the rules."

"Oh."

"Try to focus," she tells me gently. I read between the lines. *Focus on yourself for once, not on Noah and what he is doing.*

"Remember how this all works?" she asks me.

I make some sort of incoherent mumbling noise, my throat tight.

"What is it?" she asks.

"Will . . . will Lilah's family be there?" I'm embarrassed to ask, to be so selfish, but the thought of having to face them makes me want to turn and run.

Grosvenor frowns slightly. "Her mother has been called as a witness, you'll see her then, but just look ahead and keep your eyes on the judge or the witness in the box. Do not look into the public gallery, do not look for the victim's family. It's the last thing anyone needs and will only be upsetting to everyone involved," she warns.

"Okay. What else?"

"Slimy old Dodgson goes first. I won't lie to you, I've worked with him before and he's going to go big and he's going to play dirty, so you just need to stay calm and remember we get our turn afterward. Anything he says, no matter how frustrating, we will grit our teeth and counter when it's our turn."

"We will counter," I parrot, my voice wobbling.

She nods, her lips set firm, and turns on her black heels. I follow, feeling like a lamb to the slaughter.

"It is the prosecution's belief, Your Honor, that Claire Arundale attended Lilah Andersson's house with the full intention of causing her great harm, and therefore we will be pushing for a conviction of murder with a life sentence," Dodgson states, sitting back down.

Grosvenor rises from her seat.

She holds her own, looking firm and confident, and I stare fixedly at a split end in my hair to disguise the nervous tension that is making me tremble.

"It is the defense's case that Claire Arundale accidentally killed the victim, Lilah Andersson, in a moment of provocation with low culpability. Miss Arundale was previously a blameless member of society with no previous convictions. We shall therefore be pleading for a charge of manslaughter by reason of loss of control, Your Honor." She sits back down, patting me under the table to reassure me. We've gone through this several times, and she assures me that, if her plea bargaining is successful, I'll only be sentenced to a couple of years in prison. She's told me it's the best I can hope for.

The judge peers at me closely and I look back down at the floor, not wanting to appear confrontational in any way. After a moment, Her Honor Abigail Black nods.

"The first witness the prosecution call is medical examiner Dianne Campbell, who carried out the autopsy on the victim," Dodgson bellows.

I try to swallow, but my throat refuses to function.

FORTY

April 5, 2025
Dear Diary,

I've been so busy at work recently, trying to impress everyone and avoid any stupid slip-ups, but now I can breathe a sigh of relief because Noah and I are going on holiday together today. I know I've been droning on about it for a while but it's finally here and soon enough I'll be basking in the Italian sunshine. We've been talking about where to go for a while and it was actually Noah who chose Venice—he said it would be romantic. I've never been before, but I can't wait! He said we can think of it as a celebration of my new job, which is so nice. It feels like a great time to become even closer as we take our first trip away together.

In the morning (I'd barely slept, I was too excited) he surprised me with some prosecco and orange juice in bed. It felt like Christmas, when Mother would pop a bottle open and she'd have Buck's fizz and I'd have just orange juice, but it would feel fancy in a champagne glass.

And then I got ready for the airport. Usually, I just travel in leggings and a jumper but I wanted to look nice for Noah, so I made more of an effort, wearing a (still comfy) cute cotton jersey day dress and some sandals. I added a slick of red lipstick last-minute, because it felt very glam and appropriate for Italy.

When we were boarding the plane, I was a bit self-conscious. There were loads of other British couples like us, but there were a few beautiful leggy Italian girls among us, too, and I couldn't help but feel a bit pale and dumpy beside them. And underdressed—lipstick aside.

But Noah was such a gent, he didn't even look their way but kept his hand in mine the whole time, chatting away to me and making me feel relaxed and cared for. I hate the intrusive thoughts I get, Mother's voice hissing her nasty words at me. They make me feel like I'm never good enough, force me to compare myself to other people when I know it will be to my detriment. Noah says that my differences are what set me apart and drew him to me in the first place, but sometimes I wish my differences were a bit more . . . conventionally beautiful.

Mother was always beautiful—on the outside, to make up for the poison inside. When I was little, I used to wish I looked more like her. Whenever somebody complimented me on my thick chestnut hair or said how lovely my brown eyes were, Mother would soak it in as though they were praising her. "Yes, that's my Claire! A true beauty!" But when we were on our own she'd say to me, "Don't get a big head, Claire, darling. Your eyes are lovely, they're like mine but a bit murkier. And you can thank me for your mane of hair, though the color is a little dull in comparison to mine."

Anyway, I don't know why I'm sitting here writing about Mother when I'm on my way to Italy with a gorgeous man. I'm going to write a list of the things I want to do so that when we land we can look at them together and work through the checklist.

1. *Have some great red wine*
2. *Have a great pizza*
3. *Have some great pasta*
4. *Have great sex (obviously)*
5. *Visit an outdoor market*
6. *Go on a gondola*
7. *A sightseeing tour?*
8. *Visit Doge's Palace*
9. *A sunset cruise*
10. *Walk over Rialto Bridge*

And can you see the weird red smudge on the side of the page here? I somehow cut my finger open when I was trying to open a dodgy can of fizzy aranciata from the airport shop. The metal must have been old because the part you pull open just basically crumpled and ripped in half and cut my finger. Noah took it to the counter and complained and they gave me a plaster, but it's bled through. We joked about it and said it's probably an omen that something terrible and gruesome will happen to me when we get there, some sort of tragic boating accident where I'll lose a limb next!

Things can't stay perfect forever, after all.

Claire

FORTY-ONE

DR. DIANNE CAMPBELL

The jury is silent as each of them takes in the injury documents and photographs that Dodgson has submitted to the court. Grosvenor tries to turn her body away from me, to shield me from seeing the photographs in front of her, but I catch the flash of crimson and I remember standing in that perfect cream room with Lilah's skull caved in, bleeding out onto the carpet.

I feel momentarily lightheaded and grip the table with my hands to stop myself from swaying.

"Have some water." Grosvenor slides a cup toward me, her voice uncharacteristically gentle. "And try not to look at the photographs."

I close my eyes, gathering myself, as Dr. Campbell begins to speak, her thick Scottish accent making me frown in concentration.

"You can see here," she says, pointing at a medical illustration that I refuse to look at, "the skull has been dented at the pterion, just by the temple. This was the main injury that would have led to death by bleed on the brain."

"Is it common for this sort of injury to occur?" Dodgson asks her.

"It is not an uncommon head injury, and in fact there is an artery that runs right below the pterion here"—she points again—"which means that any sort of traumatic impact to the skull in this area can very easily lead to aneurysms or hematomas."

I'm trying to follow as best I can, but the medical language is throwing me and I'm not sure what's going on. I look to Grosvenor for reassurance, but she's scribbling away on a pad as though it all makes perfect sense to her. I risk a glance at the jury and can see a few frowns as they try to keep up.

"And so you're saying that the cause of death was an injury or impact to the skull?" Dodgson confirms.

"I am, yes."

"And do you think it possible that the injury stemmed from the victim knocking her head against the mantelpiece as shown?" he asks, a picture of the crime scene appearing for those in the court-room to assess. The mantelpiece looms in the center of the room, and all I can think is how sharp the corners look, how hard the marble surround must have felt when Lilah hit her skull against it.

"Yes, I do think that if a person were to hit their head on the corner of this mantelpiece it could very easily impact the skull hard enough to cause the brain to bleed," Dr. Campbell confirms.

"Can you tell us about her other injuries?" Dodgson asks.

I take a deep breath—this is the evidence I am most concerned about.

"We found some light bruising on the right shoulder that would indicate a hand pressed against it," she says.

"Can you show us what you mean?" Dodgson asks, and I won-der for a moment if he's specifically trying to make me have a break-down in public. I draw another deep, shaky breath.

A photograph of Lilah's tiny little shoulder appears before us, a light lilac palm print visible on the exposed flesh.

"This here is a match for a palm shape," Dianne explains.

"So it's fair to assume she was pushed?" Dodgson confirms.

"Yes, it is my professional opinion based on the outline of this bruise that the victim was pushed on the day of her death."

"An action violent enough to cause her to fall and hit her head?" Dodgson asks.

"Yes."

"Leading to her death?"

"Yes."

*   *   *

"I can't believe you would even suggest I don't love you," Mother wailed hysterically, tears streaming down her face. I was thirteen, and it had been one of our first proper arguments, the first time I'd really dared to speak out and tell her how I felt.

"Well, you don't act like it," I told her sullenly, teenage angst roiling in me and refusing to back down in the face of her crocodile tears.

"Claire, darling, I *love* you. You are my first and only child, is that not proof enough?"

I narrowed my eyes at her. "That doesn't prove anything. It just proves you didn't want another kid."

"Why would I, when the one I have is perfect and fulfills me so much?" She sobbed, hunched over to make herself seem small and vulnerable.

I bit my tongue on all the retorts that stirred in me then: the fact that she never told me she loved me unless it was to manipulate me; the fact that she never behaved as though she wanted a child; the fact that she always put herself and her feelings first. Instead, I clenched my fists and remained silent.

"I am telling you that I love you, Claire, and that should be proof enough," she insisted, her tears drying and anger leaking into her voice.

I shrugged and replied, "Okay."

Inside, I was imagining pummeling her vengefully, screaming at her. *Do you still love me now, Mother?* I'd ask, feeling her flesh quail beneath my pounding fists.

I breathe in slowly as Grosvenor stands, Dodgson shooting me a smug look, his eyebrows raised just a fraction as he saunters past me to take his seat.

Grosvenor makes confident eye contact with me for just a split second, and I feel like she's trying to say to me, *Don't worry, we're going to be okay.* I nod back, the tiniest lowering of my head.

"Dr. Campbell, can you confirm that the pterion that was fractured, causing the bleed on the victim's brain identified as the primary cause of death, is in fact the weakest point in the skull?" Grosvenor asks, keeping her voice light and matter-of-fact.

"I do confirm that it is the weakest part of the skull," Dr. Campbell replies.

"So it would be fair to say that it did not require a huge amount of force to cause this injury? That it is hypothetically possible that the victim merely tripped and sustained the injury without any external force causing the fall?" Grosvenor asks.

"It is possible for a person to trip, hitting their head, and then to suffer a bleed to the brain with no external force applied, yes."

"Thank you," Grosvenor says, and I hear whispering among the members of the jury that makes the hairs on the back of my neck stand up.

"Order," the judge reprimands, and I am thankful.

"And to confirm: the partial print on the victim's shoulder could have been caused at any point and by any person in the twelve hours prior to the fatal head injury. There is no conclusive evidence that it was inflicted by my client in the same time frame as the estimated time of death?"

"It is indeed possible that the bruise could have occurred before the defendant went to the victim's home, and the partial bruise is not identifiable as Claire Arundale's print."

"And when looking at the expert report we can see that the victim's blood samples revealed she was in fact very anemic at the time of her death?" Grosvenor continues. I look up. I was unaware of this and am unsure of its potential significance.

"Yes, blood samples did confirm that Lilah Andersson was anemic at the time of her death."

"And am I correct in understanding that anemia can cause people to bruise particularly easily? From less force than it takes to cause the average person to bruise?" Grosvenor asks.

My eyes widen.

"I would agree that the victim was more likely to bruise than someone who was not suffering from anemia."

"So to summarize: You agree that the victim required less pressure than the average person to cause her to bruise? That it is impossible to be sure the palm print in question was caused by the defendant? And that it is entirely possible that the victim merely tripped in her own home and had the terrible luck of hitting the weakest part of her skull, leading to her accidental death?"

I blink.

Dr. Campbell shifts in her seat, but she's already nodding slowly. "Yes, that summary is accurate," she concedes.

"No further questions, Your Honor," Grosvenor says with a glance toward the judge.

My counsel turns to face me and she is smiling.

For the first time I find myself thinking that, thanks to Grosvenor, I may actually have a fighting chance of clearing my name.

FORTY-TWO

LAURA THORPE

Dodgson has called his second witness to the stand. My heart begins to race as soon as I see the face of the woman who is trotting up the aisle. It's Laura Thorpe. She flicks her hair over her shoulder and bats her lashes at the jury. I have not seen this woman in thirteen years. Thirteen years since she last tormented me and she's somehow been found from the rubble of my childhood and presented in court today. I feel white-hot rage take over my entire body as she sits down primly, still with that same annoying smirk on her face she wore constantly at school.

"Mrs. Thorpe, is it accurate to say that you were a school friend of Claire Arundale from the ages of eleven through to fifteen?" Dodgson asks.

How did he find Laura?

I slide a note discreetly to Grosvenor across the table. It reads: *WTF?*

She slides one back. *He's trying to paint a picture of who you are. Stay unfazed.*

That's easy for Grosvenor to say. Her decades-old archnemesis isn't a witness for the prosecution, trying to get her convicted on a murder charge.

"Well, I wouldn't go as far as to say we were friends," Laura replies in that same snide singsong tone I recall from years ago. I bristle immediately, feeling like a teenager again, wanting to hide away in the art room from her and her bullying friends.

"But you were in the same tutor group? Spent a lot of time to-gether?" Dodgson rephrases.

"Yes, I'd say that's accurate," she agrees, and shoots me a look that is so smug I want to slap it off her face.

I glare at her, full of resentment and fury that she is here, in this courtroom, trying to ruin me, again.

"And tell us, what was Miss Arundale like at school?" Dodgson asks.

Laura makes a show of batting her eyelashes, chewing on her over-plumped lips before answering. "Well . . . Claire was quite . . . quite unpopular, really," she says, pulling a sorrowful expression. But she has the same spiteful eyes that she did as a teenager, and I can sense her relishing this unexpected opportunity to make me feel awful about myself.

"Unpopular in what way?"

"She didn't really have many friends, she kept herself to herself. She was a bit strange. I think people didn't know how to behave around her," Laura says.

I didn't think it was possible for me to feel fifteen again, but she's managing to make it happen. For some bizarre reason, I feel my self-loathing begin to reemerge, see myself through her eyes: a sad, pathetic virgin loser. It makes me hate her the same way that I hated Mother.

"What do you mean by *strange*?"

"I don't know, really. Just different from the rest of us. She spoke to herself sometimes, and she lied a lot too."

"Lied?"

"Yes, like fibbing, you know? So, there was this one time when I'm pretty sure she was following me home one day after school. I could just, like, feel her watching me, and every time I turned around, she'd pretend to be looking at something else?"

I wring my fingers together behind my back. *How can she still be so conceited?*

"So then, anyway, eventually I turned around and asked her why

she was following me and she said something about going to someone's house, but I lived on Westmont Street, which is a private road,
and I knew all the kids on that street, so I knew she was lying about
visiting a friend. Just silly, weird things like that."

I cannot even bring myself to look up, I am so embarrassed. This
was years ago. Kid stuff. Nothing big, nothing important! I had just
wanted to see where the girl who was making my life a living hell
lived, so I could try and be the sort of person she'd leave alone. This
has nothing to do with Lilah.

"And why do you think she followed you?" Dodgson asks.

"I don't know—to make herself fit in better, lie her way into
making some friends maybe," Laura suggests dismissively. "I tried
to be her friend once," she goes on. "I reached out to her, asked her
if she wanted to go shopping with me after school, but she never
turned up," she says with a shrug. But this time, she looks me dead
in the eyes, because she knows, and I know, that I turned up that
day after school. And I waited for her and her friends for forty minutes in the food court before realizing I had been stood up. The next
day they were all laughing about it, about how sad Hairy Clairy had
actually believed Laura and had gone all the way to the city mall,
waiting for them to turn up.

"She's lying," I whisper to Grosvenor, unsure if I'm about to
launch myself over the counter to strangle Laura or burst into tears.

Grosvenor simply holds up a hand to silence me.

"And how did this solitary lifestyle affect her? Was she quiet . . .
shy? What was her personality like?" Dodgson probes.

"Objection, Your Honor! Speculation," Grosvenor says, standing up, and I let out a sigh, releasing the tension I did not know had
been building up. Grosvenor has bought me a moment to breathe.

"Okay, let's rephrase that: What was Miss Arundale's general behavior like at school?"

"Well, it was bad. She would be very angry sometimes, with me
and the other girls especially. It must have been from jealousy. She
always sat in the back of the classroom on her own, hunched over,

and wouldn't talk to anyone. And whenever the girls or I would try to speak to her, she'd snap and lash out. She could be quite nasty."

"What do you mean by *snap and lash out*?" Dodgson asks her.

"Well, one time, she tried to hit me. We were in the girls' toilets and I was just putting my lip gloss on and she came out of nowhere and swooped down on me. I tried to move out of the way but she nicked me on the neck with her fingernails. She was almost suspended, but her mum talked the head out of it. Claire got away with a detention," Laura says primly, rubbing her neck as though it's still sore over a decade later.

I glare at her. I did try to hit her that day in the toilets, but it wasn't like she's saying. There were three of them in there and they jumped me when I came out of a stall. They tipped my bag over and Laura picked up one of my lip glosses and was trying it on. Mother had bought it for me. I told her to give it back and she refused. After a year of being picked on by her, I snapped and tried to hit her. And I'd do it again. Though I think maybe I'd better not say this to Grosvenor or the court.

"Is it fair to say that your experience with the adolescent Miss Arundale was one of discomfort, aggression and strange behavior?" Dodgson asks.

"Yes," Laura replies primly, sticking her nose in the air.

"Objection! You're putting words into your witness's mouth," Grosvenor says, on her feet again.

"No further questions," he replies smugly.

Grosvenor stands to take Dodgson's place and cross-examine Laura.

"Mrs. Thorpe, is it fair to say you have not seen Miss Arundale in over a decade? That you have maintained no contact at all with my client?" she asks.

"Yes, that's fair. I don't keep in touch with people who are vicious," she says pointedly.

"So is it fair to say that you actually do not know the Miss Arundale of today at all?"

Laura pauses, looking unsure of herself. She glances at Dodgson for direction, but he's unable to help. "I suppose not. I was answering questions about our days at school."

"And have *you* changed since you were a teenager?" Grosvenor asks.

"I don't know what you mean," Laura replies.

"Well, I can see from police records that you were arrested for shoplifting at the age of fourteen. From school records, I discover you were suspended for bullying aged sixteen. That you dropped out of university in the first year, but lied in social media posts to say you were still attending. You then had another brush with the law for drunk driving, aged eighteen. Is all this correct?" Grosvenor asks, her voice breezy, almost playful.

Laura looks outraged, her face bright red. She is rubbing her manicured hands together. I am biting the inside of my cheek to stop myself from laughing.

"Yes, that's correct," she eventually grinds out through her teeth.

"And then you had two children with your husband and the record goes quiet. You have become a family woman, focused on raising your children well?"

"Yes," Laura replies, nose in the air, shifting in her seat.

"So it's fair to say that you have changed a lot since your teenage years, and my client, in the same manner, is very likely not the same person she was at the age of fifteen?"

"I have changed," is all Laura says.

"What would you do if someone tried to take your child from you, Mrs. Thorpe? If they denied you the right to be with your children? Would you push them, or worse?" Grosvenor chances her arm.

Laura looks affronted and Dodgson shoots to his feet. "Objection, Your Honor! Relevance," he calls out. "And pretty much every other ground," he mutters under his breath.

"Sustained," the judge replies, allowing Laura to avoid answering the question.

"That's all." Grosvenor smiles.

The judge gives a nod and Laura is escorted from the room. As she walks past, we both refuse to make eye contact, but her strong perfume wafts over me and I feel like vomiting. It stings my throat.

I wonder how much more of this I can take; how many more horrible memories are going to be unearthed; how many more twisted truths and bare-faced lies are going to slap me in the face throughout the trial. It feels like they're trying to break me in court, but they don't realize Noah already has.

FORTY-THREE

We're in the consultation room and Grosvenor has been preparing for the next witness while I've tried to block out intrusive memories of my terrible school days and Laura Thorpe.

"Listen, don't worry about that witness. It was bullshit, just Dodgson trying to fill a quota," Grosvenor assures me. "Nobody gives a shit about some childhood bully from however long ago. We all have a Laura in our life."

I wonder who Grosvenor's Laura is and try to imagine the strong woman in front of me being picked on as a child. It's impossible.

"Who's the next witness?" I ask.

"Sukhi Dhillon."

I close my eyes in relief.

"Have you spoken to her much? Heard anything from her?" Grosvenor asks me.

Guilt floods through me. "We've written a few letters. She's tried to visit but . . . I can't bring myself to see anybody while I'm locked up on remand. Least of all her. It's embarrassing. I'm so ashamed of being in this situation," I admit.

"Claire, I just want to make clear and remind you . . . Sukhi is being called in by the prosecution, not us. So just be aware that you may not like what you hear," Grosvenor tells me, gravely.

"Sukhi wouldn't drop me in it. She's my friend," I say firmly.

Grosvenor says nothing.

SUKHI DHILLON

"How long have you known Miss Arundale?"

Sukhi glances at me, chewing on her lip. "Around fifteen months."

She's wearing one of the suit dresses that I've seen her in at the office for client meetings and looks good in it. She gave me a warm smile when she walked past me to the witness stand, her eyes filled with sympathy. It made me want to weep, the fact that my friend was here, had been dragged into all of this, and was still offering me her support and not turning her back on me.

"And you work with her?" Dodgson asks.

"Yes. I work in PR, Claire is on my team, which is how we met." Sukhi throws me a brief, supportive smile, and I bow my head to her in silent thanks.

"Mrs. Dhillon, is this the CV Miss Arundale included with her job application?" A copy of my CV flashes up on-screen. Sukhi frowns down at her own paper version, before nodding. "Yes, I believe it is, though it was a while ago so I can't be certain."

"We can see here that the last job Miss Arundale claims to have had was another role in PR, at Baker Rise Public Relations?" he says.

"Yes. That is where she worked before she joined us."

"Because I rang the HR team at Baker Rise PR, and they have no record of a Claire Arundale working for them in this time period. In fact, they had no record of a Claire Arundale ever having worked for them."

Sukhi frowns at me and I feel my skin begin to itch with shame. It was such a stupid thing to lie about, but I had *so* wanted the job and didn't want to embarrass Noah after he went to all the trouble of helping me apply.

Sukhi turns back to Dodgson, her voice hard. "Is that a question?"

"No, merely an observation." He smirks back at her.

"Lying on a CV isn't a crime, is it? If that is what you're imply-ing. PR is competitive and hard to break into. I won't comment on how she got her job, that is for HR to look into," Sukhi adds.

"So you acknowledge Miss Arundale may have lied? May indeed be a chronic liar?" Dodgson thinks he has the way in he was angling for. But Sukhi will not give an inch of ground.

"No. I will not comment further on this, not having spoken to Claire about her CV nor personally hired her. In our personal inter-actions, I have never known her to lie."

Dodgson raises his eyebrows at the jury, stopping short of rolling his eyes.

"You have *never* caught her out in a lie?" he pushes again.

"No." Sukhi's voice is unwavering.

Dodgson allows a painfully long silence to drag out, and for one crazy moment I want to burst out laughing as I watch Sukhi glare at him, refusing to back down.

"Thank you, Mrs. Dhillon," he drawls eventually. "No further questions."

"What a waste of her time," Grosvenor whispers to me, giving my shoulder a tiny squeeze as she stands and takes Dodgson's place.

"Hello, Mrs. Dhillon. Can I just confirm Miss Arundale's role within the team?" she asks.

"PR assistant. An entry-level role."

"And your position?" Grosvenor asks.

"Her senior—a senior executive. But she doesn't report to me or anything. We're on different accounts; she is lifestyle, I'm in litera-ture."

"Did you interview her?"

"I didn't, no. Our boss, David, hired her but I did have some input about the candidates at CV stage. He said she interviewed well so I vouched for her as a good option. It's important in PR that you leave a good first impression."

"And did Claire?" Grosvenor asks.

"Yes, she did. She's knowledgeable and a hard worker, shows initiative, and was always last to leave the office and first to arrive. She'll be a brilliant publicist one day."

I feel a small glow of pride at being defended so warmly.

"And outside of work, did you spend much time together? Or speak about things unrelated to the office?" Grosvenor asks.

Sukhi darts her gaze at me again, and I'm finding myself mortified that one of the only people I might be able to call a friend has been dragged into this mess, forced to speak up for me in front of a bunch of strangers. I give her another little smile, as though trying to thank her telepathically for being here, to apologize for involving her in any of this.

"We spent most lunchtimes together and spoke a lot about our personal lives. I would consider Claire Arundale to be my friend and not just a colleague," Sukhi says, looking directly at me. For some reason, I feel my eyes begin to water.

"Good to know." Grosvenor pauses to let this sink in and then resumes. "And what did you know of Miss Arundale and her personal life?"

"She is a kind, caring person," Sukhi replies.

"Did you ever see her lose her temper? To use the previous witness's phrase, 'lash out' at all?"

Grosvenor turns to the jury, raising her eyebrows to demonstrate the importance of this question.

"No, never. I never heard her raise her voice, even after everything that happened with Noah," Sukhi replies firmly.

"And what did you know of Miss Arundale's and Mr. Coors's relationship?" Grosvenor asks.

"I knew they were engaged."

"She told you this?"

Sukhi doesn't falter. "She spoke about him daily. Just little things: mentioning going home to him, what they were doing at the weekend . . . She had a photo of him as her phone wallpaper, I saw it once when she was ordering a takeout lunch and asked to take a closer look. She was happy to show it to me. I knew he had a fancy job, that they had been on holiday together and that they had hopes of traveling some more." She trails off. "Lots of things, really. It was lots of little things that would come up when we chatted, which sort of built up a picture of her life, rather than one big conversation about her time outside of work." I'm nodding along. It's true, I don't speak about myself often. All that Sukhi knows of me is probably from her paying attention and picking up bits and pieces from different conversations and comments made.

"And did she have an engagement ring?" Grosvenor pushes.

"Yes, she wore a ring that he gave her," Sukhi confirms.

"So you got the picture that Miss Arundale was overall a very kind, caring person who was in love with her fiancé and in a happy relationship?" Grosvenor summarizes.

"That's correct," Sukhi says.

"And can you run us through Miss Arundale's reaction when you visited the Pulitzer Haas office on the nineteenth of September last year?"

"Well, obviously, it was all a horrible surprise for Claire, finding out her fiancé didn't work where she thought he did. She basically went into a state of shock, I had to get her some water and sit her down . . . It was a lot to take in."

"We have CCTV footage of this whole interaction," Grosvenor states, and grainy footage from the Pulitzer Haas foyer begins to play. My face heats up.

"She looks quite distressed," Grosvenor comments, shooting a glance at the jury.

"Well, yeah, anybody would be," Sukhi exclaims. "I couldn't believe it myself, and I'm not engaged to the guy! I felt awful for her, the poor thing."

I stare at the ground, embarrassed to be reliving this terrible moment in front of so many people, so many strangers.

"Did she reach out to Mr. Coors to find out where he was?" Grosvenor asks.

"She was in a state of shock, as I said, but I know that once she
had recovered enough to try to call him, she did. I believe she also
sent a text, if I remember rightly. But I mean, you never go looking
for bad news, do you? I was there and she could barely speak to me,
let alone the man who caused all this. She didn't *deserve* to have this
happen to her," Sukhi says quite sharply, with a fierce glance over at
the jury.

"And then later you were there when she confronted Mr. Coors
in a club?"

"Yes, I was there, and once again, all things considered, she acted
more calmly than I would have done," Sukhi replies, and I am taken
aback by the defensive tone of her voice. This woman is protecting
me. I have the urge to grab her in a huge hug, apologize to her for
not being a better friend. This is a loyal woman, who is standing by
me, despite only knowing me for fifteen months. A tear rolls down
my cheek and I brush it away with my hand.

"We had discovered Noah was at this club by searching on Facebook: I found his page and he'd been tagged at that location."

"And you told this to Miss Arundale?"

"Yes, I went round to her home and showed her his profile. And
it was awful—she was blocked from his Facebook so she couldn't
see it. Her own fiancé had blocked her, so she couldn't find out what
he was up to. He was clearly living some sort of dirty double life that
he was trying to hide!" Sukhi sounds so outraged on my behalf, I
feel another pang of love for her.

"Objection! Speculation," Dodgson drawls.

"Sustained," the judge confirms.

Grosvenor continues. "So you showed her the page that you
found, and accompanied her to the club?"

"Yes, and we saw him there, with Lilah Andersson. There was
no denying it—they were all over each other. Well, Claire was very
dignified in the situation, much more than I would have been! She
took off her ring, told him it was over—and then I threw water over
him for good measure. Not Claire, me. There are witnesses, I'm

sure, who can corroborate that. I don't want her to get the blame for his soggy suit." She folds her arms as though daring the jury to disagree with her, and I hear a few muffled chuckles. I'm starting to think Sukhi should have been a lawyer too.

"And how did they react? Mr. Coors and Miss Andersson?"

"Well, as you'd expect! Noah looked like he'd seen a bloody ghost when she walked in, couldn't believe he'd been caught out. He even asked what she was doing there, I couldn't believe the audacity of it! As for Lilah, she looked pretty ashamed of herself, but I wasn't really concentrating on her. The other woman usually gets the blame, but in my opinion it was all on Noah. He was the one cheating, after all. He sat there gaping like a goldfish, didn't argue or anything, even when I threw the water."

"And Miss Arundale just . . . left the club?"

"Yes, I took her home. I believe a glass was thrown, but I don't know who did that."

I blink. Sukhi has just lied on the stand for me. She knew I threw the glass and she's betting on the fact that the CCTV footage was too frenetic for the precise sequence of events to be visible. I cannot believe she has just done this! I look at the floor, unable to stop the thumping in my chest. It's one thing to defend me, another to put her own liberty and reputation on the line and outright lie for me.

"Yes, we can't make that out on the footage clearly, a lot of people move in after the drink was thrown and obstruct the camera," Grosvenor agrees. "So you left after that?"

"Yes. She was in a terrible state, shaking the whole way back in the cab, and when we got home she was just crying and crying. I was really worried about her," Sukhi admits.

"So you saw her in a state of significant distress?" Grosvenor asks.

"Yeah, definitely. She was hurt and upset," Sukhi says.

"But still showed absolutely no violent tendencies, made no threats or gestures that might be found intimidating, such as a shake of the fist?"

"No, nothing like that. She seemed broken and sad."

Grosvenor gives a small smile and nods to her. "Thank you, Mrs. Dhillon."

"Claire is a good person," Sukhi adds, and I have to swallow the lump in my throat.

FORTY-FOUR

On our lunch break I sit quietly, thinking about Sukhi and her testimony. I didn't expect to feel so overwhelmed by emotion, but I am, and with no warning, I realize I am sobbing.

Grosvenor looks up, startled. "Claire? Claire, are you all right?"

I shake my head. "She is just such a nice person, I don't deserve her," I manage to croak through more snotty sobs.

"Who? Sukhi?"

I nod feebly, hunching over so I can cry more heavily, my hands going up to my face to hide myself away and afford myself some privacy.

Grosvenor says quietly, "You take all the time you need to pull yourself back together." I can hear the rustling of paper, which indicates she's going to ignore me and my emotions and go back to work.

I continue to sob, overcome with emotion at the idea that someone who has only known me for a few months has defended me so loyally, in a situation where there is nothing to gain for herself. She must like me, care for me even. It's something that I have been starved of, apart from when Noah was in my life.

Claire is a good person, Sukhi said. It hit me in the chest like a bullet, the notion that someone could think that of me. I realize, with a sense of shock, that after decades of being told I wasn't good enough by Mother, that I was a bad person, I had come to believe it. The fact that someone as kind as Sukhi saw enough in me to believe I was good, even though I obviously lied to get my job . . . I feel like a fraud, like perhaps she just doesn't know me well enough yet to see the true Claire. I have deceived Sukhi about more than my CV.

I was seventeen and had been in bed with a crippling migraine. I started suffering from them when I was fifteen, after my periods started. My vision would blur at the sides and then a cracking pain in my head would start to build, until it felt like someone with a drill was splintering my temples with it. Occasionally I would vomit from the pain. The only way to cope was to pop some codeine, lie in a dark room and sleep it off. Luckily, they weren't too regular, but I remember on this occasion I was lying in my room, clutching my temples and writhing in pain, when my bedroom door opened.

"Claire, darling, I need you to help me with my hair. It won't go the way I want it to and you're so good at braiding," Mother said, sweeping in and perching herself on a corner of my bed, oblivious to the fact that I was clearly in no state to be helping with her hair.

"Mother, I can't. I have such a migraine," I groaned, rolling over feebly in bed to emphasize the fact that I couldn't move properly. My eyes were still squeezed shut. I was afraid that if I opened them to the light it would cause nausea to roil in my belly.

"Oh, it's just a little headache—come on! It will only take you five minutes," she replied, getting up from the bed.

"Mother, please. Why do you need your hair braided right now?" I tried, hoping that she would realize it was unimportant.

"For the event this evening, darling, I want it half-up, half-down, with just one French braid down the side. Just one, it really won't take long," she pressed.

I sighed, trying to remain calm. "Your event isn't until later, Mother. Please, let me sleep off this migraine, and I promise that when I wake up and the painkillers have kicked in, I'll come and do your hair. It will be done before you need to leave," I reasoned.

I heard her suck her teeth and braced myself for what was to follow.

"Claire, I'm not asking a lot: It will take just five minutes. Don't be so selfish. You know I can't do it myself. I don't want to be in a rush later!"

"Mother, I told you, I *will* do it, just not right now. My vision isn't good and it will come out badly. You don't want that, do you?" I tried again.

"Claire, open your eyes when you're speaking to me, don't be so rude," she hissed.

I cracked my eyes open and the light entering the room from the door behind her sent blades of blinding pain right through my head to the back of my skull, which instantly began to throb. I winced.

"Don't be so dramatic." Mother rolled her eyes. "Honestly, Claire, you are such a horribly selfish person. I don't ask for much, do I? A bloody braid in my hair is all I want, and you're acting like I'm asking for one of your lungs!"

I didn't reply. My head hurt too much.

"Fine. Be a horrible, selfish daughter. I'll just have to try and do it all by myself, and then I'll look awful at the party and it will be *all your fault.*"

She turned on her heels and slammed the door shut, but before doing so, she flicked the light switch on. A final parting punishment. The light hit me like a train and I vomited into the plant pot by my bed.

I wondered how Mother would like it if she felt as if she had shards of glass rattling around in her skull. I imagined my hands holding the sides of her head and shaking it violently, setting the sharp fragments dancing, so she could feel exactly how I felt.

I collect myself and Grosvenor sprays some sort of mist onto my face, meant to reduce redness and puffiness. It smells like talcum powder.

"I thought it was good for the jury to see me looking pathetic." I sniff as she sprays me liberally.

"Don't worry, Claire. I assure you, you look pathetic! But you don't need to be blotchy as well," she replies. I look up at her, surprised to find her giving me a small smile.

"I didn't know you could joke?"

"Only on special occasions. We lawyers have a strict ten-joke-per-year quota to fill." She winks at me. "You ready?"

"No."

"Tough luck," she replies, holding out her hand to help me up from my seat.

FORTY-FIVE

June 12, 2025
Dear Diary,

Noah and I have had our first proper argument. He was meant to be meeting Sukhi for the first time, she's been dying to see him. So anyway, she booked for us all to go to dinner, Noah and me, Sukhi and her husband, Fateh. Sukhi and I headed to the restaurant after work together and met Fateh there. It was my first time meeting him, and he was lovely. Very polite and funny. He had this easy banter with Sukhi that I could tell came from all their time together. She was totally herself around him.

So we wait, and it's getting later and later. We've ordered drinks because the waiter kept coming over to ask, and I'm calling Noah to no response. So then eventually he texts me and says he's sorry but he's got wrapped up in a work meeting and can't make it after all—when we've already been waiting there for thirty minutes. I was mortified!

Fateh was so nice about it, but I could tell that Sukhi was unimpressed, although she was polite and said she was sure it was something important that was keeping Noah away. I had so wanted him to make a good impression on her, and for him to like my new friend. I'd sort of envisioned all of us hanging out as a four, doing double dates together. So I was fuming. I couldn't even really enjoy the meal, and when I got home I told him as much. I said he'd embarrassed me and that I felt he wasn't respecting my friends' time, and that he should want to spend time with my friends and get to know them the way I want to get to know his.

To be fair, he looked like he felt guilty about it, and then I began to get a stress headache and had to go to bed with a wet flannel, and he came in looking even more sorry. He ran to the shop to get me painkillers and told me he understood why I was so upset and that he didn't mean to put work before our relationship. He massaged my aching temples until I fell asleep, and in the morning I hadn't the heart to continue being angry at him.

Claire

FORTY-SIX

EMILIA WATERSON

"Next to the stand the prosecution calls forward Emilia Waterson," Dodgson announces.

I watch as a slightly built elderly woman with dyed red hair permed into ringlets steps up to the witness stand, holding on to the handrail and giving a nervous nod to the judge. She avoids looking in my direction and exhales heavily as she sits down. She looks harmless, a little old lady, the sort I'd probably stop and offer my arm to if she was trying to cross a road.

"Can you tell the jury your relationship to the victim, please?"

"I'm her neighbor," Emilia replies. "I've lived in the house opposite Lilah for years, been there since the day she moved in. Lovely girl," she adds with a sorrowful shake of her head.

Lovely enough to steal my fiancé. Still, I shouldn't think ill of the dead.

"And where were you on the day of her death?" Dodgson asks.

"I was at home, gardening. Perfect weather for it, you know. I was sorting out the pebbles around my path and weeding the flower beds by the windowsill . . . Dratted weeds pop up there every year."

This triggers a vague recollection of a flourish of red hair tucked between the bushes across the road when I approached number 48 to speak to Lilah.

"Had you ever seen the defendant before that day? Did you recognize her at all?"

"Well, to be honest, that day I didn't recognize her, no. She's not very memorable," adds Emilia, unnecessarily. "But then when all of this was on the news, I realized that I *had* seen her before! So I told my son when he was visiting and he helped me to check my archived doorbell camera footage to be sure, because my eyesight and memory aren't quite what they used to be, and sure enough, there she was! She had come round a few days before the incident, but late at night. I have footage of this lady"—she points a shaky, gnarled finger at me—"sneaking past my front door on the driveway and then standing behind a tree for a bit. Then she leaves the frame."

"You say sneaking. Why is that?" Dodgson asks. To my horror, the doorbell footage is now playing for everyone to see. To be honest, I look sneaky. I'm twitchy and glancing behind myself frequently. I resist the urge to bury my head in my hands.

"I assume she was trying to use the tree in front of my home to keep her out of sight?"

"Objection! Speculation." Grosvenor stands up to intervene.

The judge nods at her and she sits back down. I dare a glance at the jury but their expressions seem confused, as though they can't work out what to think. A few of them are writing notes. I catch the eye of one man and quickly look away before I can register his expression.

"Thank you, Mrs. Waterson, this goes toward showing the attack on Miss Andersson was premeditated—that the defendant had been in the area, watching the victim's house, at *least* once ahead of the attack, and quite possibly on other occasions that were not caught on camera." Dodgson walks back to his table, chest puffed out, conscious this is damning evidence. His skin looks gray under the strip lighting.

Grosvenor stands slowly and walks around the desk, her footsteps echoing in the silent courtroom.

"Ladies and gentlemen of the jury," she says loudly, and I flinch. Grosvenor then turns to Emilia, giving the old lady a little nod before facing the jury again. "I remind you that the heart of this case is whether or not, on the morning that she visited Lilah Andersson in her home, my client intended to cause her serious harm, as required to prove a charge of murder."

Members of the jury eye each other sidelong and I hear murmured comments.

"Order!" the judge calls again.

"Ladies and gentlemen of the jury, please concentrate on the events of Saturday the twentieth of September 2025. What did you see *on the day of the victim's death*?" Grosvenor asks the witness.

"I saw this woman knocking on Lilah's front door," Emilia answers.

I resist the urge to shrink back and instead remain totally still, trying to keep my face blank. She's not a sweet old granny after all.

"And how was Miss Arundale behaving when you observed her arrival?" Grosvenor presses.

Emilia shrugs. "Like any other visitor."

"Nothing to cause alarm? You didn't think she was *sneaking*, to use your own word?"

"No," Emilia concedes.

"You said she was knocking on the victim's door? So not banging loudly or bringing undue attention to herself?"

"No, it was just a normal knock. She was not raising her voice. I couldn't hear what was being said between the two of them once Lilah answered the door. I only remember that the interaction between them seemed strained. Lilah looked like she didn't want to let her visitor in, she wouldn't open the door fully. I assumed this was one of those door-to-door canvassers, you know, collecting money for charity or asking the occupant to fill out a questionnaire or something. They can be a real nuisance."

"So my client didn't appear aggressive, over-emotional or otherwise out of control before she entered the house?"

"No."

"And it was in fact Lilah Andersson who was behaving strangely?"

"To me, who knew nothing about the situation, yes. Lilah's behavior seemed nervous and Miss Arundale was calm in her delivery when she spoke."

"But you didn't hear what was being said?"

"No, my house is across the street and I was weeding behind some shrubs."

"And the time Miss Arundale visited before this, where you suggest she was 'sneaking,' is it possible that she was in fact there to see Noah Coors, not Lilah Andersson, and was taking precautions so as not to be seen by his other girlfriend?" Grosvenor pushes.

"Well . . . well, yes, that's definitely possible. I don't know that she was watching Lilah specifically," Emilia admits, the reply sounding weak.

"No further questions from me. This highlights the fact that there was no visible anger or emotion apparent in my client's behavior on the day of her encounter with Lilah Andersson immediately preceding Miss Andersson's death. It also dispels the idea that she was stalking the dead woman. None of this proves any element of premeditation. Thank you, Miss Waterson," Grosvenor tells her.

I watch Emilia shuffle away from the witness stand and wonder how much of a help her reluctant observations will be toward convincing the jury that I did not go to Lilah's house with the intention of harming her.

After this evidence, the judge calls for proceedings to end early.

I am ushered back into one of the small, beige consultation rooms behind the courtroom by my assigned security. Grosvenor and her junior are waiting for me and she is pacing up and down excitedly.

"An early finish! It's a good sign. We're rattling Dodgson, debunking his argument that you were angry and emotional when you arrived at the house. He's going to spend the rest of today looking for another angle to pursue," Grosvenor tells me enthusiastically. It's the first time I've seen her look so alive, brown eyes shining and her thin mouth curved up in a Cheshire cat grin.

"What do you think he's going to try and say tomorrow?" I ask warily.

"Whatever it is, we'll have rebuttals," she tells me confidently, pouring herself a cup of water from the dispenser in the corner. She takes a long sip before leaning over her documents. "Let's get to work, team."

"My mother is coming," I said smugly to the little girl standing next to me. Our teacher was busy securing my ridiculous lion headdress. "She can't wait to see me because I'm the lion," I added, as though it wasn't obvious.

The girl nodded but I was sure she couldn't possibly understand. After all, she was just a chorus deer. I was the lion, with lines to say and everything.

I was nine and it was the school play: a strange story written by our drama teacher, set in a jungle where a pride of lions decides to become vegetarian and live in harmony with their neighbors, the dancing deer. In hindsight, it was a way for her to push her own vegan agenda, but at age nine, invited to take one of the most coveted parts, I didn't care. All I cared about was that Mother had promised to be there and had spent a surprisingly undramatic afternoon helping me make my costume. I couldn't wait for her to see me up on that stage, performing, being successful. She might even be proud of me.

So the lights went down and I waited nervously backstage, hopping from foot to foot and fiddling with my fake paws.

The zebra had gone out and introduced the play and I waited until it was my first moment onstage. I marched out proudly, swinging my butt a little to give my tail some impetus. I tried to look out into the audience but the spotlights were blinding and the audience one dark mass of unrecognizable silhouettes. I decided to ignore it.

Mother was out there, I knew she was. So I carried on regardless, and gave it my all. I roared and I sang and I leaped and I laughed, and the audience clapped and I imagined her clapping along, perhaps nudging the couple next to her and saying proudly, "That lion there, that's my daughter!"

But at the very end when the house lights came up and we were on our final song—in which we interacted with the audience, running down the aisles and throwing confetti on everyone—I saw a couple of newcomers stumble through the doors at the back and my heart sank. I heard a shrill giggle and knew for sure it was Mother. A few of the other parents turned and shot disapproving frowns in her direction. She deflected them by exaggeratedly shushing her companion, a man I had not seen before. I stood onstage blinking, unsure what to do. She didn't even notice me, staggering along a row to protests from the other parents as she tried to find two vacant seats.

When the song was over, everyone rushed out to meet their parents, praise and laughter filling the air. I sat at the back of the hall behind the costume rails, my arms folded, not wanting to see her. She had missed the entire performance.

Eventually, she came looking for me. She reeked of alcohol and cigarettes, and was stumbling a little in heels that were higher than any of the other mums had been wearing. Her date stood back a little awkwardly, nodding to me.

"Darling!" she called musically, loud enough for the parents nearby to turn and look. "Oh, Claire, darling, you were just wonderful! What a fantastic little cougar you were!" She laughed a little too loudly, teeth bared as she did so.

"Good job, kid," her date added.

"I was a lion," I corrected her quietly, but she hadn't heard me. She hadn't seen me at all. All this praise was not for my benefit. I had trusted her when she'd promised to come, trusted that she would be there to support me. But instead she had gone on a date, got drunk and forgotten all about me until it was too late.

I decided that day that I wouldn't trust her again. If you don't trust people, they can't let you down.

Now I study Grosvenor's determined expression and feel a flicker of fear in my belly. I'm having to trust her, this random woman whose only loyalty to me comes from her paycheck, to prove I did not murder Lilah.

FORTY-SEVEN

The next morning our start time is postponed several times until it's fixed at 11:30. We're told this is at the request of the prosecution. "Dodgson could just be trying to rattle us or to buy himself more time because he's so concerned about the evidence," Grosvenor tells me conspiratorially.

The delay makes my stomach roil in nervous anticipation, and even though she remains outwardly calm I can tell by the way that Grosvenor keeps shifting pens on the desk before her in the consultation room that she, too, is concerned.

By the time the trial resumes I'm a jumpy, nervous wreck, desperate to know what prosecuting counsel's new line of attack will be.

When I see the next witness walking down the aisle, I recognize her instantly, and know for sure that this round of questioning is not going to go in my favor.

MAGGIE THURNWALL

Maggie is slowly walking down the aisle in the courtroom, taking her time, as though my entire future isn't hanging in the balance. Bloody Maggie, the receptionist who caused a rift between Noah and me. One of the very few times we quarreled.

She is wearing a plain gray dress suit, similar to the one she used to wear when she prevented me from visiting him during working hours. She gives me a look of open disgust, wrinkling her nose in disdain, before taking her place and nodding to the prosecution to begin, as though we're all here at her command. As though she's the judge. It annoys me, how uptight and pretentious she is, but I'm hoping we can get this over with quickly. In and out. I'm not sure how much more I can stand to listen to before my ability to remain calm and detached is tested too far. My jaw tightens.

"Mrs. Thurnwall, please will you share with the courtroom how you came to know Claire Arundale?" Dodgson says, one polished brogue tapping lightly on the floor as though to hurry proceedings along.

"I worked at Pulitzer Haas as their receptionist for three years. Before I left, I came to know Claire around October of 2024. She was infatuated with one of our employees, Noah Coors."

Oh, so I'm on trial for loving my fiancé? I refrain from rolling my eyes.

"What do you mean by infatuated?"

"Well, at first she didn't actually come in, you see. But I noticed her loitering around outside the building. It's my job to notice things like that, suspicious behavior in and around the premises, you know. I noticed her particularly because she had this bright red peacoat she always wore and so it stood out. Anyway, the first time she was just sitting outside eating her lunch, nothing special. But then she came back every day after that. A lot of people eat in the courtyard outside the office, of course, but it was the way she sat facing the entrance every day. As though she was waiting for someone, looking for someone."

Am I on trial for eating my lunch now? I clench my teeth.

"How long did this go on for?" Dodgson asks.

"A few days. And then she started coming by at the end of the day as well, when all the bankers would clock off," Maggie goes on.

"Did you think she knew someone there?"

"At first I did, yes. I thought she must be dating one of them. They get around, those boys, you know."

"Was she ever bothering anybody, speaking to anyone?"

"Well, no. That's why I left her to it. It was strange, yes, but she didn't seem to be doing any harm. Some people just like to have lunch in the same spot every day. I thought maybe she was one of those routine-obsessed types, you know? But then eventually one day she came into the foyer. And she had brought a plastic bag with her, a branded one from the taco place around the corner. She came right up to the desk and smiled at me and said she was dropping off lunch for Noah Coors. I thought it was strange, the wording was a bit weird, you know? Like she was a delivery driver, when she wasn't? It wasn't that she was having lunch with him, she was just dropping it off, like a mother would for their child who'd forgotten their lunch."

This time I do roll my eyes. Just because this woman doesn't deign to bring her partner lunch doesn't mean there's anything odd about someone who does. So what if I want to drop my hardworking fiancé off a little treat on his lunch break? What's weird about that?

"I call up Noah and tell him he has a visitor. He comes downstairs and she's sitting there. She waves when he comes down as though she knows him, holding up the bag and pointing at it. She tells him she's got him some lunch. And what's strange was how he reacted, because he asked her why she would do such a thing. Now, I had someone else waiting to be dealt with at the desk, but I'm a nosy old bird and just had to keep one ear on their conversation. It felt like an episode of *EastEnders* happening in front of me."

This draws a few chuckles from the courtroom and I find myself becoming annoyed. Why are they giving this crazy lady any airtime at all?

"So what happened after Mr. Coors asked why she had brought him lunch?" Dodgson tries to bring the atmosphere in the room down a notch.

"Well, he looked awfully confused but thanked her, and she leaned in and gave him a kiss on the cheek, which he looked a little surprised about, and then left. He took his lunch up with him, so I assumed maybe he did know her after all, that perhaps she was a client."

"I see. And do you believe that he was in a relationship with her or that it was some other sort of connection?"

"Well, to be honest, it's never been clear to me whether he did know her or not. All I know is that she came again a couple of days later, the exact same scenario: a lunch bag with her and asking to leave it for Noah. But this time when I called him, he told me to get rid of her, that he didn't want lunch and to make up an excuse. In fact, he told me specifically not to let her into the building to see him again. He sounded quite annoyed, as though it was my fault! I told Claire I was very sorry, Noah was in a meeting and could not come down, and that it was best that, unless she had prearranged it with him, she did not come again."

"And how did Miss Arundale take this news?"

"Well, not very well at all. She got quite enraged with me, called me an old cow and said that she could see her fiancé any time she damn well pleased. She slammed her hands down on the desk and caused quite a scene."

I remember this interaction differently. I admit I did call her an old cow, and I don't regret that. But I didn't slam my hands down on the desk. I believe I called her an interfering old cow and told her I would be speaking to Noah about it when I got home, but I was still wary of causing a scene and embarrassing him at work so kept it relatively low-key. Of course, when he got home that night we argued about it, I even raised my voice slightly, but he darted around the topic of me dropping off lunch and somehow convinced me to agree not to visit him at the office without checking with him first. He said it distracted him from his work. In hindsight, perhaps that should have been a red flag that he was hiding something from me.

"Were you afraid of Miss Arundale at any point? What was her behavior like?" Dodgson asks Maggie.

"Well, I was intimidated, yes. She was very upset, her voice was raised and she made a scene. Pulitzer Haas is not the type of place where that sort of behavior is often seen, and people waiting in the reception area were all looking over. So I pressed the security button and waited for them to escort her out. She was getting really up close and personal, kept trying to grab the phone out of my hand, demanding to speak to Mr. Coors, and then she was saying that he would be getting me fired. Threats being thrown about left, right and center! It was very upsetting. I'd been in that job for years and never had any sort of confrontation like that before. So then security came and hauled her off!"

She's exaggerating!!! I write on a piece of notepaper, sliding it across to Grosvenor. She glances down momentarily but does not react otherwise.

"Hauled physically?" Dodgson is saying.

"Yes. They picked her up under her arms and marched her out of there."

"Why did they pick her up?"

"Because she was resisting . . . She was screaming and kicking and demanding to see her fiancé."

I tap the note on the table, but Grosvenor still refuses to engage with me.

"And after all of this had occurred and she was out of the building, then what happened?"

"Well, I had to file an incident report. I told security to keep an eye out for her, not to let her in if they saw her again. And then I spoke to Noah and he confirmed that he did not want her coming in to see him without an appointment. He said he thought she was someone trying to get a job. I couldn't get my head around it, to be honest, the idea that this woman was so adamant he was her fiancé and he was so adamant he didn't know her. It was bizarre."

"It's fair to say that Miss Arundale came across as quite unstable, then?"

"Oh, yes," Maggie replies. I stop myself from narrowing my eyes at her.

"Objection! Leading question," Grosvenor counters, standing. The judge nods at her.

"Do you think, from what you experienced on that day, that Miss Arundale is the type of woman to lose her judgment when it comes to Mr. Coors?"

"Yes, she came across as obsessive and clingy, very controlling if she *was* the girlfriend, I'd say. Couldn't blame him for trying to hide from her at work!"

I let out a hiss between my gritted teeth and try to count to ten in my head, Grosvenor patting my knee beneath the desk.

"Thank you, Mrs. Thurnwall," Dodgson tells her, his voice slimy as a slug trail.

Grosvenor blows out a long breath and closes her eyes for a moment before standing up and striding purposefully toward Maggie, who blinks at her.

"Mrs. Thurnwall, when Mr. Coors told you that he did not know my client, despite the fact he had accepted lunch from her mere days earlier, did you believe him?" she asks, straight to the point as usual.

"Well, to be honest, I wasn't entirely sure, because you know what men are like—I had seen Mr. Coors meeting a few different ladies at the end of the working day outside the office. Some of them he did look pretty cozy with . . . But it wasn't my business. He worked in the building and my job was to see he wasn't disturbed unnecessarily. End of."

"So what you're saying is: It's possible my client truly was just a girlfriend being treated poorly by an unfaithful partner who was, to use your words, 'trying to hide from her at work'?"

Maggie hesitates, eyes flicking quickly toward Dodgson before she answers Grosvenor.

"Yes, it's possible."

"And is it also fair to say that many people eat in the courtyard outside Pulitzer Haas's office building, and that to sit there and do so every day is not so very unusual?"

"I suppose not," Maggie says now, her voice wavering.

"So really, the only evidence that you are bringing to the table is that Miss Arundale had lunch a few times in a courtyard, dropped off lunch once to Mr. Coors, who accepted it, but then later told you he did not know her and not to receive any more food packages from her?"

"Well, yes, that is what happened."

"And at any point when Miss Arundale was becoming upset and had to be removed by security, did she waver from saying that she was engaged to Mr. Coors and within her rights to visit him?" Here I have to bite my cheek to stop myself from smiling at how quickly Grosvenor has turned this around for me.

"Yes, the girl seemed so sure, so confident in what she was saying, and so I did suspect there was more to it than met the eye . . . but as I said, I had to do what I was told. If he didn't want her there during the day, it was my job to go along with it. I didn't care what happened outside of working hours and the building, that was his problem."

"And did you see Mr. Coors with any other women after these incidents?"

"Yes, I did. At the office Christmas party he turned up with a blonde on his arm, very leggy and young-looking, said they'd been together for years. Again, I thought it strange, but it wasn't my place to get involved. To be honest, I avoided them for the evening because I knew for a fact he had been on a date with a different woman right before that."

I draw in a breath, a sudden sharp oxygen surge that feels as though it's cutting through my airways. *Another date?* I rack my brains to remember if he took me out just before his Christmas party, but I can't be sure.

"How did you know this?" Grosvenor asks, sounding unsurprised by the information that is overturning my world.

"I have access to their calendars, you see, for arranging meetings if necessary. And I had clocked that Mr. Coors had a few dates with someone called Mads logged in for evening hours. One date was days before the Christmas party, and then on that night he turned up with this blond woman. Now, of course, I know it was Lilah Andersson, but at the time all I could think was, *You're not Mads from the calendar.*"

"And how did you know that?"

"Well, I admit, I was guessing and stereotyping, but the name accepting the calendar invites was Mads Choi."

"A Korean name," Grosvenor states.

"Yes."

"And when Lilah Andersson turned up on Mr. Coors's arm that night for the Christmas party, you put two and two together: that Lilah was not of Korean descent and ergo most likely not the woman he'd been meeting recently in the evenings?"

"Yes," Maggie confirms.

"And would it be fair to say that your perception of Miss Arundale was that she was perhaps one of many girlfriends Mr. Coors was seeing?" Grosvenor asks.

"Yes, I believed that she definitely knew him in one way or another, but as I said, Mr. Coors had several women hanging around. The three most prominent in my experience were Claire, Mads—who I never met but saw in all the calendar invites—and Lilah," Maggie confirms.

"So to counter your previous statement, if we look at all the facts together, Miss Arundale actually did not come across as unstable? Nor was her behavior particularly controlling?"

Maggie thinks for a moment. "I suppose I may have been a bit harsh on her, if it turns out he *was* stringing her along," she admits.

"Thank you. No further questions." Grosvenor turns on her heel and strides away from Maggie, who shoots me a side-glare.

I feel my face heat up. I imagine myself through this woman's eyes. A sad, pathetic loser on trial for murdering my boyfriend's other lover. For the millionth time, I wonder how my life has panned out this way. And then the painful realization hits me: Maggie will leave court today and forget about me, perhaps occasionally bringing me up as a piece of dinner-party entertainment, an anecdote to laugh at. The thought that I am worth nothing more than that makes me feel hollow inside.

FORTY-EIGHT

It's funny, the things we remember. You remember a film character, but not the name of the film. Or a landmark, but not when you visited it last. My childhood feels like a strobe light. Flashes of memories and then darkness, no context or framing, often leaving me confused and unsure if what I remember is the whole story. Am I misremembering or was it as bad as it now seems?

For example, I remember being ten, crying in my room after Mother had shouted at me. That's the light part, but beforehand all is dark. I can't remember what we argued about, what she said to trigger my tears. I can't remember if it was my fault or hers. But what I do remember is hearing her next door to my bedroom, on the phone to a friend. I tried to stifle my sobs, embarrassed that she had the power to reduce me to a weeping little baby. And in the moment when I'd swallowed the last of them, I heard Mother say, "She's having a tantrum as we speak . . . Yes, I know, you'd think she'd have grown out of that by now. I'm so bored of her crying all the time, but I leave her to it and eventually she exhausts herself."

I remember hearing her say those words so clearly that it's as though she's standing next to me right now, whispering them in my ear. I recall how my tears dried almost instantly, to be replaced with venomous loathing for her. Mother had a total disregard for anyone else's emotions. She certainly didn't care in the slightest about my feelings. There was never any apology after a fight, never a conversation or compromise after an argument. All there was for me was shouting, followed by tears, followed by silence. I was ten when I decided that I wouldn't give her the satisfaction of seeing me cry anymore. I'd set my jaw and curl my fingers into tight fists and tell myself that if she didn't care about my feelings enough even to check on me, then I would just have to take care of them myself, and that meant not allowing myself to cry.

Of course, I'm human. I have cried since then. I cry at the Battersea Dogs Home advert on television. I cried reading that book about the little girl with cancer. I cried watching the news when the war broke out in Ukraine. I cried when Noah proposed. And again when he left me. But I didn't cry over Mother again. Not while she was alive anyway.

FORTY-NINE

After the judge winds up proceedings for the day, Grosvenor tells me she's going to pull an all-nighter to rework her strategy to match Dodgson's, which she feels is now to paint me as an unstable woman who can't control her own actions.

I spend my time outside the courtroom torturing myself with what I have learned. Thoughts circle round and round in my head. Why did Noah lie to Maggie about me? Who the hell is Mads? Was she truly his girlfriend, or just another innocent woman who has been dragged into this messy, demeaning soap opera?

Why would he take Lilah to his stupid Christmas party instead of me? I imagine her swanning around in a glitzy sequined dress, his hand on the small of her back as he guides her around the room, introducing her to his colleagues. Her head would be thrown back in laughter and his colleagues would be eyeing her closely and playfully asking Noah where he got her from and if she had any sisters.

The reality of my situation hits me so hard then that it hollows me out. Noah is embarrassed about being seen with me.

My skin crawls with the utter humiliation of realizing that the fiancé I am so proud of is utterly embarrassed by me. To the extent that he wouldn't even introduce me to his colleagues, and took his more beautiful and talented mistress to meet them instead. I expect to cry, but I don't. I no longer can. I am such a poor excuse for a woman that he hid me away. I drove him to lie because of how terrible I am, how embarrassing my existence is. So far, this moment of realization has been the worst, even more painful than the realization that my fiancé was living a double life. This one feels so deeply personal that every interaction I have ever had with Noah is now tainted by the notion that part of him would always have been noticing all my flaws. And he packed them away until they reached a point when he decided that his wife-to-be was such an embarrassment he was unwilling to be publicly linked with me. He may as well have stabbed a knife through my heart.

I was fourteen. I arrived home from school and there was a box on my bed, wrapped with a silk ribbon. Mother was standing by the door beaming at me, watching closely for a reaction.

"What's this?" I asked, trying to make my expression one of excitement rather than apprehension. For a single unsettling and bizarre moment, I considered the theory that there was a decapitated human head bleeding out through the box and onto my bedsheets.

"A gift!" Mother announced. I glanced at her and did not see the usual darkness lingering behind her gaze, only a genuine flicker of enthusiasm.

"A gift?" I repeated, unsure how to approach the situation. "What have I done to deserve it?"

There had to be a loophole, some sort of trick. Maybe not a decapitated head, but I wouldn't put it past her to have dropped a snake in there, or some other sort of shock-factor prank, just to see my reaction.

"Nothing. I just thought I'd spoil my daughter," she said. "Go on, go on, open it!"

She flapped her hands at me and, despite my nerves, I felt myself begin to get excited. She was in such a good mood, perhaps it truly was a kind gesture? There had been a handful of previous occasions when she suddenly wanted to play the Best Mother of All Time role and would take me out for the day, spoil me, buy me McDonald's burgers and silly little gifts and laugh at everything I said. Perhaps this was one of those days.

I sat myself on the bed and untied the ribbon, taking care to fold it in case Mother wanted to reuse it, afraid to upset her, to upset this moment.

When I lifted the lid off the box, my breath was short, filled with anxiety but also with hope. I peered in and there lay a pair of stiletto heels in my size. I blinked, then remembered myself and broke into a huge grin. "Oh, wow, Mother! What beautiful shoes!"

I hated them. They were so far from anything I would usually have worn, but I took them out and made a big show of admiring them with their pointed toes and heels that were at least five inches high. "I got them for our dance class!" she announced.

My hands froze, still holding the shoes in front of me. "Dance class?"

"Yes, darling. I've signed us up for a dance class together— I thought it would be fun! A little mother–daughter bonding?"

I kept my face straight, afraid to let my emotions show. I did not want to attend a dance class, and certainly not with Mother. "Wow," I said weakly, words failing me.

"Yes, we shall go tomorrow and you can wear your new shoes. I have a matching pair!"

She looked so excited, I actually felt guilty for not being excited with her. She wanted to spend time with me. Finally, she was taking an interest in me. "Great," I told her, and she looked pleased for once when she left me in my room, shiny black shoes resting in my lap.

Of course, the dance class that followed was a shit show.

It was a Latin dance class, the teacher a sleazy bloke called Javier with greased black hair and a blinding white smile that made simps like my mother weak at the knees. She had nattered nonstop on the journey to this random hall, reapplying her lipstick before going inside. My performance was abysmal. I'd no coordination, no sense of rhythm. I flailed around pathetically, trying desperately to keep up with everyone else, to keep Mother happy, not to spoil the big day she had imagined when she'd booked the class and bought us match- ing shoes.

Javier tried to come over and help me but I saw Mother frown and so I quickly batted him away, assuring him I wanted to get there on my own. Mother told him she could do with extra help instead. As he held her hands from behind and showed her how to roll her hips, I plowed on, determined not to disappoint her.

"You're rather clumsy, Claire, darling," she said to me in a low voice, brows furrowed in reproach.

I sashayed away from her, desperate to find some hidden talent in myself that would make her proud. But minutes later my heels began to burn, and soon my feet were all I could focus on, the steps that Javier was trying to teach us going right over my head as I was distracted by the dull ache from my squeezed-together toes, the searing burn in the back of my heels with every step I took.

Eventually, I couldn't take it anymore. I paused, wincing as I peeled off the shoes. Ribbons of skin hung limply from my blistered heels. The insides of my shoes were covered in blood. I could feel Mother's glare from across the room as I dared to pad over to her barefoot, my high heels abandoned at the side of the hall. I couldn't bear to put them back on and my lacerated feet were stinging at the kiss of the cold air. My face heated at the realization that I had left bloody patches on the floor where I had removed the shoes.

I smiled at her, tried to continue as we had been before, but she tilted her face away and ignored me for the rest of the lesson. When we were back in the car, she let it rip.

"You hate the beautiful shoes I've bought you! I paid for this dance class for us but you ignored me the whole time and left blood all over the place . . . Just imagine what Javier must have thought. The absolute state of you! That's the last time I treat you to anything nice. You are so ungrateful. You're spoiled. Spoiled rotten."

The words stung at first. But their impact faded as I realized the sting in my heels was even worse.

FIFTY

MADELINE CHOI

As soon as Dodgson introduces the next witness, I feel sick. My throat is tacky and dry and I begin to tremble in anticipation. It was one thing seeing Lilah with Noah at the club, learning about her and assessing her on social media. It's an entirely different matter to have to face in court, when I am on trial for murder, yet another woman Noah has supposedly been seeing. I still cling on to the hope that this is a mistake, a misunderstanding. Mads is also a male name after all; there could be a reasonable explanation for those evening meetings.

But even if there isn't, meaning that my defense becomes easier, that I'll receive a lesser sentence, it still means I've been deceived twice over by Noah. Before I heard about Mads, I hadn't even contemplated the possibility that there were more women in his life, other girlfriends. For a start, who has the time? But then I chew on my lip as I think of all the work trips he had to take, all the late nights in the office that I thought were part and parcel of being a high-flying financial whiz kid, but which perhaps concealed something darker.

"Dodgson is pissed off about this one," Grosvenor whispers to me, leaning over.

"Why?" I whisper back.

"She's only going to hurt his case. It's brilliant for us, though," she tells me.

"So why is he questioning her?" I ask.

"He'll look stupid if he doesn't. When I requested she should appear as a witness, he was given the choice to cross-examine. If he doesn't bother then it's an automatic one–nil to us. I guess he's just going to try to pull whatever he can out of her to help his cause, but let's be honest, she's only going to make Noah look terrible," Grosvenor explains.

I don't reply.

"And you look innocent," she adds, as though this wasn't clear to me.

The sound of shuffling and bodies turning in their seats announces that the new witness has arrived. The whole room is looking in the same direction. I see a flash of white-blond hair and quickly glance away, my face hot. Is she a relative of Lilah? Or just another blond woman? As Mads steps into my peripheral vision I jolt out of my spiral of inner turmoil. I find myself fascinated by her looks, so different from Lilah yet so similar in her air of confidence, the expensive perfume that wafts from her as she walks past me to the witness stand. She is petite, around five foot two, and while Maggie was right to assume from her surname she would be Korean, I think Mads may be mixed-race. Her raven hair is pinned back with pearl clips and she's wearing a pink lip gloss that shines, making her mouth look as lovely as Lilah's, though her lips are less bowed. And she's pale—as pale as Grosvenor, another way in which she is more similar to me than to Lilah. This woman seems less supermodel, more everyday, and the realization terrifies me because it means that Noah just wanted women—any woman—to satisfy him. If Lilah and I combined weren't enough, how many more was he seeing? I grip the table tightly until the flesh under my nails turns white and I wonder if I will throw up.

"Miss Choi, will you please explain to the jury how you came to meet Mr. Coors?" Dodgson asks.

Mads clears her throat, looking directly at the jury and avoiding my eyes. "I work at the Squat Rack gym. I'm a personal trainer there and Noah signed up using his company discount. I gave him a free session, which I give every new customer to the gym, and he asked for my number. We began a . . . correspondence," she says. I wince at her word choice.

"Was this professional or personal?"

"It began as professional; I was just his trainer. It became romantic."

"Did you want it to become romantic?" Dodgson asks, raising an eyebrow.

Mads looks indignant. "I'm a grown woman. If I didn't want it to become romantic, it wouldn't have."

"And are you in the habit of dating clients?" he asks.

At this, her cheeks flush pink. "No, I am not. Noah was and still is the only client I have ever become romantically involved with."

"Do you date a lot?" Dodgson asks.

"Objection! Relevance," Grosvenor intervenes.

"Sustained." The judge nods, raising her eyebrows in silent displeasure at Dodgson, who has the decency to look embarrassed.

"Sexist pig," Grosvenor whispers to me.

"No further questions," Dodgson concedes, looking much less smug than he did at the start of his examination.

Grosvenor stands, and strides up to Mads, her chin raised.

"Hello, Miss Choi. I wonder . . . the phone number you have submitted to us, which Mr. Coors gave you and contacted you on . . . were you aware that this was a burner phone?"

"A burner?" Mads repeats, eyebrows pinching together.

"A secondary phone, a cheap one used separately from his main phone that he used for keeping in touch with friends and family."

"No, I wasn't aware of that," Mads replies, pressing her lips together afterward.

"And were you aware of his partner, Lilah, with whom he lived in Chelsea?" Grosvenor continues, twisting the blade further into Mads's chest.

"No, Noah made no mention of any other woman in his life. I had assumed, because he asked for my number and pursued me, that he was single."

"How often did you see Mr. Coors, and over what time frame?"

"We were seeing each other for around four months in late 2024, just once or twice a week outside of when he visited the gym for a workout."

"What did you do together?" Grosvenor asks.

"Just normal things. We went to dinner a lot, drinks, the cinema once . . ."

"And did you ever go back to his house?"

"No, I didn't. He . . ." Here Mads trails off, shifting uncomfortably in her seat.

"Go on," Grosvenor encourages.

"Well, we would go back to mine because all the dates were closer to my flat than his." She is turning pink.

"And who organized the date locations?"

"He did," she admits, her voice low.

"So Mr. Coors was always in charge of organizing things and could plan dates close to your residence, to cover for the fact that he never invited you back to his home?"

"Objection! Hearsay," Dodgson warbles, though he looks shaken.

"I mean, I guess at the time I just thought it made sense, and sometimes he said he had an early work meeting so had to leave me in the evening, but also I work from five A.M. some mornings for prework sessions with clients so I didn't always want him staying over . . ." Mads's voice trails off again.

"I assume, but would like the jury to hear it confirmed, that you were having a sexual relationship with Mr. Coors?"

I hold my breath.

"Yes," Mads confirms.

I deflate.

"And that you are the owner of the email address Mads.Choi@ mailwave.com?"

"Yes, that's me."

"And he sent you calendar invitations for these dates using his work calendar?"

Mads is now wringing her hands, humiliated by the details she is having to share.

"Yes, he said he kept everything in there as it made it easier to keep track."

"To conclude, Madeline: You were having an affair with Mr. Coors, and he gave you absolutely no indication at all that there was another woman, let alone two, in his life?"

Mads looks at me, her eyes full of confusion. "Yes, that is correct."

"And how does it make you feel, to know that you were one of several?"

"Objection! Hearsay, Your Honor, we don't know how many there were." Dodgson looks like he is about to have a stroke, a bead of sweat trailing down his temple.

"How does this make you feel?" Grosvenor repeats to the witness.

"Like shit. Sorry! I don't know if I'm allowed to say that. I feel bad. I feel angry with him for being so deceitful, and upset with myself for wasting my time on him," she says, shooting me a meaningful glance.

"And if you were to see Mr. Coors today, do you think you might be annoyed to the point of giving his shoulder a little push?" Grosvenor asks.

Mads looks bewildered. "I . . ."

"*Objection! Speculation!*" Dodgson roars, his face now pink as gammon.

"No further questions, Your Honor," Grosvenor says breezily, her mouth curving into the tiniest of smiles.

As she walks past, Mads glances at me with what looks like a hint of apology in her eyes.

Two women fooled by Noah Coors.

Two fooled women, one dead mistress and one lying fiancé. I feel my heart break with every fresh confirmation that he is not the man I thought he was.

FIFTY-ONE

We've broken for recess and I'm sitting with Grosvenor in silence in the little consultation room that has come to feel more familiar to me than my own flat, and I'm afraid. Afraid of this trial continuing. Clearly, I have been living with a man who wasn't who I believed him to be at all. And it scares me that I could have been so easily fooled.

Mother always liked meek men. Quiet, obliging men who gave her the praise and attention she wanted. Men who could lavish gifts on her, or else admiration. She liked to dominate a room, to jerk the strings of all those around her like a master puppeteer. There was only one time when she didn't pick a meek man. He is one of the few I remember. His name was Jack, and she met him at a routine doctor's appointment. In fact, he was her doctor. He was charming, handsome, wore his sandy hair parted to the side and swept over like a movie star. Of course, she flirted with him immediately. She had gone in for a prescription and waltzed out with a date.

After that he took her out for dinner a few times. I would hear his convertible pull up outside the house late at night and hurry over to the window to check what state she was in when she left his car, so I could work out what mood she would be in over the next couple of days. They would kiss, and he would walk her all the way to the front door, and often she would be wielding a bouquet of flowers. She'd giggle girlishly, and this was a version of my mother that I

was so unused to seeing that I would feel wrong-footed, unsure how
to engage with her. I wondered if he, as a medical man, was somehow healing her, making her a better, newer version of herself.

Things moved very quickly. Within a few weeks he was basically
living with us. Mother was over the moon, and I heard her bragging
to friends on the phone about him, what a catch he was, how he
spoiled her . . . oh, and did she mention? He was a *doctor*. He was
nice to me as well. Not that she cared. But he would always smile at
me, make an effort to engage me in conversation, and when she
would direct his attention back to her, he would give me a knowing,
apologetic smile before turning her way. It was as though in those
short few weeks he had learned how to maneuver her—something
that had taken me years. He knew not to rile her, not to show too
much interest in me, while nevertheless being polite and kind
enough that she praised him as the Perfect Man.

After a few more weeks, I began to envision a new life for myself. Jack would bring Mother the happiness I never could. She
would be this shiny nice new version of herself, and I would have a
father figure. Someone distant enough to keep her happy, but close
enough to make me feel like I had a family unit. Someone to screen
my future boyfriends and drive me places if I needed a lift. Someone
to slip me a sly ten-pound note with a wink, just to treat myself with
because now we were connected. I think Mother was envisioning
the same thing. A life where she could give me even less attention
because he would cover that part of parenting, a life where she'd
move into a bigger suburban home and drive his convertible around,
a life where he would come home from a long day of touching ailing
bodies and fuck her in their bed.

It was a slow transition. He began looking at her phone when she
wasn't in the room. I caught him doing it twice and both times he
winked at me, as though it was our little secret. He would throw out
clothes of hers that he didn't like and tell her she must have lost
them when she went searching. He would maneuver her to go out
less, which at the time I thought was his way of setting a good ex-

ample, making her into a mother and partner before other things. In fact, he just wanted to spend time alone with her, with nobody else involved.

Then one night I heard him screaming at her, telling her that he was sick of the way she looked, of how men looked at her. For me, it had come out of nowhere. He called her a slag, and then he hit her. I heard her body hit the floor with a soft thud, and then she was screaming at him, bellowing at the top of her lungs. "Get out! Get the fuck out of my house! I never want to see you again, you fucking psychopath!" she yelled. I'd never heard her scream so loudly and ferociously at anybody who wasn't me.

"How fucking dare you put your fucking hands on me? I'll have your medical license if you ever set foot near me or my daughter again!" she continued, full of rage but with a tremor in her voice.

"Good fucking riddance!" he roared back, slamming the front door with such force that all the lightbulbs rattled. I had remained rooted to the spot in my bedroom. Mother did not come in to see me, nor did I check on her.

Jack tried to apologize. I knew it from the bouquets of flowers that kept turning up at the house and the way that Mother would let her phone ring out after a glance to see who was calling. But we never saw Jack again, and we never mentioned him either. It was as though we had wiped the slate clean. And the following week, when a friend asked her what had happened to the handsome doctor she was dating, Mother replied, "He fooled me entirely. But I shall never be fooled like that again."

"Look, I know that was hard on you. I'm sorry," Grosvenor tells me, putting a hand on my shoulder, and I look up to detect genuine feeling in her eyes. "Men are awful," she adds quietly.

"I never had an inkling of any other women before I found out about Lilah. Even when I learned about her, I honestly never considered that there would be *more* of them. Does that make me stupid?" I ask, my eyes starting to tear up.

"No, it makes you a trusting woman who was taken advantage of. I'm sorry," she says again. "I have something that might cheer you up." She pulls out a letter and places it in front of me. "Arrived at my office yesterday addressed to you."

For a moment, I think it's from Noah, and my heart skips.

I look at my name, carefully printed on the envelope, and my heart sinks. This is not Noah's handwriting. His strange spidery script is far away from this careful rounded lettering. I close my eyes for a moment to compose myself, allow myself to grieve the loss of that fantasy. Of course it's not from Noah. I doubt he's even allowed to write to me, with Lilah's trial still ongoing. I rip the envelope open at the top and pull out the letter, my eyes scanning it quickly.

Dear Claire,

It will never not be strange to be writing to you in this situation, but I'm glad I can give you some comfort and support. I can't begin to imagine what you're going through. I hope you're okay, and that they are treating you well. I'm trying to be positive, and not to worry about you in there all alone, but it's hard. I imagine when I next see you for the trial, it will hopefully bring me some peace.

I think about you every day. The media went quiet for a while but it's busier since the trial began. You've been in the news often. They haven't used the best photo of you, I'll be honest . . . In fact, the media have been horrible about your whole situation. I think when you get out you should really avoid newspapers and sites. Definitely don't google yourself!

But you will get out, Claire. I know that's not you, the person the media are making you out to be, and I'm happy to testify in court to say so. I know it was an accident. I'm sorry I wasn't there for you. I should have checked in more often, made sure you were okay. Maybe if I had gone to see Lilah with you, this could have ended differently.

But I check in with your lawyer's junior often and she has kept me

semi up-to-date and assures me that you are not guilty of murder—
though I didn't need a lawyer to tell me that!

I suppose what I'm trying to say, Claire, however incoherently, is that
I believe in you. I believe what you have said, I trust you and I am here
for you. I'll be following the trial every day, and remember—whatever
you need, whether it's someone to listen while you cry and rage, or just to
forget all of this and talk about the latest work gossip (Fiona from
marketing snogged Brian from tech!!!), I am here for you, and I'm not
going anywhere. I'm so sorry you are going through all of this.

All my love,
your friend, Sukhi x

P.S. If you want anything, magazines, etc., let me know and I'll get it
sent if you can tell me how. Or maybe call me? Or write to me,
whatever you want. Or don't. Whatever's good for you.

My eyes have welled up and I hastily shove the letter back into its
envelope so that I don't cry all over it and smudge the writing. I sit
in silence for a while, overcome with emotions that I struggle to
identify, reminded of the stakes for Sukhi as she sat up there and
defended me in a room ready to hate me and anybody on my side.
Gratitude for all of her lovely thoughtful letters, and the reminder
that there's something waiting for me on the outside. Awe that
someone I've known for a relatively short time is so trusting of me.
Love that I didn't know I had, for Sukhi and her kindness. These
are all positive emotions, so I don't know why I feel so mournful, so
undeserving. I feel like this kindness is too much. The fact that
someone would even sit down and take time out of their day to
hand-write me all these letters, knowing I haven't replied to most of
them . . . it feels baffling. It feels as though it's something that happens to other people. To the Lilahs of this world, not the Claires.
The Claires don't deserve kindness or love. But then again, I suppose the Lilahs of this world don't deserve death.

FIFTY-TWO

June 15, 2025
Dear Diary,

Noah and I have put the Sukhi argument behind us. He's promised to schedule another time to meet her and Fateh, and said he'll set an entire day aside in case we want to do something fun like go to the zoo. I think he knows that seeing cute animals is my weakness and I won't be able to say no.

At breakfast yesterday I found he'd made me a little zoo of paper animals, all with apologies written on them.

> Sorry I'm shit!
> Sorry I am flaky and rubbish
> Sorry I work too much
> Sorry I didn't get to meet your friend
> Sorry! Sorry! Sorry!
> Sorry! Let's go to the zoo? Sukhi can come?? (A better zoo than this one . . .)

He'd made them a pen out of five forks and had put the origami animals inside.

He makes it so difficult for me to stay annoyed with him.

Claire

FIFTY-THREE

I do not want to return to that courtroom. I am exhausted. My headache is now a constant distracting thrum, and we have fallen into an unspoken ritual whereby whenever we have a break, Grosvenor silently slides two ibuprofen over to me with a glass of water. I think she's noticed how I'm constantly massaging my temples, trying to ease out the months of stress that are reverberating painfully against my skull.

For just a moment, I close my eyes and wonder if there is some way that I can hide the ibuprofen from her, put them under my tongue temporarily, hoard them up and then end this quickly. But a memory stirs, some sort of documentary I must have watched sometime, and I'm sure the quantities it would take to kill me would be impossible to squirrel away. As though on cue, a streaking pain almost blinds me, ripping through from the back of my skull, and I find myself acknowledging that I would be totally incapable of turning down any painkiller offered to me, even if death were the reward. I squeeze my eyes shut and begin to massage my temples, already reaching for the glass of water in front of me.

"Migraine?" one of the prison guards asks.

"Mmm," I grunt back.

"Killer," he replies.

FIFTY-FOUR

MAJA ANDERSSON

Today I have to focus, because Maja, Lilah's mother, has arrived as Dodgson's next witness. She looks terrible. This is not the woman I saw lounging on an obscenely expensive bouclé sofa with a glass of champagne in her hand and not a care in the world. This version looks haggard and frail, deep shadowed lines beneath her red-rimmed eyes, hands wrinkled and with a tremor. She's lost her shine, her once-golden aura now a sad, murky gray.

I wonder if my own mother could ever have lost her sparkle as a result of losing me. In the entirety of her life, despite all the broken-down relationships I witnessed, I never truly saw her lose that. Instead she would plow straight on and dismiss the offending person from her mind, blink them away and move on to the next as though nothing bad had happened. I wonder, had I been the one to die first, if she would have blinked me away, continued with her life while using the loss of her daughter as another of her dramatic tales to garner attention and sympathy.

I find myself curling my fingers in anticipation. As Maja takes the stand, I notice her chest shaking sporadically and realize she is holding in sobs.

She is wearing a sharply tailored navy blazer, with a string of pearls around her neck. The white shirt beneath is so crisp I cannot see a single crease. A delicate gold chain decorates her wrist as she holds up her shaking hand to take the oath. Lilah's mother is a wreck; that much is clear. She has been broken by the loss of her daughter, and I feel a sharp and unwelcome stab of jealousy at the sheer amount of love Lilah had in her life. I imagine her setting the table alongside Maja, both of them laughing companionably and sharing affectionate anecdotes. The realization that Lilah will be missed so much more than I would ever be swarms over me and sends a prickling sensation through my chest.

I shake it away as Dodgson welcomes her to the stand to say her piece.

"We'll keep it short today, Mrs. Andersson, as I'm aware this is difficult for you," he tells her, with a pointed glance at the jury.

She mouths *thank you* at him silently, as though fearful that using her voice will result in howls of grief.

"Did your daughter Lilah ever mention the defendant to you?"

"Yes," she replies, voice thick.

"Can you tell us about it?"

"Well, she didn't tell me her name or many details. I don't think she wanted me to worry." Her voice sounds cracked and scratchy, as though her throat has given out, and her accent retains a Scandinavian edge. "She had mentioned that a woman had become obsessed with Noah, but she said it flippantly, as though it was just an irritation rather than anything *dangerous,*" she continues. "I would have told her to come stay with me immediately had I known there was any possibility of harm coming to her. I spoke to her almost every day and she only mentioned it that one time, as a by-the-by comment."

"Do you recall when this was, the date when she mentioned the accused?"

"Yes, it was not long before her death." She pauses to adjust to this idea. "I believe they'd had a run-in with each other at a club."

Lilah's face flashes before my eyes, the way she flinched when I threw my engagement ring at Noah in the booth. Sukhi's presence bolstering me as she chucked a drink at him. The way I threw that glass at Lilah, the shattered shards of glass behind her.

"And this was the first you'd heard of her?" Dodgson asks.

"Yes, though not by name, as I said. Lilah just called her some strange, obsessed woman."

I bristle.

"And what did you know about Mr. Coors?"

"Well, everything, just about! I've known Noah since he was a boy. They've always been a pair," Maja says, and this time her shoulders crumple and she lets out a sob. "It's been terrible, this entire trial, finding out about the man he truly was, about the other women, all these things that Lilah will thankfully never have to know but I will always live with. The knowledge that he played my daughter for a fool until her dying breath will haunt me forever."

Dodgson bows his head, allowing her a moment to compose herself, the judge offering a tissue.

"Is it fair to say that Lilah was known to the defendant, that they had already had a previous, violent altercation?" Dodgson asks Maja.

"Yes, that's fair. Apparently the accused threw a glass at my daughter, which I would classify as violent."

"Objection! Hearsay!" Grosvenor interrupts. The judge nods in agreement.

"But it would come as no surprise to you that she would seek your daughter out again for a second confrontation?" Dodgson continues.

At this, Maja stiffens. "Nobody *saw* this coming."

"Apologies, I misspoke. What I meant was, they were known to each other and there was a possible motive for a clash?"

"Yes. As Noah explained to me, the woman was unstable and clearly disturbed about him being with Lilah."

I bite my lip so hard I can taste blood.

"And your daughter knew you were worried about her?"

"Yes, of course. What mother doesn't worry about her daughter?"

I feel a stab in my gut, a loss of breath as though I've been punched.

"And is it fair to say that Lilah mentioning the altercation was . . . a big deal? That she wouldn't have worried you for no reason?"

"Yes, I suppose now, in hindsight, I should have probed more, asked more questions. She must have been shaken by it to have mentioned it to me in a call."

"Thank you, I have no further questions."

I take a shaky breath as Grosvenor steps up to take her turn and question Maja.

"Mrs. Andersson, considering what we have discovered about Mr. Coors's womanizing in the course of this trial, is it fair to say that when he told you that the defendant was 'unstable,' he could have been covering his own back? Distancing himself from her to avoid your daughter finding out about another affair?"

Maja frowns, one shaking hand tweaking at her lower lip absentmindedly. "Yes, I suppose that could be possible." She turns to look at me, and though she says nothing, I can see it in her critical glance. *Why would Noah cheat with that pathetic woman when he already had my Lilah?*

I force myself to blink and slowly look away, not let her see that I can hear her thoughts and they hurt me.

"And is it also possible that when your daughter said Miss Arundale was obsessed with Mr. Coors, in fact this could have been something made up entirely by him, to avoid any possibility of their affair being discovered?"

"Yes . . . it is possible," Maja admits slowly, realization beginning to dawn on her, and alongside her, the jury. They have begun to look at me directly, as though unsure what they believe and wanting to see if they can work it out. Work *me* out.

"So what you're accepting is that you have no proof whatsoever that what your daughter or Mr. Coors said about the defendant is true. That this entire testimony has been essentially a case of he said/ she said?" Grosvenor challenges her.

"Objection!" Dodgson stands up, looking indignant.

The judge nods to Grosvenor and waves a dismissive hand at Dodgson. "Objection overruled."

"No further questions," Grosvenor finishes up.

I press my lips together to keep myself from smiling.

FIFTY-FIVE

HARRY BARTON

It's the final testimony of the day and I'm the most exhausted I've been so far, my eyes swollen and puffy and the ever-present migraine ripping through my skull. Every time I think about Noah, it seems to drill deeper.

"Mr. Barton, how long have you known Mr. Coors?" Dodgson asks.

The young man on the stand looks laidback, his stance straight, shoulders relaxed. I know him, though he hasn't yet made eye contact with me. Noah's best friend, Harry. He is pale, his normally dark skin dulled. I wonder if he is always so sickly-hued, or if it is exhaustion from staying up while comforting Noah.

"Twenty-two years, sir."

"And in this time, you've known Mr. Coors's girlfriends? His crushes?"

"As far as I'm aware, I have known everything from his first weeklong crush in year seven through to his relationship with Lilah."

"Why do you say *through to* when referencing Lilah Andersson?"

Harry Barton shrugs lightly, as though it's obvious. "Because she was his last proper relationship. They've been together ages." He recognizes his error and winces. "They *were* together ages. He was going to marry her."

I stare at Harry, then shrink back in surprise when he glares right back, entirely unfazed. He is the first witness who has seemed totally in control of their emotions, their hatred of me. It makes me want to burst into tears, because he seems so *real* up there, so completely within his rights to be angry with me, to hate me. Yet still, he lies. He *had* to have known about me, the way I knew about him. I admit, I haven't met him in person before, but Noah mentioned him in passing to me several times: Harry was a major presence throughout Noah's teenage years. Surely as a major presence in his more mature life, I would have been mentioned by Noah in my turn? Or perhaps not. Perhaps he was lying about that, on top of everything else, when he told me his friends were pleased he was settling down with me. I don't know what to believe anymore.

Realizing the levels of deceit that have been practiced for so long, not just in Noah's dealings with me, but with his friends and family as well, hits me like a double-decker bus, the notion that he could have lied to us all, broken my trust so completely, kept me a secret and led his double life behind my back. There *must* be a logical reason for it all. My hopes are resting on this trial ending with a light-bulb going on over my head, a resounding explanation for all of this madness, the final comfort of clarity and understanding. I am owed that much at least. How can one person play so many others for fools?

"And so despite your close and long-established friendship with Mr. Coors, there was never any hint he was conducting a relationship with this woman? That he was cheating on Lilah?" Dodgson nods over at me, a faint smirk on his mouth that I want to slap away. Because the smirk says it all. *Obviously Noah Coors did not date this pathetic excuse for a woman. Look at the state of her.* It's as though it's an inside joke they're all in on, that blatant curl of his lip a cruel sting to my wounded pride.

"I never heard of Noah engaging with Claire in any way," Harry replies, his voice free from the slightest tremor. I pick up on that carefully worded answer, and judging by the way Grosvenor lifts her head, she has too.

"Did Mr. Coors ever speak to you about this woman in any other context, outside of a sexual or romantic relationship?" asks prosecuting counsel.

"Yes," Harry admits. My eyes dart toward him. *He spoke about me. I knew Noah would have mentioned me, have shared something about me with his closest friend. I knew it!*

"He told me he met her at Morrisons." Harry falters for a moment as though treading water. My heart lifts at the memory of Noah's eyes locking with mine across the aisle.

"Well, *met* is a strong word . . ." Harry retracts, trailing off with a frown.

"What do you mean by that?" Dodgson asks.

"Well, he did *meet* her, I suppose. He spoke to her. Once, at the supermarket, about wine."

I frown, unsure where he is going with this, fearful of how this warm memory I have of our love-at-first-sight moment is going to become twisted in his account of it.

"And then, apparently, she became obsessed with Noah. Began stalking him. I mean, I didn't know it was *Claire*." He glances over at me and swallows, the first sign of nerves. "I didn't know it was this woman," he clarifies. "I just knew that he met *a* woman, in the supermarket. He told me about it at the pub over a pint, and we had a bit of a laugh about it. I didn't take it too seriously, you know? It was just a bit of banter to me, my pal being supposedly stalked. And I didn't know what she looked like or her name or anything until all of this came to light, and then it clicked. That they were the same person."

I feel as though my stomach is falling out of my body. *Obsessed? Stalked?*

"And that was the only time she was mentioned?" Dodgson asks.

"Yes, we didn't speak about her after that night."

"And what was Mr. Coors saying? About their relationship?"

Harry pauses to scratch the back of his head, his nose wrinkling slightly. "Well, not much, to be honest. Look, we were a couple of pints in, I can't remember it too clearly. He just said some weird girl he'd spoken to in Morrisons was stalking him on social media."

But I didn't even have him on social media! I thought Noah hated social media?

"Did Mr. Coors seem concerned, or worried about his and Lilah's safety?"

"Nah, like I said, it was just a bit of a laugh over pints. That's why I didn't bring it up again, why I forgot until all of . . . this happened. I mean, all the girls fancy Noah, it's not weird for someone to fancy him and follow him online. He didn't seem bothered, definitely not *concerned* about it, or we wouldn't have made a joke of the whole thing. He didn't even mention Lilah in this conversation, as far as I can remember. It was just an anecdote, a funny story."

I can tell from Dodgson's expression that this is perhaps not what he wanted to hear, and he soon wraps up his questioning, Grosvenor stepping up to take his place. I find myself wondering if it's worse to be seen as a stalker or a joke. A gimmick. An anecdote.

I was sixteen and standing at the vending machine in the school playground, reaching in for the ice-cold can of Coke I'd spent my spare change on. One of the few luxuries I allowed myself, as I was intent on saving all my spare cash to move out as soon as I turned eighteen. I turned, frowning, when a chorus of laughter washed over me. A gaggle of boys from my year were lingering nearby, shooting glances over at me, laughing. I smoothed my ugly school skirt down, tried to keep my chin up as I cracked open my can of Coke. I could feel my skin warming, and prayed I wasn't reddening visibly.

"Oi, Claire! Over here, Claire!" one of them, Marcus, called over to me. I considered them. This had to be a wind-up. But the ones looking my way were smiling, the others uninterested, talking among themselves or kicking at the ground. I looked over my shoulder, unsure what to do.

"We don't bite, Claire! We just want to ask you something!" another boy yelled. Embarrassed by my own insecurity, I forced myself to walk over to them and they quickly enveloped me, closing me in the middle of their circle.

"Good Coke?" one asked.

"Fine," I replied with a shrug, trying desperately to seem cool and collected, unbothered by this bizarre display of attention.

"Right, so the thing is, Claire, Stevie here has something he wants to ask you," Marcus said with a laugh, shoving Stevie toward me. He, to his credit, looked just as uncomfortable as I felt at that very moment, shooting Marcus daggers and chewing on his lip with oversized front teeth.

"Yeah, so, er, I just wondered if you wanted to go to prom with me?" he asked. He blurted it all out in one long sentence and I blinked at him, unsure if I was understanding correctly. His friends had all burst out into laughter and jeers, shoving one another in their excitement like a pack of monkeys. Internally, I was reviewing all the details that attending the prom would involve. I'd need a dress, which was something I didn't want to spend my money on. I'd have to dance, which was something I had no interest in doing ever since that awful Latin dance class with Mother. I'd have to spend the evening with Stevie, which was not a prospect that particularly excited me. And I'd have to tell Mother, who would undoubtedly find some way to make it all horrible for me.

"Oh my God, she's actually *considering* it!" one of them bellowed with exaggerated laughter.

"It was a joke, Claire," Stevie said, rolling his eyes as though it was obvious. I flushed furiously, my chest tightening.

"Claire thought Stevie wanted to take her out!" one of them yelled with glee, and then they were all laughing as though it was the funniest thing in the world, a couple of them actually doubled over and dramatically clutching their stomachs.

I shoved my way through their horrible, sweaty bodies, escaping them as I hurried away, but their laughter chased me, and above it all, I heard one voice shout: "As if she thought anyone would ask her out unless it was a *joke*!"

"Mr. Barton, I believe you did not answer one of Mr. Dodgson's questions earlier," Grosvenor says, going straight for the kill. I knew she'd noticed the same thing I had.

"Excuse me?" Harry asks, but I see his Adam's apple bob as he swallows.

"Mr. Dodgson asked you if you knew of a relationship between Mr. Coors and the defendant, Miss Arundale, which you denied, but also if Mr. Coors had ever cheated on the victim, Miss Andersson. You only answered one of these questions." She raises an eyebrow at him knowingly, and Dodgson runs a hand through his hair.

"I mean, you know . . . Noah got a lot of attention from the ladies, he's a good-looking lad . . ." Harry's voice trails off and he rubs the back of his neck.

"Mr. Barton, I ask once more: Did you know of Mr. Coors having sexual relationships with other women besides Lilah Andersson?"

I watch in fascination as Harry Barton turns an astounding shade of puce, and then, bringing a hand to his face and lowering his head, admits, "Yes. Yes, I am aware of Noah cheating on Lilah."

Gasps from the public gallery and I hear a door slam. I wonder if it is one of Lilah's relatives.

I can tell Grosvenor is holding back a triumphant smile. "How many times would you say he had cheated on Lilah?"

"I don't know. I didn't keep count."

She pounces on that. "So it's fair to say there were so many women that you were unable to keep track?"

"I didn't say that!" Harry looks more flustered by the second. "It wasn't that many—I tried to stay out of it, that's all. It wasn't my business!"

"Did you ever hear about a Madeline? Or Mads, as Noah called her?"

"No, no, Noah never told me about them really. Never names, they were just, like, flings, I don't know. I think he was just trying to let loose before he got tied down, before he married Lilah," Harry says. I can hear the fight has left his voice. He knows he has fucked up, that he's painted his best friend as a lying, cheating scumbag who failed his dead girlfriend in every possible way.

"So you didn't know about Miss Choi, who we all know through her testimony was seeing Mr. Coors semi-regularly, for quite a decent period of time. Would it be fair to assume that there were quite likely to be other women you did not hear about?" Grosvenor asks.

Harry sighs, defeated. "Yes, I suppose. There were several."

"And he'd meet them where?" Grosvenor pushes.

"Bars, after work. I'd be there sometimes with him. He made me swear not to say anything to anyone, in case it got back to Lilah. I'm sorry. I feel awful. I thought I was doing right by my mate, I didn't ever think . . . If I could go back and change . . ." It looks like he might even cry.

"So is it in fact entirely possible that Mr. Coors met my client in a Morrisons supermarket, chatted her up, and she began what she believed was a friendly relationship with him, by following him on social media?"

Harry swallows, and the delay in his reluctant response is palpable. "It is possible that Noah lied about it, yes."

"And then after that, is it also possible that they began a romantic correspondence and Mr. Coors refrained from sharing the ins and outs of this with you, as you seem to have only been given a partial picture of his other romantic entanglements?"

"I suppose it could have been like that," he concedes.

"That's all, thanks," Grosvenor says, spinning on her heel.

FIFTY-SIX

JOSEPH MILES

Our first witness to the stand today is Joseph Miles," Dodgson announces the next day. He says it as though it's a grand event, a celebrity meet'n'greet. Joseph is tall and gangly, with curly dark hair and bushy eyebrows. He's young, perhaps in his late twenties.

I realize with a sinking heart that I know this man. I know him, but my head is foggy and I can't quite seem to place him.

"Mr. Miles, is the Claire Arundale sitting over there"—a nod toward me—"the Claire Arundale that you know?" Dodgson asks.

Joseph glances over at me for the first time, his eyes quickly darting away.

"Yes," he confirms.

"And will you tell the court how you know her?"

"From Morrisons, sir," he replies.

Ah, yes. He works at my local Morrisons. That's where I recognize him from, although seeing him in a badly fitting suit in this setting has thrown me. Usually when I see him he is in his store uniform.

"I'm the manager there," he explains. "And Miss Arundale worked for us for a while."

Immediately, I frown.

I look toward Grosvenor but she shows not a flicker of emotion or reaction, as though none of this is fazing her. As though she knew it was coming. So I stay calm on the outside. On the inside, I'm wondering what the hell is going on, why this man is here speaking for the prosecution.

"And when did Miss Arundale stop working for you?"

"September the eighteenth 2024, sir."

I freeze. That's not right.

"You seem sure of that date?" Dodgson asks.

"I am, sir."

"Why?"

"I had to fill in a lot of paperwork about it, sir. With HR," Joseph clarifies.

"And why was that?"

"Well, because there was no notice period or anything. She just left halfway through her shift and didn't come back," he explains.

I'm frowning so hard that it feels as if my forehead may split at any moment, because I do not have a single clue what this man is talking about. He works at Morrisons, yes. But I certainly didn't, not in 2024.

I lean over to Grosvenor.

"Shhh!" she hisses at me before I even open my mouth, and I recoil like a scolded puppy.

"Is that unusual?" Dodgson asks, turning to raise his brows at the jury knowingly.

"Well, yes," Joseph replies. "Usually you would hand in written notice to say you're resigning, and work for another couple of weeks while we found a replacement. Claire's contract had a one-month notice period she should have fulfilled. And I've never before had a staff member leave mid-shift without giving any sort of reason."

That's because it's *weird*. Who would leave mid-shift at work without saying anything? I certainly would not do something like that. None of this makes any sense . . . My head is starting to ache, a dull pain deep in the back of my skull, and I imagine little bugs crawling out of the crevices of my brain as I try to compute what is happening.

"What was Miss Arundale like to work with in general?"

"Well, she was a very good employee—she worked with us for years," Joseph admits, glancing at the jury. "She arrived on time, she was polite, helpful with customers. Didn't require much training, she picked things up quickly. Covered people when sick, always up for a bit of small talk in the aisles between tasks when things were quiet . . ." He trails off, as though unsure if he's saying the right things.

"So you would say it was out of character, for her to leave randomly mid-shift?" Dodgson asks.

"Absolutely." Joseph nods vigorously, as though pleased to have been asked a question he can answer wholeheartedly.

"And no member of your staff knew why she left? There was no obvious incident? No family emergency of any sort?"

"Not that I heard of," Joseph replies carefully. "I asked everyone, obviously, who was on that shift with her, but nobody knew of anything at all. She seemed fine when she came in. But I know that her mother had died just a week before. Miss Arundale hadn't wanted any time off, said that they weren't close, that she wanted to keep working . . . to stay busy." He chews his lip.

"We have some CCTV footage of her final shift that we'd like to play for the court. After viewing it, will you please confirm that the footage is authentic and is from your place of work?"

"Yes." Joseph nods.

A tape is produced, pulled from a clear, creased evidence bag. And on a screen that has been set up for the jury flashes up CCTV of Morrisons. The wine aisle. And there is Noah, and there am I, on the day that we met.

"Objection! This is new, last-minute evidence," Grosvenor begins, but the judge quickly cuts her off.

"Overruled."

For the first time, Grosvenor looks shaken. This footage is obviously something that she did not know Dodgson had access to.

I blink at the grainy CCTV footage, the ache in my head creeping forward to a point in my forehead. Grosvenor is still as a hawk beside me, her hands folded carefully in front of her as the footage sits in a mocking freeze-frame in front of us.

"Please note the date and timestamp here," Dodgson explains, pointing to the bottom right-hand corner of the footage: September 18, 2024, 5:07 P.M.

The day I met Noah.

"Before we play this footage, can you confirm the timings of Miss Arundale's scheduled shift that day?" Dodgson asks Joseph.

"Yes, I have a copy of the timetable from that day. Claire was in to work at two 'til close. Ten P.M.," he clarifies.

"I'd also like to establish that the two people we see in this footage are, quite clearly, Claire Arundale and Noah Coors." Dodgson points his finger again at the screen and then the footage begins to play.

I'm standing in the wine aisle, and I'm wearing a Morrisons uniform, sorting out the bottles on the shelves.

"This is . . ." I whisper to Grosvenor, but she cuts me off with a raised hand, eyes not leaving the screen. I'm not even sure she's breathing, her chest is so still.

I try not to fling myself across the room, the desire to cover the screen with my body suddenly overwhelming me. Instead, I sit back and watch Noah approach me on the footage. He looks gorgeous. Seeing him on-screen like this makes him look like a movie star. And to be honest, this bizarre fictionalized setting is only adding to the cinematic quality of what I'm seeing. We appear to speak, though there is no sound. I watch myself walk him halfway along the aisle and hold up a bottle of red wine. I appear to be speaking about it and Noah smiles and takes it, adding it to his basket. Then, I show him a white wine bottle and he takes that, too, still speaking to me. I watch as he strolls off-screen.

A new crack of pain slices its way through my left temple. Moments later, the me on-screen picks up another bottle of wine and follows him, leaving the frame.

The footage then cuts to the storefront and we can see Noah leaving, having paid for his bags of shopping. A minute later, there I am, appearing to follow him out. The wine bottle is now gone from my hands, discarded somewhere between leaving the wine aisle and exiting the store. The footage stops.

"And that was when Miss Arundale left?" Dodgson asks Joseph.

"There's no footage of her returning that day. So I think she left at that point and did not return, yes."

"And is it fair to say that from the footage we have just seen, it seems Miss Arundale and Mr. Coors had a professional interaction, and Miss Arundale then followed him out of the store uninvited?" Dodgson continues.

"It could appear that way, yes," Joseph replies.

"No further questions." Dodgson resumes his seat.

Grosvenor stands. "Just one question from me." She smiles at Joseph warmly and I see his shoulders visibly drop as he relaxes.

"There was no audio on the tape," she comments.

"Correct. Our CCTV records without audio," Joseph confirms.

"So it is very much possible that when we watch my client speaking with Mr. Coors and handing him the wine bottle, he has asked her to leave and meet him at a nearby coffeehouse?"

"Yes, that is always possible." Joseph nods.

"Thank you, Mr. Miles. That is all."

He nods at me, a small smile on his face as though we are friends, and leaves the stand. My entire body is tense, but to my great alarm I notice that beside me, for the first time, Grosvenor is just as tense as I am.

FIFTY-SEVEN

laire, this next part is going to be the hardest for you, okay?"
Grosvenor is speaking to me in a soothing tone of voice. I look
at her and notice that the dark purple rings beneath my eyes are
reflected on her face, and her hair is sticking out at the sides. She
looks like she hasn't slept. I wonder if this trial has been keeping
her awake at night like it has me. The thought touches me briefly,
the idea that someone would care about me so much that my possible fate keeps them awake. But I remind myself it's her job, and
the real thing that's keeping her awake is concern for her own reputation. The CCTV footage from yesterday rattled her, I know it
did. I must accept that I am, largely, alone. I was alone before I met
Noah, and now I find myself alone again, deceived by the man I'm
in love with.

"Noah is going to testify, and it's going to be incredibly difficult
for you to listen to. It's going to be emotional and altogether shit. I
can't sugarcoat this for you," Grosvenor tells me.

My eyes are welling with tears already. I'm so afraid of what I
will hear my fiancé say about me, about us and our relationship.
"He'll be talking about you, and he'll be talking about Lilah, and it's
not going to be fun for any of us. You have to remain composed,
okay, Claire? Can you do that?"

I nod because what else can I do?

"At least this is the end for Dodgson's team. Noah is the last witness, and Dodgson will make his closing statement and try to paint

you as a murderer, but we're going to ignore everything he says because it's all bullshit, okay?"

"Bullshit," I agree feebly, with a nod.

"And then we are called in by the clerk and I close off and that's it, it's out of our hands. We'll have done all we can, and it's down to the jury."

I'm so scared I think I might genuinely wet myself, my stomach unbearably twisty-turny, my breath coming out short and sharp.

"You're not a murderer, and you are not going to be convicted as one. Not if I can help it," Grosvenor tells me.

I nod, but it's because I want to believe her, rather than because I *do* believe her.

"Claire? I have to ask you . . . why did you not tell me you were working in Morrisons when you met Noah in the wine aisle?" She's watching me carefully.

I swallow. "I didn't really think it was relevant, I suppose. It happened how I told you, aside from the fact I was an employee."

She says nothing, and I can't read her expression. Her eyes are watching me so intently, I feel like she's reading my soul. I stare back, entranced, until she blinks, and the moment is over, and she's barking orders to her junior.

I resist the urge to vomit and get ready to go back into that courtroom, knowing that, perhaps as soon as tomorrow, I will either walk free or be sent behind bars for at least the next decade of my life.

FIFTY-EIGHT

NOAH COORS

My breath catches in my throat when Noah walks into the courtroom. He is so devastatingly handsome, his suit cut perfectly to flatter his broad shoulders and chest, the lines of his cutaway shirt collar mirroring his chiseled jawline. I realize, with a shock, that I have not seen my fiancé in person for many months and yet I can see no change in him. I reach for my glass of water with a shaking hand. Grosvenor nudges me under the table and hisses, *"Don't look at him,"* through gritted teeth, and I fight with every instinct in my body to wrench my gaze away from him. Then I feel a pang because he isn't looking at me. He has avoided my gaze for the entire walk through the room, and as he seats himself at the podium he stares ahead as though I don't exist. A strangled sound escapes me, somewhere between a cry and a gasp, and Grosvenor nudges me again, harder this time. I take another shaky gulp of water. I thought I could do this, but I can't. It's too hard. It's too hard seeing my boyfriend up there and having so many questions I'm unable to ask him.

I should be angry, should be consumed with rage, but instead all that emotion is manifesting as panicked desperation, a feral need to know what the fuck is going on. Why did he do this to me?

"Mr. Coors, have you met this woman before?" Dodgson asks.

I straighten slightly in my seat, and my left index finger twitches in anticipation.

"Yes, I have. We met at Morrisons." His voice is raspy, drained by exhaustion and filled with such bitterness that it hurts me to hear it.

"And what was the exchange?"

"She was working there, I was shopping. I asked her for a wine recommendation. She gave me one, I bought what I had gone there for, and left."

"And that was the entire exchange when you first met?"

"Yes."

"You did not invite her for a coffee afterward?"

"I certainly did not."

I feel my blood boiling. My fingers tighten around the sides of my seat as I try to retain my composure. I focus on my breathing but I'm so angry, so *let down* by the lies, lies, *lies* he is telling. Why? And for what? To retain his already-dashed credibility as a one-woman man?

"How would you describe the interaction?"

Noah does not even pause before answering, as though this question has been rehearsed with Dodgson a thousand times. "Fleeting."

I breathe in slowly, letting all the memories of us flash before me, reminding myself of why I love him, of what we have. Pouring me hot coffee in the morning, the crooked smile that I would wake up to when the smell of roasted beans grew too strong to resist. Laughs and easy conversation at our dinner table each night, often followed by whispered sweetness in the evening, his arm wrapped around me in bed. There was nothing contractual or professional about our relationship, nothing fleeting about us. Something must have happened to Noah that I don't know about, to make him go back on all of this so cruelly. There has to be a logical reason for his about-face.

"And what happened after you left Morrisons? Was that the end of your contact?"

"No. She sent me a friend request on Facebook a few days later. I recognized her from the profile photo."

"How did she have your name?"

"I don't know. I didn't give it to her."

I stiffen in my seat, frowning. He's lying. On oath.

"Did you accept her friend request?"

"No, I did not. I felt uncomfortable that she had added me . . . about the circumstances surrounding it."

"And was that the end of your interactions?"

"No. Over time she added some of my friends, who unknowingly accepted her, thinking she was a random requester. Eventually, one of my friends got in touch with me. She had been added by Claire, and when she had gone onto her page to see who she was, had noticed that there were photographs of me on her page. Photographs that Claire must have taken from my social media accounts and shared as though they were hers. And in some, she had even doctored herself into the image."

The photograph of us both on Las Ramblas is projected onto a white screen. Beside it is another image, identical except that I am missing, Noah standing alone and smiling at the camera. I feel sick. I look to Grosvenor and she is unnaturally still beside me.

"How did this make you feel?"

"Creeped out! That was when I told my friend Harry about the situation, but I just sort of played it down, laughed it off. It felt weird to take it all seriously. Obviously now I wish I had," he adds at the end, pointedly.

"And what did you do after your Facebook friend flagged this behavior to you?"

"I blocked Claire. I made all my accounts private and blocked her on everything, even LinkedIn. And I told all my friends who were Facebook friends with her to block her. I also warned Lilah. I didn't want her to stumble across a photoshopped image and think it was real, or anything like that. It was embarrassing."

My ears redden.

"Was this your first conversation with Lilah about Miss Arundale?"

"Yes. I hadn't had any reason to mention her before: She was nobody to me."

I suck in a breath as though I have been slapped. Nobody? *Nobody?* I was his fiancée! He was my partner, my *everything*! I feel myself fight the urge to sob hysterically. I begin trying to hyperventilate as discreetly as I can.

It was April. I was sitting with Sukhi in the office, rain pattering outside and confining us to the depressing "breakout" area, sad sandwiches in hand and a couple of packets of crisps between us.

"Shit weather," she commented.

"Shit day," I countered with a weak smile. She returned it, then paused for a moment before placing a hand over mine.

"I'm sorry about your mum, Claire."

I stared very hard at the tabletop, forced myself to feel nothing. "It's fine. It was a long time ago," I replied after an awkwardly long pause.

"I know, but that doesn't make it any easier," she told me, patting me on the hand.

It was seven months since Mother's death, and after much back-and-forth with solicitors about probate, her money was to be released later this month.

"At least you can use some of your inheritance to get on the London game of Snakes and Ladders—buy a property," Sukhi tried to joke.

"No inheritance," I replied.

"No? What do you mean?" Sukhi frowned. "I thought you said that it would all automatically go to you as she had no other close blood relatives?"

I forced a shrug. "I didn't get any money in the end."

"I'm sorry, Claire. That's a real kick in the teeth. I reckon the way I burn through money, my future kids won't have any either though, bless their hearts." Sukhi laughed determinedly, trying desperately to lighten this conversation I seemed determined to keep darkening.

"She had money. She chose not to leave me any."

"What do you mean?" Sukhi lowered her sandwich, brow furrowed in total disbelief. "She left it to someone else?"

"Yeah. She left it all to some charity for donkeys. Said there was 'nobody else' to leave things to, apparently . . ."

"Jesus Christ, Claire, that's . . . Well, look. I don't want to comment on your relationship with your mum, but that seems rotten and I'm sorry to hear about it. I'm sorry she didn't think of you."

I shrugged, though I felt a dull ache in my chest. "Yeah, well. I guess I'm just nobody."

"You're not nobody, Claire. Don't say things like that. What did Noah say?"

"He told me she's rotting away in hell and we don't need her money anyway. That I have him even if I don't have her, and that I'm his whole world and she didn't deserve me."

"Sounds about right," Sukhi said, nodding.

"And as far as you recall, that was the end of the harassment? After the social media blocking?" Dodgson asks Noah.

"No. She got my phone number somehow, kept leaving me weird voicemails, so I switched off the messaging option and left my phone ringing out. I don't even know how she got my number—it must have been online somewhere for work or something. She even came to my office. I told the receptionist not to let her in again. I gave security photographs of her. I even gave some to Lilah to give to her own office, in case Claire went after her as well."

"What do you mean by *went after*?"

"Well, I didn't know what she wanted—whether she was after money, or if she was unhinged, or what."

He pulls at his tie, and I wonder if he is about to choke on all his lies.

"And so she was now blocked from all your social media, banned from your office, and that was the end?"

"Well, I also got some emails through to my work address, but I don't know who they were from. The email was anonymous, and the address was a mix of random numbers and letters. To be honest, I didn't even get them for ages—they were going into my spam folder. But then one day I was looking for something and I found them all, hundreds of them. They were short, saying things like *I love you,* and *See you at dinner.* I was so confused, but I assumed someone just had the wrong email address. Now I am convinced it was her."

"Hearsay!" Grosvenor objects, standing up, but her voice wavers in a way I haven't heard before. My eyes are closed; I can't bear to look at anyone in this room.

"And *that* was the end of the interactions?" Dodgson asks, rolling his eyes at Grosvenor in a way that I would find incredibly offensive were I not busy loathing my fiancé for the first time in my life.

"Yes, for a while. I had begun preparing a log for use in requesting a restraining order by this point, but I hadn't heard from or seen Claire again, so I figured she got the message and was done with me."

"At what point did you begin to feel concern for your safety, enough to keep a log?"

"When I saw the photoshopped images of us together online. Lilah convinced me it was too far, that I had to put an end to it. I did it to keep her happy—I didn't really want the hassle." Noah's voice wavers when he says her name. My knuckles whiten.

"We even put a deposit down on a guard dog, just to make Lilah feel a little safer."

Rosie's Rottweilers was to protect them from me? I want to laugh, but I want to cry even more.

"You felt you were in enough danger to require a protection dog?" Dodgson asks.

"Well, no, I never thought it was *dangerous.* But Lilah was just so weirded out about it all and I wanted to do anything I could to make her feel safer in the house, especially as we were trying for a baby. If she was pregnant, I'd have wanted her to have someone at home to protect her while I was at work. The dog seemed like a good choice."

The blood is bubbling in my veins, hot and molten.

"And still you chose not to go to the police?"

"Lilah wanted to," Noah admits, running a hand through his hair and looking down. "Obviously I regret not doing so now," he says, and his voice breaks. He wipes a tear away.

"Why did you not?"

"Because I didn't want my affairs to be discovered. I was worried that if they began to look into this woman and her interactions with me, then more would be uncovered. Relationships that were real affairs, and I didn't want Lilah to find out," he admits, breaking into a sob, one hand covering his face.

"And the affairs that were raised, Miss Choi's testimony—do you have anything to say about that?"

"They happened, and I'm sorry, but they have nothing to do with this trial, or with what happened to Lilah. If I could take back ever speaking to any of those women and get Lilah back, I would."

My eyes are boring into his, *willing* him to look at me, even for just a second. But he doesn't, and I know why. Because he can't. My fiancé cannot bear to look me in the eye while he lies, lies, lies through his teeth, to get me locked up. I hold my chin a little higher, as though daring him to glance my way, to unravel, to break and tell the truth to this jury, to this *world* of people who have been fed lies from his entire circle, his entire fucking contacts book.

But, of course, he doesn't.

Grosvenor calls for a recess, and that's when I know I'm screwed.

FIFTY-NINE

No tears leaked from my eyes as I faced the coffin, a bunch of white lilies clutched before my chest. I stared at the dark polished wood resolutely. This was my final goodbye to Mother. It seemed odd that such a huge force, such a violent and brutal part of my life, was now in a narrow box. I'd never realized before quite how petite she was, she had always seemed larger than life to me. Behind me was a room full of people I didn't know, faces I vaguely recognized, most of them men. I hadn't arranged a fancy funeral. She hadn't deserved an expensive final send-off.

But I had booked a slot at the local crematorium and put a notice in the local paper, in case she'd had any local friends I hadn't known about. Apparently she did, because many more people turned up than I had expected. I was the only family there, though. Not that I'd have known, because she never introduced me to her relatives—having been cut off from them since she was a teenager. I didn't know who my father was, and looking around the room I wondered, for a split second, if there was any chance that he was in the midst of the mourners. But I shook the thought away. I was never destined for family life. Never destined for loving parents, for mischievous siblings, for marriage or children. It would always be just me on my own. Just Claire.

"Claire, why did you manipulate those photographs of you and Noah?" Grosvenor is asking me once we're back in the consultation room. Her voice is unnaturally gentle.

"I . . . I didn't," I reply.

"You did though. The evidence was up there on the screen and it was checked by an editing expert," Grosvenor says, holding up the court notes. "Do you know how to use Photoshop? Is that what you used to edit them?"

"I . . . I use Photoshop for work, I design press releases, but I don't do photo editing at work," I try to explain. My head is buzzing, everything hazy.

"Claire, are you okay?" Grosvenor asks.

"I don't know," I reply. My chest is seizing. I feel like I can't breathe.

"Someone get a paper bag," Grosvenor is saying, but her voice is distant and echoing as though she's underwater. I grip on to the edges of the table and feel like I might die. I want to curl up into a ball and hide, escape everything that is happening to me right now. I want to be anywhere but here.

The last time I had a panic attack was the day I got the phone call to inform me that Mother had died.

"Is this a joke?" I asked, assuming she had roped someone into calling me as a prank, one of her friends from the pub perhaps. It was exactly the sort of thing she would do, trying to cause me distress and then passing it off as a joke, telling me I'd overreacted, laughing at my distress.

"I'm sorry, Miss Arundale, this is real and we will require you to make some decisions regarding the body. We can refer you to a brilliant funeral home who can take care of everything you need . . ."

The voice trailed off as I began to hyperventilate, dropping the phone onto the ground. Mother was dead. Mother had died of cancer and I hadn't been there; she had died alone in a hospital and I hadn't been visiting because I didn't believe her, because I thought she was trying to punish me for leaving home, for losing contact with her. If I hadn't left home, I would have been there with her. I would have been there to care for her and maybe she wouldn't have died so young.

My chest ached with a sharp stabbing by my sternum. My eyes clenched shut as I curled up and tried to control my breathing. Mother was dead and it was my fault. The guilt was suffocating me, and I was rocking where I sat, trying to sob but nothing was coming because I barely had enough air in me to breathe, let alone sob, and why were there no tears? How could I be so cruel as not to cry when news of my own mother's death arrived?

It was the first time I had experienced a panic attack, and for months afterward, even after meeting Noah, I jumped and felt my heart quicken every time the phone rang, waiting for more bad news to arrive. I ended up setting my phone permanently to Do Not Disturb, I was so afraid of bad news reaching me again. Would Noah die next? I had begun to spin out of control after she died, my emotions ruling me and dictating all of my actions. Sometimes I felt as though I was a ghost, looking at Claire from the outside. Sometimes I felt something rotten in my core crawl out, nasty thoughts and words plaguing me. Sometimes I felt nothing at all, as hollow as a coffin.

One night, I screamed into a pillow. It wasn't from grief. It was fury that she had died, a selfish slice of rage at the fact that she had dared to leave this world before I had the chance to tell her the truth about how I felt. About how she had hurt me, how there was something wrong with her and I had been the one to suffer for it while I was growing up in her care. I screamed loudly into a pillow until I was sure my throat was bleeding, then I passed out. The next morning I went to work, and met Noah.

I scold myself for being so selfish that the thought of going to prison can instill the same visceral reaction in me as finding out I caused my own mother's death. Such a selfish murderer I turned out to be.

The closing statements and verdict were delayed because we had to wait for a doctor to sign me off after my panic attack ended.

Then, Grosvenor made me speak to my psychiatrist, Dr. Pye, again, with the trial on hold until I was medically signed off. We spoke for an entire week, almost all day long. Just me and my painful, traumatic memories playing on a never-ending loop.

"Look, Claire. You don't *need* to lie. You did not go into that house to murder Lilah, you did not intend for her to hit her head when you pushed her. You are *not* a bad person," Dr. Pye tells me one day as I repeat Mother's words to her through my racking sobs.

I am a bad person.

SIXTY

JESSICA PYE

Dr. Jessica Pye steps up to the stand. She looks too young to be a seasoned psychiatrist, too inexperienced for my entire future to rest on her testimony, but I know from our conversations that she's switched on. I like her, if I'm being honest, after spending hours with her recounting and sharing so much of my life and thoughts. She is very serious, her full lower lip occasionally protruding when I speak, the only sign I can identify that means at least something I've said is of interest. She frowns occasionally, but this is often paired with a comforting nod, which leaves me unsure what she is thinking. Is she agreeing with me or am I just highlighting something she already suspects?

When I last saw her she was in a cream dress, but today she's wearing a black dress and blazer, looking substantially more professional and imposing than she did at our last session. I gulp and hope for the best. This woman is so impartial that I can't help but feel hopeful that she can intervene and end this entire charade. I'm hoping that the worst that can happen today is that Judge Black finds there is no case to answer in relation to murder, leaving only the possibility of the lesser charge, manslaughter. After all, I didn't mean for Lilah to die. I never in my wildest dreams imagined that one little push could have brought us all to where we are today.

"The court invites Dr. Jessica Pye to speak," the judge intones.

"Following several conversations and assessment of all the key parties, it is clear to me that Claire Arundale cannot by any reasonable person be found guilty of murder," she says.

My eyes widen and I exhale loudly with relief. I sink my head into my hands, allowing myself to luxuriate in the comfort of this woman, this *stranger,* finally defending me. Finally backing me.

"While we psychoanalyzed Miss Arundale immediately after her arrest, I'm sorry to say her mental capacity has deteriorated further since then. We were called in by her legal team, who believed she had begun to show signs of mental health issues, and I have spent the past week reevaluating her under the new circumstances. Following my new assessment, I also argue she is not mentally capable of standing trial, and this has been backed by several other psychiatrists following an examination of all court and psychiatric assessment transcripts."

I jerk in my seat and frown, looking over at Grosvenor, who seems to be nodding in agreement. Not capable of standing trial? What does that mean?

Slowly, she slides me a note.

I'm sorry, Claire. You are not a murderer: This is the best route out for you.

I stare at it, my blood running cold as realization begins to dawn.

"During my examination, I found overwhelming evidence that Miss Arundale suffers from a severe case of delusional disorder by way of psychosis. It is, in fact, the most extreme case I have come across in my years as a professional. The defendant is unable to distinguish reality from fantasy, and her unshakable belief she is engaged to Mr. Coors illustrates that she is not living in the real world and so cannot tell fact from fiction. It is my understanding that they did indeed meet in Morrisons supermarket on the eighteenth of September 2024, but that it was a brief and professional encounter, as per Mr. Coors's testimony. Following this encounter, the defendant followed him to a coffee shop, where she learned his name and place of work from a lanyard hanging out of his backpack. She then began to construct a double life for herself, which she quickly spiraled into, unable to understand what was real and what was a construct of her own mind. The difficulty of this disorder is that, largely, it will not impact a person's day-to-day life. She is able to work, to function and to socialize, but the depths of the disorder are hidden away within the recesses of the mind and it is not until you begin to dig that you realize just how severely delusional a patient is."

I feel sick, a sense of hot dread sweeping over me.

"It is my personal belief that her disorder, while largely genetic, has been fueled by the environment in which she grew up, over which as a child she had no control. She was raised by an abusive mum, who I believe to have had cluster B narcissistic personality disorder. This induces extremely volatile behavior and heightened emotions, affecting the same side of the brain as psychopathy or sociopathy. Being raised by someone with this type of personality disorder is proven to leave offspring with severe emotional neglect and trauma wounds, which can occasionally evolve into psychosis if the patient is already genetically predisposed to the condition. After hours of conversation with Miss Arundale, it is clear to me that her childhood left her completely devoid of emotional stability, love, nurturing or security, which I believe to have triggered her psychosis in later life following the passing of her only parent.

"Furthermore, Miss Arundale's delusional disorder fits perfectly into the category of erotomania, in which a person believes someone is in love with them. This will often lead to the stalking behavior we have heard described, and which we have heard instances of from some of the witnesses in the trial. In her defense, these delusions can also lead to irritability and mood swings, which would have been escalated by the defendant's alcohol consumption in the week leading up to Lilah Andersson's death. It is clear to me that the defendant is a victim of her own mental health, that she has been suffering from an undiagnosed psychosis for a quite astounding length of time, completely unmedicated, and that she cannot in consequence be held criminally liable for the death of Miss Andersson nor stand trial as a result."

"I invite the defense to make a statement," the judge is saying, but again the words sound wavy and watery as my chest tightens and I feel myself closing down.

"We have cross-referenced entries from Miss Arundale's personal journal and have found various discrepancies between her understanding of reality and what actually happened," Grosvenor begins. "On September the twenty-second 2024, for instance, she wrote about visiting an Italian restaurant with Mr. Coors after an interaction on the street, while CCTV footage shows Miss Arundale never actually entered the restaurant, instead watching Mr. Coors through the window while he ate with Mr. Barton. On April the fifth the following year she wrote about a trip to Venice, but airline logs prove that only Miss Arundale was booked to travel on that flight, with Mr. Coors accounted for at work in the UK the same week that she wrote about their being on holiday together. In February when she wrote about becoming engaged to him, he has a solid alibi, being present at a client party the entire evening. Her ring, we believe, was purchased by Miss Arundale herself from a local Christmas market. The receipt was found in her home, folded into an origami rabbit, beside a bizarre notebook filled with ramblings relating to Mr. Coors, his family and friends. It is clear to me that the events described in Miss Arundale's journal represent the truth as she saw it and not the objective truth. I believe that this is evidence enough of the psychosis Dr. Pye has diagnosed her with and ask that my client be discharged from trial on the grounds of mental incapacity."

I stand, my legs shaking uncontrollably, and vaguely hear Grosvenor telling the court we need to adjourn because I am ill, but her voice is echoing strangely and the next thing I know I am on my knees in a fluorescent-lit court bathroom, heaving into a toilet while two people stand guard over me, and tears are streaming down my face, and all I can think is that this is wrong, wrong, WRONG, and how I wish that Noah would step in and stop it from happening.

SIXTY-ONE

Diminished responsibility due to an abnormality of the mind. That was how the trial concluded, with all the witness testimonies thrown out. All that emotional trauma was a waste of time and energy. I never should have stood trial in the first place, apparently.

The court noted that my ability to understand my situation and conduct was hugely impaired and had led to a loss of self-control when I believed Lilah was having a child with Noah. Noah is not my fiancé. He is never, according to them, going to be my husband.

SIXTY-TWO

I am wringing my hands together in my lap, my eyes fixed on my feet. The disgusting slippers they make you wear here were once white, but are now an off-putting murky beige.

"And, Claire, how about you? How have you been getting on this week?"

I jolt upright at the sound of my name. The team leader, Daisy, looks at me carefully with an encouraging smile on her face. She's not really a team leader. She's a psychiatrist. But they make us call them team leaders, as though it makes it all less serious. I take a shaky breath, pairs of eyes peering at me curiously from around the circle we're sitting in. Some patients, like me, like to keep their gaze fixed on the floor. One woman is muttering to herself under her breath, but she does this so often that it has become a strange comfort to me: a reminder of what true mental illness is. Some of the others are flitting their gaze about restlessly, impatient and bored. But many watch me, interested. And so I begin.

"This week has been . . . tough. Honestly, it's been quite shocking. I've now been here long enough that my new medication has worked its way into my system . . ."

Murmurs around the group of understanding and empathy. "And now I guess I'm just coming to terms with what I've done, who I really am and how I've ended up here." My shoulders sag at this point.

Daisy beams at me as though I've told her she's won the lottery. "That's *brilliant,* Claire. Really good self-awareness and progress! And how are you feeling about these revelations?"

I sigh. "Honestly? Tired." I get some chuckles around the circle at this, vigorous nods of understanding and camaraderie.

"I guess it all stems from my childhood, my relationship with my mother. I need to work through all that I went through then, and my unhealthy attitude toward being loved, as a first step." Daisy is now nodding so enthusiastically that she reminds me of those bobbleheads in cars, and I worry hers may fall off her neck entirely.

"And how about your emotions? What have you been feeling this week? I know the last time we spoke there was a lot of anger." She's frowning at the memory.

"Yes, well, I'm still angry, I'll be honest. I feel betrayed by the court system, even though I suppose it kept me out of prison."

"Barely!" someone heckles.

"Prison is entirely different and much worse," Daisy counters crisply. "Claire, carry on, please."

"You're right. Prison is entirely different. At least here we have our own toilets!" It's only half a joke but falls almost entirely flat.

"Anyway, I wish they'd diagnosed me sooner, prepared me for what was going on. I felt ambushed by my own lawyer. And as part of the psychiatric evidence, they shared my diary entries. Those private, personal memories in my own handwriting . . . I felt so humiliated," I admit for the first time. That was the final kicker, those diary entries. The last trace of any sort of pride I might have retained, dashed as my innermost thoughts, secrets, wishes and horrors were shared with a bunch of strangers. I feel my face flush at the memory, the complete horror of the diary becoming part of my case notes, typed out letter by excruciating letter.

"And what about Noah? His friends?" Daisy asks.

I keep my face carefully neutral. "I can't be angry with them: They only went up there and spoke the truth—anybody would have done the same. But I am sad every day about what happened to

Lilah, and I wish it hadn't." I look at the ground again and swallow down the lump in my throat. I feel tears spring to my eyes and hurriedly wipe them away. Nobody is laughing now, the circle around me grown quiet. Even the muttering woman has reverted to shaking her head furiously and silently.

"And that's what we're here to help you work through," Daisy says gently, watching me with pity in her eyes. "Let's move on. Jacob, how are you getting on with your outbursts of anger this week?" She turns away from me and I relax just a fraction. I've said my piece. Now I just have to sit through the rest of this session and then I can go back to my awful little box room and reflect on what I've learned in my journal. A journal that, hopefully, will *remain* private.

The horror of the court logging my most personal, private feelings as evidence of my mental health was palpable. I thought the trial could not get any worse for me after Noah's and Jessica's evidence, but somehow it did. Since then, I've had a letter from Grosvenor checking in on me, asking me to call her, but I've declined. I don't want to speak to her, and I don't want to kid myself that our relationship was anything other than professional. She'll get another client soon enough and forget I ever existed. Sukhi, however, I do still speak to.

We have weekly phone calls and write letters. She's pregnant now—she sent me some copies of her scans in a letter. That was hard for me, I'll be honest. I'd had a low week and felt so empty and alone. And eventually, after speaking with Daisy in a one-to-one session, we realized I was also afraid. Afraid that I would be replaced by this baby and abandoned by Sukhi, our friendship redundant as she assumes a new role. I've since acknowledged that I can never compete with a baby for Sukhi's attention, but that I can offer her a different sort of relationship, one that the baby couldn't compete with me for, either. And that's okay. I can accept that, and I can look forward to having this special friendship with Sukhi where we are tied together by the bizarre experience that she, in a way, lived through with me. Of course, there is also the pain of not having my own child, and the fact that it will be a long time before I will be able to have one, considering I am now almost thirty and very much alone. But Daisy has assured me there are several options by which I can conceive naturally, and that my eggs are far from dried up just yet. So that's a small silver lining, and something that helps encourage me to get better and get out of here. The quicker I'm happy and healthy, the quicker I'm free; and the quicker I'm free, the quicker I can go back to rebuilding a normal life and, hopefully, someday, having my own family.

Alongside the medication, weekly group-therapy sessions and phone calls with Sukhi, I am having extensive therapy sessions relating to Mother and my feelings about her. These are an almost daily occurrence and I have three different therapists. Daisy for my usual CBT chats, a hypnotherapist who is trying to draw out the darker memories my brain has locked away from me, and a therapist who specializes specifically in narcissistic personality disorder and how it affects any offspring.

It's been eye-opening for me to realize that there are other women like me who have endured a similar upbringing. It's also been enlightening, though difficult, to take in that none of it was my fault. It was never about me. Mother would have behaved the same way whoever her child was, because she was ill and her way of seeing the world was distorted. She was the main character, always. In her eyes, I was an adjunct who had no feelings, no emotions of my own, only there to support her and drive her forward. And in a way, I feel pity for her. What a sad way to live her life: without any real relationships, without any way of feeling true love or human sympathy.

She must have been as lonely as I am now.

EPILOGUE

Elmswood Psychiatric Hospital
September 11, 2026

Dear Diary,

*Today was a better day. We had our group session, and I think it went
well. Daisy seemed pleased, anyway. And that's what all of this is about
really, isn't it? Progress. That's the focus. Small steps a day at a time
that will eventually culminate in one huge, impressive advance. Once
they realize how far I've come, they'll let me out, because I won't be a
danger to the public or to myself.*

*I'm less angry today. The courts may have betrayed me with their
appropriation of my journals, but at least I am not in prison. I have a
fair amount of freedom, lots of activities I can indulge in. I'm getting
quite into painting. Most of my block-mates are okay. There's one girl
who is super shy but seems sweet. She's in for arson, but I reckon she'll
be let out to a rehabilitation unit soon, as nobody died. Sukhi writes me
letters, which remind me that there's a life outside this place to aim for.
I'm trying to work out what that life will look like for me once I'm out.
Will anyone hire me? Will I ever get that family I've so longed for?
These are things I worry about frequently, but the staff here have
assured me that when I "graduate" from here and am sent to the public
rehabilitation unit, I will be assigned social workers whose whole job
will be to look after me and make sure that I can get back on track with*

things like work and socializing. So that is what I'm focusing on for now.

Of course, I still have my secrets. We all do, after all. My first secret is that I haven't been taking the drugs they give me. I know that they're designed to make you foggy, so they can keep you locked up here even longer, make out that you're too unfocused to be ready to leave. No, not for me. So I pretend to swallow them, but I hide them under my tongue and spit them out down the toilet later. If I can't spit a tablet out, I swallow it but keep it lodged as high as I can in my throat and then throw it up later. Sometimes it doesn't work, of course, and I just have to suck it up and swallow it. But I'm trying to make sure that there's never enough of them in my system to get into my bloodstream and alter my thoughts or moods. Because that's what they want—to make us all little sheep that they can herd around. I don't belong here because I'm not fucking crazy. I'm not! I know the truth, and all of those dirty lying witnesses know the truth, and I cannot let them treat me and drug me like I'm a psychotic who is dangerous to society. No. So I pretend to take the pills, keep my wits about me, say the things they want to hear in my progress sessions and await the day they let me out.

My second secret is that I don't belong in this hospital, but I do belong in prison. Because (and this is funny) the truth is that Lilah didn't trip and hit her head. And I didn't push her. No, I held her shoulders with my two hands and I slammed that bitch's skull into the mantelpiece, and I would do it again if necessary because she stole my fucking fiancé and then my life.

Now all I have to do is keep pretending that I know I've done wrong, and I'm sorry, so they will let me out and then I'll be reunited with Noah again. I can't wait. I know he's out there, waiting for me. I hope I don't keep him waiting too long.

I have to flush this paper now, in case they find it. I always make sure to fold my new diary entries carefully, into paper birds, before drowning them in the toilet. But I feel better already. Maybe there is something in that whole "confess your sins" idea. Maybe Noah and I can convert to Catholicism when we're reunited. Maybe I just like writing, releasing my thoughts into the ether. Either way, I'm coming home, Noah. I promise.

Love always,
your Claire

AUTHOR'S NOTE

The author acknowledges that courtroom procedures have been fictionalized for dramatic representation and are not true to life or research.

ACKNOWLEDGMENTS

It has taken a whole host of people to get me to where I am today, and thanking everyone in such a small space is going to be difficult, but we grind.

First, a huge thank-you to my agent, Camilla Bolton, as well as Jade Kavanagh and all of Darley Anderson for championing and believing in my book. Cam, I honestly thank my lucky stars every day that you met me for that lunch and took a chance on me. I'm so lucky to have you as my agent; you've made dreams come true and honestly changed my life.

A mega thank-you to my incredible editors Emily Griffin and Claire Simmonds for seamlessly making my book come to life, alongside all of the Century team, especially Hope Butler, Rhiannon Carroll, Lucy Thorne and Katya Browne. From publicity and marketing through to production, sales and art, I know it takes a mountain to produce and sell a book and I am so thankful to each and every one of you.

And across the pond, thank you to my US team, especially Jesse Shuman. I'm unbelievably lucky to have such talented editors!

Shout-out to Sara Nisha Adams and Chris Bridges for your writing support through the drafts. A huge thank-you to my friend Sukh Ojla for your help in bringing Sukhi to life on the pages.

Thank you to all my closest friends and family—you know who you are and I know some of you will see yourself hidden in the pages of this book (some less subtly than others, Amy Grosvenor!)

and I just want to say thank you all for being the friends I need and the family I love so much. You all inspire me every day.

To my husband, Steven, for always supporting me in my dreams and being my number one cheerleader, and Betsy, the light of my life. God I love you, you weird little dog.

Thank you to anyone who supported me from day one when I wrote those first terrible, awful books that should never see the light of day—you have to write some crap to learn what's good (or in my case, how to write at all), and I can't believe you guys supported me through the crap! Anyone who read my first fantasy—I can only apologize. Especially Katie Civitelli. I hope you enjoyed this book much more—your encouragement and support in those first books helped get me to where I am now.

And thank you to all the people I have probably forgotten to include by name—you know what I'm like, and to be honest writing the acknowledgments was harder than writing the book.

ABOUT THE AUTHOR

CALLIE KAZUMI is a British Japanese writer who started work on her first book after being given Stephen King's *On Writing* by her father. She lives in London with her husband and her bichon frise, Betsy. *Claire, Darling* is her debut novel.

callieuntitled.com
Instagram and X: @callieuntitled

ABOUT THE TYPE

This book was set in Granjon, a modern recutting of a typeface produced under the direction of George W. Jones (1860–1942), who based Granjon's design upon the letterforms of Claude Garamond (1480–1561). The name was given to the typeface as a tribute to the typographic designer Robert Granjon (1513–89).